LICENSE

To Cher,
Live, Love, Dream
Diane Rivoli
(11/23/19)

LICENSE

A Novel

DIANE RIVOLI

COVER ILLUSTRATION BY JOSH RIVOLI

To Joseph, who makes all things possible

TABLE OF CONTENTS

Chapter 1

DRIVER'S LICENSE

Dixie had followed Arizona all the way down to North Creek and then gotten on the highway. The sun shining through the windows was like an elixir leading her away from her frumpy beginnings towards the bonanza of a new day.

She had left so early, her family still sound asleep; no coffee brewing yet, no eggs frying, no bacon. Her stomach gurgled. Every license plate she passed reminded her of food! APL-Apple, CKE-Cake, BNS-Buns, FGG-Egg Foo Yung. She had to stop somewhere before she started picking around in the seat cushion seams searching for stray crumbs!

She got off the highway at the next exit (a small town called Bunderby) and stopped in front of Fitzpatrick's, a little diner with a large poster board out front, the specials written in crayon.

Bowl of New England Clam Chowder – $3.00

Baked Macaroni and Cheese with Tossed Salad – $7.00

Boneless Chicken Breast Smothered with Provolone Cheese and Sautéed Peppers and Onions; Thick Cut French Fries and a Cherry Tomato Salad – $11.00

Dixie dashed in and practically fell into the booth right next to the door. Aaahh, the smells wafting from that kitchen! Her mouth watered and her stomach gurgled even louder.

A smiling waitress with a tail of dark flowing hair bouncing behind her started towards her booth but before she was even half way there, Dixie blurted out her order. "I'll have the chicken breast special, a large coffee and a large glass of water."

"Sounds like someone's really hungry! I'll get that out for you in a flash, Honey." and the waitress hurried back into the kitchen with Dixie's order.

Luckily for Dixie's tummy, her lunch really did come out in a flash.

"Here you go, just like I promised. And my name's Pam. If there's anything else you need, you make sure and let me know. We aim to please."

She was such a friendly, effervescent waitress! Dixie grinned and dug into her meal. Minutes later the last little tomato passed through her lips. Everything was gone. She had practically inhaled it.

Then she noticed the big plate of donuts beckoning to her from under their glass domed cover on the counter.

"Are those donuts fresh?" she asked when Pam came to refill her coffee.

"The freshest!" Pam enthused. "We pick them up every morning from Eversweet Bakery just a couple blocks down the road. They come off the line, into the box and into our hands. The apple-stuffed are my favorite. Just delicious. Would you like one?"

"I can't resist!"

Delicious did not begin to describe that donut. Tender, chunky apples just touched with lightly sweetened syrup and a dusting of cinnamon sat surrounded by a sugar sprinkled dough that was so soft and fluffy, it nearly melted in her mouth. It was heaven! It was bliss! A perfect end to a perfect lunch for an awesome new beginning!

With her stomach content now, Dixie relaxed and stretched in her seat. What a cute place Fitzpatrick's was. It was decorated in shades of ecru, sage and burgundy with a rooster theme. There were ceramic roosters, fabric roosters and wooden roosters. There were big roosters and small roosters. There were rooster plaques, rooster pins, rooster paintings and rooster mugs. And all the roosters were for sale.

As she stood at the cash register to pay her bill, Dixie selected a brightly colored rooster pin - A souvenir to mark the beginning of her journey to freedom.

"How much?"

"Honey, the pin's on the house. You take care now, you hear? Make sure you stay safe."

Was there something about her demeanor that made Pam guess she had just left home, that she was a young woman out on her own, that she might need safekeeping? Or was that just something she said to everyone? No matter. She was a smart, observant girl. Everything was going great. She had no worries.

Dixie tucked a generous tip for Pam under her empty plate, and left the diner in a state of euphoria - her stomach pleasantly full, her rooster pin attached to her purse strap. She knew she had not made a mistake in leaving her family behind. She knew she was headed for something wonderful. The world was full of promise. As she got back in her little Jetta and drove away, the rooster flag hanging by the diner door waved a cheery goodbye.

Dixie's life really hadn't been bad. It was just a nothing remarkable blah life. She wanted something more. Something more than the dead end job she had as a cashier at The Dollar Store. Something better than her loser boyfriend with the purple dyed hair who played in a loser band at the bar every weekend and slept all day.

She loved her Mom and Dad and her younger brothers, Owen and Gabriel, but her parents expected so much of her. She had to mow the lawn and stack bundles of firewood next to the garage. She had to do all the laundry and help her father power wash the deck. Worst of all was that they enforced a curfew and she wasn't a kid anymore. She was twenty years old!

And her brothers! They were always fighting or running around like apes and climbing all over the furniture. They did devilish things like hiding chicken bones under her pillow or stuffing her purse with raw cookie dough.

She just couldn't stand it anymore! Change was what she need-ed: excitement, adventure, independence! So change was what she was going to get.

Life was a gamble wasn't it? She was flying down the road, her azure blue Jetta matching the blue of the sky.

Chapter 2

LICENSE ON A GLORIOUS DAY

Could her day have started out any worse? Her bathwater had been lukewarm, her high fiber cereal wasn't producing the desired effect, and she had found Boyd passed out on the kitchen floor like a whiskey embalmed cadaver awaiting the scalpel of a medical student.

Pam gave Boyd a none too gentle kick with the toe of her shoe. Now that produced the desired effect! He grumbled and sputtered and sat up, rubbing his face with his hands. He flashed her a goofy grin and stood up on wobbly legs.

"Pam!" he uttered, his voice as wobbly as his legs, "You look fabulous!" He lurched towards her then, wrapped his arms around her neck, and tried to kiss her.

"Cut it out Boyd! Don't go trying to get frisky with me now, Mister Dragon Breath! What the hell were you up to last night?"

"Oh, Pam. Remember? I was out with the guys. You know, celebrating! Cause of Tony's promotion! We saw a movie at Cinema Flicks and then we went down to Dexter's. I had the best burger! And we threw back a few, well maybe more than a few, beers and, and some shots!" Boyd explained with slightly slurred words, his brain and his tongue not quite in sync.

He flashed that smile again, a scoundrel's grin, inhabited by the sun. Bright enough to melt the toughest resolve. It certainly melted her heart. She could never stay mad at Boyd for long. She led him over to the kitchen table and guided him into a chair, got a pot of coffee going and gave him a tall glass of water.

"Drink this," she advised, her voice softer and more caring than before, "You need some hydration. Listen, I've got to get to the restaurant. Want me to get you something to eat before I go? Some eggs? Some crisp buttery toast? How about a bowl of Captain Crunch with some nice ripe bananas on top?"

"Ughh, no way, Baby. Just the thought of it's enough to make me wanna puke. Thanks though. I'm just gonna climb in bed and crash for a couple more hours. What time you working till?"

"Till four. Unless Eva's late for her shift, like usual. She was probably at Dexter's throwing back a few last night too!"

"Hey, you know what I'm gonna do? I'm gonna make you dinner! It'll be all ready when you get home. We'll eat out back on the patio, under the gazebo!"

"Sounds great, Boyd. I'll call if I'm going to be late. Make sure you drink that whole glass of water now, you hear?" She kissed his check and walked out the door into the summer morning.

Pam had one rule – Never leave the house in a bad mood. Nothing good ever came from a bad mood. But if you were bright and sparkly and friendly and pleasant, why, good things just seemed to come your way! Other people smiled back. Other people held the door for you or let you get in front of them in line at the bank.

If other people were sad or depressed, her smile seemed to rub off on them and lift their spirits. Making someone else's day a little happier was almost more important to Pam than being happy herself.

And, besides all that, if you were bright and sparkly, friendly and pleasant, customers gave bigger tips!

Maybe her day had started out poorly but then Boyd had given her his roguish grin and promised to cook dinner. The sun was shining. Doves were cooing. Robins, sparrows and chickadees were frolicking about in the trees, singing their morning songs. Her dahlias were coming up next to the fence and the marigolds and begonias were blooming along the walkway. No one could be in a bad mood on a day like this! Especially not effervescent Pam. Rules were made to be broken, but not Pam's rule and definitely not on a glorious day like today!

She walked over to her good old Firebird, waiting patiently in the driveway, and got in. Pam had nicknamed it the Red-Winged Blackbird because of its black exterior and red interior. She had inherited it from her father and she treasured it dearly.

"Off we go, Blackbird. The roosters are calling!" Pam backed out onto Elm Street and whizzed down the road toward the city, her Firebird glistening in the sun.

Chapter 3

PARENTAL LICENSE

"Bye bye, Dixie," Lainey Andrews whispered as she peaked through the curtains and watched the blue Jetta back out of the driveway and head east.

She sat on the edge of the bed and smiled. Her Dixie, off on her own. Her Dixie, she was so proud of her! Her Dixie, her brilliant, beautiful Dixie. She had been such a tiny bundle when she was born. Where had that tiny bundle gone? Suddenly she was sobbing, tears streaming down her cheeks.

"Lainey? What's going on? What's wrong?" her husband mumbled sleepily from the other side of the bed, the sheets rustling as he kicked them off and sat up.

"Dixie just left. She's gone, Joe. Our baby's gone."

Joe scooted over next to her, wrapped his arms around her tenderly and kissed the top her head. "She'll be alright, Lainey. Don't worry."

Lainey pulled a tissue from the box on the nightstand to dry her tears and then snuggled into Joe's warm body, letting him rock her gently back and forth as he tried to comfort her.

She really wasn't worried about Dixie. That wasn't it at all. Dixie was a sensible girl. Smart and capable. She had never given them a moment's trouble. Maybe Lainey was biased, but she thought her daughter was extraordinary!

She was an avid reader. She loved to write too. Poems mostly but short stories as well, stories with such emotional insight and depth that Lainey wondered how someone of Dixie's tender years could have written them. She'd had several sizzling editorials published in the town paper that had garnered incredible amounts of feedback and a call from the local Rotary Club asking her to speak at one of their luncheons, until they found out she was only fourteen at the time. And then there was that short, somewhat bizarre film that she had written and produced for one of her college finals – Marzipan Fever!

Mrs. Baxter, Dixie's Media Studies professor at Duckwood Community College, had given her an A Plus on the project and told Dixie that she was immensely talented, that the film had the touch of genius!

Dixie had made all the costumes and props herself out of recycled materials – old clothes, bits of fabric, newspapers, empty cereal boxes, egg cartons, coffee cans, milk jugs – whatever she could get her hands on.

Lainey had played the part of an elven princess with gold painted eyebrows. Joe was a biker dude and had to flex his muscles a lot. Owen and Gabriel had been elks with old fan blades tied to their heads like antlers. And Dixie's purple haired boyfriend, Greg, had been the hero - a cave explorer who saved the day. It had been such crazy fun! That Dixie! And then Lainey was sobbing again.

"I'm just going to miss her so much, Joe," she blubbered through her tears.

"I know, I know, Sugar. But it's not like she's traipsing off to Europe or Africa. She's only going to be a few hours' drive away. She'll come home for holidays and we can take a weekend and go visit her in her new apartment."

Lainey still wasn't convinced.

"You want to throw on some clothes, hop in the ATV and go chase her down? Give her one more hug and kiss before she gets too far from home?"

Lainey stretched for another tissue from the box, her blubbering turning into chuckling as she wiped her eyes and blew her nose. "Are you kidding? Dixie would think we were complete idiots!"

But for one moment she was actually tempted to do it.

"Well, at least it'll be a little quieter around here. You know, how does that song go? One less person, one less door bell, one less egg to fry…"

"Now I know your joking! Quieter? With Gabe and Owen still here? The bedlam twins?" Lainey started laughing and suddenly they were both laughing (quietly of course so as not to wake the boys), holding their sides and rolling around on the bed.

They rolled right into each other's arms, staring at each other with bright, smiling faces.

"I love you, Joe."

"I love you, Lainey."

Yes, Lainey really was going to miss that girl. But kids grow up. Kids leave the nest. Joe was still here. And in the end, it was Joe who was her world.

Poetic License

TINY BUNDLE

Where did that tiny bundle go?
The one I held so tight.
The one I showered with kisses and hugs
And comforted during the night.

Is she in her highchair?
Is she in her big girl bed
With her thumb in her mouth
Clutching her blanket with the silky edge?

Is she out at the bus stop
Waiting for the bus
To take her to kindergarten
To learn letters and numbers and other important stuff?

Or perhaps she's out with her father
Learning how to drive.
Or in the bathroom shaving her legs
For the very first time.

No, no
There she is now!
Walking across the stage
In her cap and gown.

Now her car is packed full
And the house seems so empty.
She's off on her own.
"Don't forget to call me!"

Where did that tiny bundle go?
She grew into a woman.
But I still remember her sweet baby smell
And the touch of her little hand.

Chapter 4

LICENSE TO BE BROKEN

Emma Baxter knew she wasn't perfect. She was sometimes quick tempered and quarrelsome. She let other people walk all over her. She had a tendency to daydream and was inclined to be overly thrifty. She didn't need Caleb to point these things out to her.

Why couldn't he point out her good qualities instead? Like that she was lively and energetic. That she was a good cook. That she was friendly, smart, reliable and helpful. That she told funny jokes.

Caleb complained that she hadn't gone after her dream, that she had wasted her talent. Emma was a gifted storyteller. She had dreamed of becoming a novelist and writing young adult fiction. But once she met Caleb, her dream had changed. Instead of spending her free time writing, she wanted to spend her free time with Caleb. She wanted to marry Caleb and raise a family with Caleb. He had been all for that then. Now he seemed to hold it against her.

And how could he even say that? That she had wasted her talent. It's not like she had stayed home and sat on her butt watching soap operas and eating potato chips all day. She had become a well-respected and popular professor at Duckwood Community College. She loved teaching! And she loved her students too. She was as proud of them as if they were her own kids, especially since having a family had never worked out for her and Caleb.

Her favorite class to teach was 'Movies – Reflections of Life: Past, Present, and Future'. For the final project, she always assigned her students the task of producing their own movie. Topic, technique, style - all up to them, no restrictions. Except that it could be no more than 30 minutes long. And nothing X-rated, of course!

Emma was always amazed at what those kids came up with. Such creativity! There was the murder mystery that one young man had done using dogs and cats as his actors. One student had combined live action and animation, switching every six minutes between the two to hilarious effect. And there was the one that had probed death and clutched her heart, the entire thing filmed in a closet using nothing but a flashlight for lighting.

But the movie that always stood out the most in her mind was the thought provoking other worldly fantasy 'Marzipan Fever'. Dixie Andrews had been the bright young mind that had come up with that masterpiece. What a promising young woman. She was someone to watch alright. There was a brilliant future waiting for that girl.

But anyway, what about Caleb? Had he gone after his dream? He had been quite an artist. His favorite subject had been Emma. He drew Emma with a bunny on her lap and Emma snuggling with her cat. There was Emma by the pink flowering dogwood tree and Emma sleeping at her desk. He had dreamed of illustrating his own line of greeting cards. Now instead, here he was, a manufacturing engineer at Dunbar and Bexley Eco-Systems. And he hated his job!

She knew he was under a lot of pressure at work. Stress could be like an aphid, sucking the life juices right out of you. It could make you irritable, ornery and depressed. So she tried to be extra happy and cheerful, hoping that some of her cheerfulness would rub off on him. She'd put on his favorite music and try to get him to dance with her.

He'd just push her away, scoffing, "What's the matter with you? Stop acting like a silly child. All I want is some peace and quiet."

And instead of her cheerfulness rubbing off on him, his sour mood ended up rubbing off on her. She was so depressed.

Caleb hadn't always been like this. He used to be lively and fun, sweet and romantic. He used to sneak up behind her, grab her around the waist and swing her about till she was dizzy. He'd set her down, twirl her to face him and give her a big kiss smack on the lips.

"How's my angel faced girl today?" he'd ask. And then he'd kiss her again, his eyes sparkling, his face beaming.

She'd laugh and laugh.

He'd say silly things like, "Don't despair! I are hair!"

Or he'd say, "A Caleb a day keeps the doctor away!"

These days he said stuff like:

"Your casserole's bland. You should have added more spices and more salt."

Or "I can still see the spaghetti sauce stain on my shirt. Did you put stain stick on it like I asked you to?"

Her sweet and wonderful Caleb, the love of her life Caleb, would resurface occasionally and it would make her heart sing. She'd come home from work to find him with a big smile on his face, wearing her apron and making fried chicken and corn bread or a chocolate cake.

He'd grab her around the waist and swing her around, just like he used to, and plant a kiss on her lips. "Emma! I'm so glad you're home! Isn't it a beautiful day? Guess what? I'm cooking us dinner!"

Sometimes he'd come home hiding something behind his back, a hesitant smile playing at his lips. "I love you Emma. I'm sorry I've been such a pain in the ass lately," he'd say apologetically. "Can you forgive me?"

And out would come a dozen red roses, all wrapped up with a bow and smelling like heaven.

"Oh, Caleb! They are so lovely!" She'd kiss him and hug him, trying to keep her face buried in his shoulder or hidden by the flowers so he wouldn't see the tears trickling down her cheek.

Emma didn't think it was any coincidence that the rose was considered the symbol of love. Yes, they were certainly beautiful, just like love could be beautiful.

But the rose also had thorns.

Poetic License

BROKEN

A brief smile
A yellow glimpse
So long since I've felt this way
Too soon it will all be departed
Driving down the road
Is it Spring now or
Winter that's on the way?

A thick fog is pushing me down
Like writer's block on life
Happiness is quickly erased
Your pencil
Draws disappointment and disgust
You have seen me naked
What can I hide?

Chapter 5

LICENSE TO BE GRAPE

V inifera – That was what they called their band. Greg and his brothers, Pete and Eli, had tossed around several other names like Galaxy or The Decibels or the really lame Germ Warfare before they had come up with the way cool Vinifera.

Vinifera had to do with grapes and with a last name like Grapensteter -well, it was like Karma or something, totally awesome!

And then to make it even more dope, they all dyed their hair purple, 'cus, you know, grapes were purple!

Greg was the lead singer and also played the keyboards and electric guitar. Pete played the bass guitar and sang backup and Eli was the drummer. Greg thought they were kick ass. They had gigs almost every weekend in one bar or another. And once they had actually been hired to play at a wedding reception! They even had fans!

Their biggest fan was his girlfriend, Dixie. Almost every show, he could see her out in the audience jamming to the beat. When they took a break, she'd come running up to him all excited, with those blue/green eyes of hers sparkling and shining. She'd throw her arms around his neck and tell him he was great, that he sounded just like Chris Martin and that he had the moves like Jagger!

Of course, there were always a few hecklers in the audience. Douches that he used to go to high school with who were way more interested in tossing back a few than listening to the music. They thought they were clever as hell.

"Look, it's a bunch of sour Grapensteters!"

"Whew...smells like rotten Grapensteters around here."

"Hey, the Grapensteters of Wrath! Maybe we can have a Grapensteter stomping party later!"

Him and his bros just ignored those morons.

After a gig, him and Dixie would hop in his Malibu and drive over to The Clover and Fern Café for a late night snack. She'd usually get an egg salad and alfalfa sprout wrap and a cup of herbal tea. His preferred grub was the double decker "Here's the Beef" burger with fries and a beer.

"That was some unreal show tonight, wasn't it Dixie?" Greg gloated as he stuffed fries in his mouth like a chain smoker. "I was on fire! I really think that someday Vinifera's gonna be big! Maybe even bigger than Coldplay or Maroon 5 or even the Stones!"

"You were totally fantastic! Rock'n!!" Dixie raved.

As she nibbled on her wrap, her elated expression turned thoughtful. "But you know, Greg, if you really want to make it big you can't just do covers. You have to sing your own originals!"

"Yah, but where am I gonna get original songs? I'm awful at song writing! You've got to come up with rhymes and melodies and stuff!"

"Don't be such a defeatist! Start with something simple, something you're interested in. Like a song about your guitar! Or even about a hamburger! How about a song about your purple hair? Or," Dixie gave Greg a sly wink, "you could write about me, your fluffy little Dixie Chickie!"

"Oh! Oh! I think I've got one!!" Greg smirked and started singing, "If you'll be my Dixie Chickie, I'll be your Tennessee lamb...."

"Cover!!" Dixie yelled.

Greg's eyes opened wide and a laugh tried to escape from his mouth. But he had just taken a sip of beer! He grabbed a napkin and shoved it over his face seconds before the beer came spewing out. Some even gushed out of his nose!

Conversation was a bust for the rest of that night. Anything they tried to say seemed hilarious beyond words. His side was aching, his eyes were running and Dixie almost fell out of her chair. It had been so insane.

Greg knew Dixie was right about the songs though. No band ever got big singing covers. And he tried, he really did! But nothing came to him. He Asked Pete and Eli to give it a try too. They were every bit as lousy at it as he was.

One night, Dixie strolled into the bar while they were setting up and pulled some papers out of her purse.

"Look!" she beamed, handing the papers to Greg, "I wrote some songs for Vinifera! Only the words so far. We'd still have to come up with the tunes but see this one here, 'Premonition'? This is the one I like best! Read it! Let me know what you think!" Exhilaration and vibrancy were practically dripping off of her. She was hopping with anticipation.

Greg read over her 'Premonition' song and a few of the others. It was hard to concentrate with Dixie watching his eyes move across the page and scanning his face trying to read him. It made him nervous. She was tripping him out.

"I don't know, Dixie," he finally said. "They're kind of lame. They don't make any sense and they sound way too girlie!"

Dixie was hurt. And mad. "Girlie? What do you mean, 'girlie'? There's nothing girlie about them! They're about dreams and feelings. Guys have dreams and feelings don't they? And dreams are bizarre. Weird. Just like songs are sometimes. And at first they don't seem to make sense, but then you listen to the way the lyrics join with the music and fuse with the emotion in the singer's voice and, all of a sudden, you get it! Come on, Greg! You sing songs. You ought to know that! Use your imagination! Don't be so thick!"

Now Greg was hurt and mad too. He knew he should have tried to smooth things over, tell her that he'd look at her songs again later when he could concentrate on them better. And he should tell her she was right! He did know about weird lyrics. He covered Coldplay all time. Their lyrics never made sense on paper. But in a song? He knew what every one of them was about. How the words were spaced, if they were whispered or shouted, if the voice laughed or cried them out. That's what made the lyrics come alive, made you feel their meaning deep down in your gut, even if you couldn't explain it in your head.

Why did Dixie always have to be right?

Instead he shot back, "I've got a right to my opinion, don't I? I don't like them. I think your songs suck!"

And when he saw Dixie's face get all red and tears start to form in the corners of her eyes, he still didn't shut that hole in his face. "And how do you know I didn't already write something on my own? I don't need you to write any freakin' songs for me! What makes you think you're so smart? You're just a nothing clerk at The Dollar Store!"

With tears streaming down her face, Dixie wrenched the papers, her songs, out of Greg's hands. "You're an asshole!" she shrieked. She turned and flew out of the bar and into the night.

After that, everything changed. Greg tried to call Dixie, but she wouldn't answer. He sent her texts but she didn't respond.

i m sorry

i luv u

i mis u

Things weren't much good without Dixie around. He felt like crap. His singing was crap. The shows were crap. His favorite 'Here's the Beef' burger was crap. Everything was crap.

When Dixie's name finally showed up on his phone several weeks later, he was so eager that he almost dropped it. And after the call, he did drop it. She hadn't called to say hello, let's get back together. She had called to say goodbye. Dixie was leaving town.

Tears started to sting his eyes but he tried to hold them off. Famous rock stars didn't bawl. Actually, they did ball! Quite a lot from what he'd heard, with all those groupies around and all. Hahaha – B. A. W. L. and B. A. L. L. What did they call that? A double entendre or something?

He smiled but only for a moment. All his smiles turned to frowns these days. All days were worthless days without Dixie. What good was anything without his Dixie? His fluffy little Dixie Chickie?

Maybe he could write a song after all. Without. That's what he'd call it. Without.

Poetic License

PREMONITION? (Lyrics)

I had a dream, an unreal dream
It was so surreal
But it was so clear
There was an apartment
Our apartment in the city
I had forgotten it was there

The morning sun
Upon my eyes
Wakes me from my sleep
I had a dream

Solid walnut trim framing ocean blue walls
Smooth granite counter tops
In speckled creams and tans and browns
A brick kitchen floor and a gleaming oak table
Muted lighting like the setting sun through a lace curtain

The morning sun
Upon my eyes
Wakes me from my sleep
I had a dream

Bullet holes in the window, in the wall
Leftovers from the spaghetti dinner
Still in the fridge
Is it a premonition?

Of life?
Of death?
I think my grandmother's waiting there
Of heaven?

The morning sun
Upon my eyes
Wakes me from my sleep
My dreams rise up like silvery smoke
Only mine to keep
For an instant?
Not this dream
This dream stayed

Chapter 6

LICENSE TO COME AND GO

Splash, splash, rub, spray, drip, splash. Odd sounds drifted into Joe's ears as he slept. They had been living in the little yellow house on Crown Cove Lane with their nutcase of a dog, Button. The house was prone to having squeaks and pings and creaks. Nighttime was the domain for sounds such as these. But the strange sounds he was hearing now were only strange because they were – normal!

Joe opened his eyes and blinked, stared at the alarm clock and blinked and stared again. Four A.M. What was he hearing? Lainey! Where was Lainey? She wasn't in the bed next to him and she wasn't in the comfy chair in the corner of the bedroom either. She'd been sleeping in that chair a lot lately when her blimp of a stomach gave her a backache and made it hard for her to sleep in the bed.

Joe groggily got up and shuffled down the hall. There was Button, all curled up in his doggie bed, with his tail over his nose, squirrel like. He shuffled a little further down the hall and there was Lainey in the bathroom, her face as bright as a sunbeam, wearing rubber gloves and brandishing a sponge. She was cleaning!

"What the heck are you doing, Lainey? It's four in the morning!"

"It's the nesting instinct! I'm trying to make things perfect for the baby. I think I'm in labor!" she said with her voice glowing.

Can a voice glow? Well, Lainey's did.

And fifteen hours later, on that April day twenty years ago, his six pound three ounce golden haired nugget was born – Dixie Margarette Andrews.

Slam, bump, stamp, zip, crinkle, stamp. Odd sounds drifted into Joe's ears as he dozed on the couch, the newspaper in his lap. Lainey and the boys hadn't gotten back from karate lessons yet and Dixie had gone out to the bar to watch her boyfriend's band. What were these sounds he was hearing? Was that Dixie home early?

He got up and hurried into the kitchen. It was Dixie, teary faced, yanking papers out of her purse, crumpling them and flinging them through the air to bounce off the wall and land on the kitchen floor.

"Dixie? What's going on?"

"Greg. Said. They. Sucked!" With each word she crumpled another page, drew back her arm and hurled the paper with all her might.

"Alright now, alright. Calm down." Joe took Dixie's elbow and guided her into a kitchen chair. "Tell me what happened."

"I wrote some songs for Greg's jackass band and he said they sucked. He wants to be a rock star. Well, he's not going anywhere! That jerk. Cause he doesn't even try! And then he said I was a nothing! A stupid loser! It's him that's the stupid loser! He's a freakin' jackass!" Dixie was livid, furious, fuming. And then she started to cry.

Joe pushed a box of tissues across the table and Dixie grabbed one after the other, wiping her tears and blowing her nose over and over again.

He began to pick up the scattered papers from the kitchen floor. He smoothed them out and set them on the table. "Well, I know one thing, Dixie. You are definitely not stupid. You are the smartest girl I know. Grapehead doesn't know what he's talking about."

"Dad, his name's Greg, not Grapehead!" And as she said it she wondered why she was defending Greg? Out of habit, she guessed.

"I don't know.... He does have purple hair. And his last name is Grapensteter. Soooo, that sounds like a grapehead to me!!" Joe teased.

Dixie laughed, just a little bit, and then she sighed. "Maybe he's right. Maybe I am a joke. The only job I can get is at the crappy

Dollar Store. Nobody else wants to hire me. I've sent out gazillions of applications, resumes and portfolios and nothing ever comes of it. Maybe I'm just not good enough."

"Dixie, that's not true at all. You're like a crucible where talent, charisma and magic have all combined together to reach their apex! You keep searching those job postings. Keep sending out applications. It'll happen. It will! And, believe me, whoever gets ahold of you will soon realize that they hit the jackpot."

Dixie blushed and grinned, pleased, yet embarrassed with all the praise. "Oh Dad. You're just saying that because you're my father. More like if anyone ever hires me they'll soon realize that they've been duped."

"Come on now. Your mother and I are not the only ones that think you are marvelous beyond words. You graduated with honors. Your teachers gave you the highest recommendations. Don't let that buffoon of a boyfriend change your frame of mind."

He took her tenderly by the shoulders and kissed her cheek. "You are a very talented girl, Dixie. Never give up. It will happen."

After that day, Joe saw a renewed aggressiveness in Dixie's job search. She was more focused, more determined. She followed up on every application, investigated every lead. Two weeks later, after a total of nine months of searching, she finally landed a job - Creative Assistant at a small television station upstate.

Joe's little golden nugget, Dixie Margarette Andrews, was leaving the nest.

Poetic License

TO GROW AWAY

A baby is born so precious and small
Unable to do a thing
Except cry when she is hungry
Or needing anything

You hold them to you closely
To love and protect with all your might
You know what you have to do
Prepare them for that distant someday
When they grow up and away from you

You teach them how to walk and talk
You teach them the colors and the shapes
Red and blue, round and square
And the sounds that the animals make

You teach them the difference
Between their elbows and their knees
And how to use the toilet
When they have to take a pee
Right from wrong, good from bad, weak from strong
How to share their toys
And how to get along

You teach them to respect and to obey
How to sort the laundry
How to fry an egg
How to save their money

For a rainy day
Because you know its nature's plan
For them to go away

And when that day arrives
As they're heading out the door
As you long to hold them closely
For just a little bit more
You'll know you've done your job
You've done what's right and true
You have taught them how
To grow away from you

Chapter 7

THOUGHTS ADRIFT LICENSE

A refreshingly gentle breeze played with Boyd's hair as he sat in his favorite Adirondack chair, mug of coffee in hand, surveying his 'estate'.

Boyd loved his yard. He and Pam had turned it from the disaster that it was into the envy of the neighborhood. They had ripped down the rotting wooden fence that had been covered in decrepit ivy, dug out overgrown bushes and shrubs, pulled bushel upon bushel of weeds and trimmed dead branches from trees.

Now, it was a wonder to behold! Something was always in bloom. An ever changing kaleidoscope of color! In the spring, the Snowdrift crabapple was like a pure white cloud in their front yard. There were purple lilacs, yellow forsythias, red tulips and the pink tipped leaves on the dappled willows. In summer, the climbing hydrangea on the new cedar fence bloomed with flowers white as snow. There were daisies and black-eyed susans, geraniums and lilies, petunias and marigolds. And in the fall, chrysanthemums, asters and the flaming red leaves on the Autumn Blaze maple. It took your breath away.

Then they had put in the patio. Talk about work! First, they had dug out the area where the patio was to go. Next, 250 wheelbarrows full of crusher run and another 250 wheelbarrows full of stone dust had gone down. Then, 330 concrete paver blocks at forty pounds each! His back had ached for weeks. But he wouldn't have done it any other way. His patio was his pride and joy.

There was nothing better after a hard day's work than to pop the top on a nice cold beer and sit on his patio relaxing in the shade.

He wouldn't be popping the tops on any cold ones tonight though! Not after last night. Oh, man, what a good time they'd had. How would he describe that movie? Raunchy. Raunchy and hilarious!

They were slapping the arms of their seats right from the start, when the proverbial 'dumb blonde' chick came rushing out the door. Her friend had set her up on a blind date and she running late. She hops in her car and goes whizzing down the road with one hand on the wheel and her eyes glued to her mirror, trying to put on lipstick and eyeliner. (Just like the idiot that had nearly run Boyd off the road the other day). Next, she's struggling to pull some book out of her purse and trying to prop it up behind the steering wheel. The book? 'Ten Ways To Trim Your Bush – From The Simple To The Elegant'.

She fumbles around in her purse again, throws her leg up on the dashboard, and that's when they really started roaring. Roaring and gaping. She was trying to shave her panty-less hoo haa. And the camera zoomed right in. Should she go for the Bermuda Triangle or the Landing Strip?

Finally she arrived at the blind date's apartment, unbelievably in one piece, and the dude asks her, "Have you ever had Italian sausage in the can?"

"I didn't know it came in a can!"

"Oh, it does. It does."

"Bottoms Up!"

Oh my god. That flick chick may have been dumb as a brick, but she sure was flexible!

Afterwards, at Dexter's Bar and Grill, they were still laughing! 'Bottoms up!' Josh would shout and they'd all down their brewskis and chasers like they were drinking water. And then they'd all burp. PJ had almost split his pants. Before they knew it, they were all totally wasted. Except Tony. He had kids to set a good example for – Daisy who was five and little Bower who was almost three. The last thing he wanted was to have his kids see him shit faced.

Tony sure did love those kids. He talked about them all the time.

Little Bower was a meat lover only he pronounced meat 'meap'. His favorite was boneless chicken strips with barbeque sauce and he could eat more of them than Tony could! Bower was always dragging the pots and pans out of the cabinet and banging on them like drums. He had a little toy lawn mower and he would go back and forth in the yard with it. 'I howp daady,' he'd say.

Little Daisy loved her stuffed animals. She would arrange them all along the back of the couch and then tell Tony the name of each one. The fawn was named Anna, the duckling was Jack and the elf was Emerson. She was always doing cartwheels and handstands and she liked to dress up like a princess.

Every night when Tony put Daisy to bed she'd ask the same question 'When will it be morning time?'

And Tony would always give her the same answer 'When you wake up in the morning, it will be morning time.' And after that, she'd fall right to sleep!

He was a great guy, that Tony, one of Boyd's truest friends!

It must have been Tony that had dropped him off home last night but he couldn't remember getting home at all. Boyd did remember spilling beer all over Josh and then laughing like a lunatic. The next thing he remembered after that was waking up on the kitchen floor and Pam calling him Mister Dragon Breath.

His Pam. The love of his life. She had fixed him coffee and asked if he wanted anything to eat even though she was headed out the door to work. And when there was work to do, she didn't just sit there watching him strip wall paper and pull out rotting tree trunks while she polished her nails and pointed at all the other things that still needed to be done. She was right there next to him, in dirty jeans and an old tee shirt, helping him get the job done.

He'd have to fix something extra special for dinner tonight, let her know how much he loved her and appreciated her and everything she did.

Sure, Tony, Josh and PJ were his good friends alright.

But his best friend was Pam.

Poetic License

A GLASS OF ALE

A load of nails
A load of hail
A load of salt
A load of mail
And a glass of ale

Hard work
Hard weather
Hard sweat
Hard bills
And aaaaaah

Chapter 8

DOG LICENSE

Owen couldn't figure out what the big deal was. He could hear his mother crying in the next room. Or was she laughing?

Owen shook his head. It wasn't like his sister Dixie had died or anything! She was just moving into her own apartment. That wasn't anything to cry about. Not like when Astrid had died.

His Mom always told the story of how she was eight months pregnant with him and Gabriel when she had walked down the street to the neighbor's to see the new litter of puppies. And when she walked back home she had a tiny black pup in the palm of her hand. That was Astrid!

Mom said that every morning when she got up she could see with her naked eye that Astrid had actually grown bigger during the night. She grew bigger and bigger and bigger until she ended up weighing one hundred pounds!

A few weeks after Mom brought Astrid home, he himself had been born. And seven minutes after that, there came Gabe! With him and Gabe and Astrid being so close in age, it was almost like they were triplets. But none of them looked the same because Owen and Gabe were fraternal twins and Astrid, of course, was a dog. Owen often wished that he and Gabe were identical though. What tricks they could play on people if no one could tell them apart! And Owen and Gabe were all about playing tricks.

Astrid was only ten years old when she had died last year but even though ten was young for a human, Dad said it was getting on in years for a big Lab/Shepherd/Samoyed/Husky mix like Astrid.

Up until the day she died, there hadn't been a day in his life that Astrid hadn't been there – helping him eat his cereal, chewing on one end of her puppy toy while Owen chewed on the other, chasing Dad's good tennis balls that Owen threw for her in the back yard or just laying still while Owen hugged her and buried his face in the soft thick fur on the back of her scruffy neck. Nothing seemed the same after Astrid died. He felt lost without her around.

They had buried her in the back yard under the tree that she liked to lay under to get out of the sun. She was wrapped in a soft old blanket to keep her warm and they put some of her favorite toys with her to keep her company. Dixie read a poem she had written about how wonderful Astrid was and how lucky everyone in heaven was to have her with them now. They had all cried their eyes out. And even days or weeks later, just when they thought they were done crying, something else would set them off again.

Like when Owen found Astrid's toy gorilla under the couch. He got all choked up and tears started rolling down his cheeks.

Mom had started sobbing when a bunch of Astrid's loose dog hairs appeared out of nowhere and went floating around on the kitchen floor like a tumbleweed. And he had found Gabe blubbering behind the shed holding one of Astrid's chewed up tennis balls in his hands.

Dad came up with the idea of hanging a plaque on the tree as a remembrance to Astrid. He found a place online that could make the plaque and they sent them a drawing of Astrid that Owen had done himself, which had looked exactly like her, along with some words that Mom had written. The plaque turned out awesome!

ASTRID

BELOVED FAMILY DOG

HER SPIRIT WILL STAY HERE IN THIS YARD
TO ROMP AND PLAY
FOREVER IN OUR HEARTS

SHE WILL REMAIN
ALWAYS OUR PUP
ALWAYS OUR GUARDIAN AND PROTECTOR

He really missed Astrid. He looked at that plaque on the tree whenever he was in the back yard.

Would he miss Dixie? Maybe a little. Who were they going to play tricks on now without Dixie around?

"Gabe! Gabe! Dixie just left!" Owen whispered loudly, kicking the upper bunk to wake his brother.

"So," Gabe mumbled sleepily

"Did you put the spiders in her suitcase?"

Gabe bolted upright in his bed and sat there, a wide grin spreading across his face. "That I did, big bro. That I did!"

"Awesome! Yah, baby, yah!"

Chapter 9

LICENSE FOR DESTINY

What was it about that young girl that made her stick in her mind so? Pam wondered as she cleared the dishes from one of the tables at Fitzpatrick's.

She was awfully cute with her blue/green eyes and honey blond hair. But that wasn't it. Maybe it was because she had been so hungry! She had devoured that big lunch and then had a donut too! And she was just a little spit of a thing. Or maybe it was because she had seemed so confident and was so vivacious and animated. But at the same time she seemed defenseless and unprotected. Whatever it was, Pam had found herself thinking about that girl all day.

She'd be waiting for a customer to decide what they wanted to order and there was that lively face in her mind's eye. She'd be carrying plates of burgers with onions rings and hot roast beef sandwiches and find herself wondering where that girl had been going or if she had gotten there safely. 'You'd think I was her mother!' Pam chuckled to herself.

Pam didn't have any kids. Not yet anyway. She and Boyd hadn't felt ready for kids when they first got married. They had purchased the house on Elm Street, which had been in a terrible state of disrepair. It was a fixer upper if there ever was one. That's the only reason they could afford it! They had done all the work themselves – stripping and painting, digging and planting, repairing and replacing. It had taken them years to get that house in shape. And then her father had gotten sick – the dreaded cancer.

She had helped as much as she could, taking him to doctor's appointments and to chemotherapy, cleaning his apartment, cooking his meals. He fought back and he fought back hard but in the end the cancer won. He had died last July, so thin he looked like a victim from a concentration camp. It was like the cancer had dissolved the flesh right off his bones. He had missed his sixty-first birthday on August first by four days.

"Pam! Pam! Your order's up! Get with it girl!" the cook yelled from the grill, snapping Pam out of her reverie.

She wiped a tear from her cheek, smoothed her apron and fixed a smile on her face. Get with it girl is right! What's up with me today? And she rushed to grab the grilled cheese sandwiches and smothered chicken specials that her customers were waiting for. Delivered with a smile! That's the way you do it!

At the end of her shift, Pam walked out of the diner and lifted her face to the sun. She could feel the sun's warmth radiate through her body all the way down to her toes. She could feel the sun's brightness reflected in the smile that grew ever bigger on her own face. Pam always felt like she had an eject button. When the sun touched her, any cares she had ejected right out of her and melted away. She scrounged around in her purse till she felt the jingle of her keys, got in her dear old Pontiac firebird and headed for home.

The enticing aroma of charcoal grilled meat tickled Pam's nose from the end of the street and when she pulled into the driveway, she could see the smoke from their backyard barbeque rising above the top of the house. That Boyd!! She had been a little leery about his promise to cook dinner. He had gotten awfully drunk out with his friends last night. But her darling man was true to his word.

"Boyd, I'm home!" she announced as she walked in the front door, down the hall, and into the kitchen.

Boyd had on the big oven mitts and was putting a muffin tray into the oven. "Hi Honey! I'm making your favorite – popovers! How was your day?"

"Busy! It always is on a Saturday." She walked over and gave him a kiss. "Looks like you're all recuperated after your escapades last night, huh?"

He put his arms around her neck, oven mitts and all, and kissed her. "Yup, all recuperated. Dragon breath is gone and everything!"

He gave her a sheepish, apologetic grin. "I'm sorry."

"You don't have to be sorry, Boyd. It's good to let it all hang out sometimes. Everybody needs to do that now and then. It adds spice to your life! But spice can be a tricky thing. The right amount adds zing and zest. Add too much though, and it just ruins it!"

"Well, I won't be adding any 'spice' to my life for a while. At least not tonight anyway! I did get a nice bottle of wine for you though. I'm just going to drink ice tea. I'll drink it in a wine glass - for ambiance!"

"Need any help?"

"Nope! It's all under control. You go get changed or whatever else you want to do and dinner will be ready in about an hour."

Pam got washed up, changed, and went out onto the patio. The patio table was set with placemats, a vase with flowers picked from the garden and even coordinating napkins. Boyd's meal was superb. In addition to the popovers, there was a grilled beef tenderloin served au jus, roasted corn on the cob with the husk all charred and smoky and some of the kernels charred too – just the way she liked it. And a fresh cucumber and dill salad. He even had the flyswatter off to the side, in case any bees or flies came around trying to land on their food and drive them crazy.

"Boyd! This is so stupendously marvelous! You never fail to amaze me!"

The evening was perfect - the wine, the food, the conversation. Boyd told Pam about the hilarious movie he had seen with the guys last night and Pam told Boyd about the man who had ordered three double cheeseburgers and about the young blond haired girl who just wouldn't leave her mind.

Afterwards, they took their traditional night time walk around the neighborhood and then settled on the couch to watch some TV.

"Boyd, I think I'm ready. Are you ready?" Pam suddenly blurted out.

"Ready? Ready for what?"

"A baby. I think it's time. Let's have a baby, Boyd."

"What?" Unbelievable! Are you serious? Ha!"

Pam couldn't decipher his reaction. His words sounded against but his tone sounded for.

"So, you think it's a bad idea?" she ventured, trying not to sound too disappointed.

"Oh! No! It's just... I just can't believe it! I've been thinking the same thing!"

"You were?"

Boyd gave her that playful, disarming grin of his. He leapt up and pulled her up next to him, hugging her close and kissing her ear.

"It must be destiny then," he whispered.

Chapter 10

LICENSE TO BE DIXIE

Sweetbriar….. Meadowbrook……. Oakview!!!! There it was!!! Oakview!!! Fifty-three Oakview!!!

Dixie parked, ran up to the door, turned the key in the lock and dashed inside, a flurry of excitement as she darted about from living/dining room to kitchen to bedroom to bathroom. She looked out every window, looked in every drawer and cabinet. She flushed the toilet, looked in the fridge, sat in every chair and sprawled out on the bed.

This was so awesome, so cool, so hers!

If she didn't want to vacuum, she wouldn't! If she wanted to leave dirty dishes and empty pizza boxes all over, she would! If she put a piece of cherry pie in the fridge to save till tomorrow, it would still be there tomorrow! There was no one to tell her to do the laundry or empty the garbage. There were no annoying brothers to scream in her ears or hide her shoes behind the compost pile.

So totally, insanely awesome!

Since Dixie owned no furniture, she had rented a furnished apartment. It even came with curtains and a microwave. Not exactly the height of fashion but it would do until she could save up enough money from her new job to be able to afford items with more panache. For now, she'd just get some things to hang on the walls, some decorative pillows, a throw, and maybe some plants, to affix her signature to the place and give it the Dixie look. And the first place she'd look would be The Dollar Store!

She went back out to the Jetta and starting lugging in her stuff, such as it was – the essentials that she would need right away. One box held a couple of pots and pans, and some dishes nestled among the sheets and towels. Another box had a few food items so she wouldn't starve till she went grocery shopping - granola bars, juice boxes, a box of Apple Jacks, Ramen Noodles and a can of cashew nuts. There was a waste basket packed with dish soap, bathroom cleaner, rubber gloves and toilet paper. Her laundry basket was filled with her lap top, I-Pod and a small 19" flat screen TV all surrounded by a protective layer of some of her clothes. The rest of her clothes were packed in a couple of suitcases. Then there was her pillow and, most importantly, Godfrey, her well-worn stuffed monkey that she had slept with every night since she was three.

Maybe she hadn't packed much, but by the time she got it all into the apartment, and after her long drive, she was exhausted. And starved! It had been hours ago that she had stopped at that cute little diner for lunch.

Dixie located the box with the food, pulled out the box of Apple Jacks and sat down at the dinette table. As she sat munching on the cereal and gazing out at the bright, sunny afternoon, she took out her cellphone and dialed home.

"Hi Mom! I'm here! Safe and sound!"

"Hi Honey! Wonderful! How'd everything go? How was your drive? Did you have any trouble finding the place?"

"Nope, no problems at all. I didn't get lost once. I even stopped for lunch at this diner all decorated with roosters and got a rooster pin. Everything's working out great!"

"Wonderful! So, how's the apartment? Is it nice? Is it clean?"

"Yeah! It's really awesome!"

"That's great, Dixie! You're probably pretty tired after that long drive, huh?"

"Yeah, but I'm just so psyched! I even got everything out of the car already. All I need to do is unpack and put things away."

"Wow! Well, it sure sounds like you've got everything under control. I should let you go so you can get yourself all settled. Listen, you take care! Don't overdo it! Make sure you give yourself time to relax. I love you, Dixie."

"I love you too. Don't worry about me, Mom. I'll be just fine. Say 'Hi' to Dad for me and tell him I love him too."

"Ok Honey. Bye now."

"Bye Mom."

Dixie smiled at the thought of her mother rushing off to find her dad to tell him that she had reached her destination in one piece, and continued her munching. The sun on her face felt like a warm caress. What a gorgeous day. And the complex really looked nice with all the trees and bushes and flowers. Directly across from her window was a little garden full of petunias of all colors - pink, yellow, orange, red, and some really cute white and purple striped ones.

Purple. Greg.

He had been so glad to hear her voice when she had called him that day to give him the news.

"Dixie?" He had been uncertain at first. Could it possibly be happening? Was she really calling him?

And then, "Dixie!" His voice had almost sparkled. She could picture his eyes lighting up.

And next, "Dixie." His voice a soft sigh of relief and redemption, thinking that Dixie was coming back and that his heart ache was finally over.

But she had been cold and to the point. "I just thought you should know. I'm leaving town on Saturday. Good bye, Greg." and she had hung up, not even giving him the chance to say one single word.

As soon as those words had slid like ice from her mouth, she felt her own heart seize up. She could picture his jaw dropping, aghast; His mouth, only moments before smiling, now curving down, an open gap in his stunned face.

How could she have been so frigid? He deserved more than that. After all, they'd been together for four years, since she was a kid of sixteen. She almost hit redial. Her finger was poised over the button. But she didn't do it. Coward.

He had made her so upset, so hurt and angry. But the fact was, she was as much to blame for their big argument as he was. She had been just as stubborn and inflexible as he had been. And then, when he tried to apologize, she hadn't returned any of his calls or texts. The old silent treatment. Infantile.

But the fact also was that she had been getting tired of the relationship anyway. It was always the same thing - him singing the same tired songs, at the same dumpy bars, with the same lame purple hair. It was the same conversations and the same positions. Greg did have aspirations but he lacked the ambition to do anything about them. Dixie wanted someone dynamic and inspired. Someone that made her feel propelled, not held back. And Greg just wasn't that person.

She should get up the nerve and call him. Apologize for her bankruptcy of feeling and tell him why it was over between them. Wish him well in his quest for the elusive stardom. Maybe she'd do it later tonight when she knew he'd be packing up after his gig at the bar.

Dixie sighed and picked up the box of Apple Jacks to take it back out to the kitchen. It would be the first thing in her barren cupboard! But wait, what was this taped to the back? An envelope! 'For Dixie', it said. Inside the envelope, a card - 'A Gift For You'.

Dixie opened the card and out fell a check - for $500!

> Darling Dixie,
>
> There will be so many things you will need to turn your new apartment from a 'place' into a 'home'. Here's a little something to get you started.
>
> Congratulations on your new job! The world is your oyster! If anyone can find the pearls, it's you.
>
> We are so proud of you!
>
> Lots of Love,
> Your Parental Units

Dixie felt a tug at her heartstrings. There were no parents more spectacularly awesome than hers. They were the absolute best! She had to call and thank them but first she wanted to get unpacked and organized.

She opened one of her suitcases and let out a shriek!

"Owen!!! Gabriel!!!" she screamed as she started hopping from foot to foot and waving her arms around her head like a crazy woman.

There were strandy webs in her suitcase! And spiders! Damn it. God damn it! Couldn't her brothers have given her a nice send off? What was the matter with them? Spiders! Horrible, icky spiders! How could they!

Dixie put on some rubber gloves, unrolled sheet after sheet of toilet paper into a huge ball and squeamishly tried to brush away the webs and squash the spiders. But the webs were only strands of cotton, and the spiders, life like as they were, were only rubbery counterfeits.

And then Dixie noticed there was a rolled up note woven into the fake webs.

Gotcha! One last time, we gotcha!

O and G

At the bottom of the note was a row of sticker hearts and goofy puckered lips.

There was that tug at her heartstrings again. Dixie smiled and chuckled, rubbing her hands through her hair and across her face. Life would be a lot less dramatic without those nutty, deranged brothers of hers around, pulling her strings and pressing her buttons.

Hey, what was this lump in her throat? Why were her cheeks wet? My god, she had only been gone half a day and she was homesick already.

Chapter 11

HONEYMOON LICENSE

'Our Honeymoon' – Lainey pulled the leather embossed album down off the shelf and began flipping the pages. The photos never failed to bring a smile to her face.

There was 'The Celebration' at port, an impressive twelve stories tall, glistening in the sun, so white against the blue ocean. "Welcome Aboard!"

There was Lainey diving into the pool. Then there was Lainey bolting out of the water, rubbing her tearing, squinty eyes, with her tongue out, spitting and sputtering. Oh no! Salt water!

There was Joe, golden, lying in the creamy sand at the water's edge. And Joe with the blue swimming goggles and snorkeling gear, holding a fishy morsel out to a sting ray. And Joe, with his foot in the stirrup trying to hoist himself up onto his waiting steed.

There they were all dressed up for the Captain's Dinner, Lainey looking gorgeous in the emerald green gown with the bows at the shoulder and Joe so debonair in his pinstripe suit. And there they were, comically oversized gloves on their hands, duking it out in the boxing ring.

There was the frog and the swan, the giraffe and the pig. Towel origami! A different animal left on their bed each night.

That was 'The Honeymoon'. Next up was 'Honeymoon #1' with a picture of them eating the top tier of their wedding cake that had been in the freezer for a year. It had, surprisingly, still tasted good! 'Honeymoon #5' had a picture of Joe and Lainey at their favorite restaurant, Emeralds, with little baby Dixie sleeping in her infant seat next to them. For 'Honeymoon #14' Lainey was in the kitchen preparing a special anniversary dinner, her pregnant belly jet plane sized, just before the twins were born.

With pictures for each anniversary, the album was much more than 'Our Honeymoon'. It was a yearly chronicle of their lives together and the progression of their family. She had new pictures ready to enter into the album now, 'Honeymoon #25', their silver anniversary!

Lainey couldn't fathom how twenty-five years could have gone by so quickly. She could remember like it was yesterday the first time she had ever laid eyes on Joe Andrews. He was walking through her friend Babs' kitchen, deep in conversation with Babs' brother, Craig.

My god he was handsome with his curly dark hair and brown eyes, his long eye lashes and his leather jacket. A thrill squeezed her stomach. Fizzy tingles zipped like electricity through her veins.

"Who was that?" She had asked, nonchalant, as if the question was nothing more than casual small talk.

But she wasn't fooling Babs! Babs had seen her face light up, had heard the wild thumping of her heart.

"You like him don't you! Is it love at first sight?"

Babs had teased her, mercilessly. But Cupid's arrow really had struck! It was love at first sight! Fifteen months later, Lainey was skipping from the church with Joe at her side, smiling and laughing, as the confetti rained down around them.

Well, they do say that time flies when you're having fun. And they certainly had plenty of fun times alright; days both simple and grand, to be remembered and cherished always. Not to say there were never any bad times. Times when they argued and bickered and the divorce word had popped into their heads and echoed around in their brains.

But echoes are only hollow imitations that peter out and disappear. Love is durable. It inks its' way into everything and colors it warm. It shoves out the bad times like an unwelcome guest that no one has an affinity for and never wants to see again.

Lainey picked up the pictures she was about to enter into the Honeymoon album and chuckled. They'd had such a good time last weekend. Gabe and Owen had been at a sleepover hosted by their karate teacher and Dixie was in her own apartment now, so the whole house had been theirs. And they had done whatever they wanted, wherever they wanted!

There was Joe (her better half) pouring champagne into the delicate green antique flutes that her parents had given them as a wedding gift. There was Lainey, eating a slice of fresh pear topped with earthy brie. And Lainey, dancing in the dappled sunlight under the maple tree.

There was Joe (the father of her children) popping the cork on the second bottle of champagne, a sly glint in his eye. There was Lainey, an 'Oh my god! I forgot!' expression on her face. And there was the garlic bread, very crisp and very black.

There was Joe (her anchor to the world) smoke billowing around him as he turned the steaks over on the grill.

And there was Joe (the love of her life) lips pursed, blowing her a kiss.

Poetic License

SILVER

The light reflected in your eyes
A silver glint

The morning dew
A silver drop on tips of grasses bent

Virgin snow in yards of white
Glitters silvery

On your head
Silver salt mixed in with peppery

Silver gold round our fingers
To mark the special day

Then till now
Twenty-five years
Our silver anniversary

Chapter 12

LICENSE TO BE GREG

Sweetbriar…….. Meadowbrook……… Oakview. Eureka! There it was.

Greg parked his Chevy and sat there, running his hands through his sandy brown hair, his eyes glued to the green door with the gold fifty-three on it.

His fingers inched towards the door handle and then he pulled them back, inched towards the key to restart the car. Again, he pulled them back.

This was a mistake. His brain must have been fried when he came up with this moronic idea. What a crock.

He hadn't seen Dixie since the argument - the argument that was the end of them and the start of everything else in his life toppling around him. And he hadn't talked to her since the day she had called him from her new place to apologize for being a heartless, frigid bitch at the end (her words, not his) and explain why it was that she didn't want him anymore. Alive, fresh, dynamic, enterprising, ambitious were the words that had flown out of her mouth to describe what she wanted and what Greg apparently didn't have.

"You want to be a star?" she had said. "You've got to get the fire up your ass! You've got to be special! Work at it Greg! I wish you well."

Depressed was not a strong enough word to describe how he had felt. It was like the nuts and bolts of him were coming unwelded, pinging and popping as they hit the floor.

And as if that wasn't enough, Vinifera fell apart as well. Pete's wife had just had a baby and Pete wanted to spend more time with his family. Eli had decided he wanted to go off to college to study law. And that had left Greg with nothing – no Dixie, no band, no life. Nothing. Because music and singing and being with Dixie were what he was all about. The only thing he still had was his boring day job - transporting specimens between doctor's offices and collection centers to the hospital for analysis.

Dixie's words echoed around in his head every day. Work at it, fired up, enterprising. These were things he had to be to get back something akin to a life. He couldn't just sit around like a zombie dope. Something had to change.

So Greg had gotten a couple of guys together and started a new band. Stump was the band's name and he was stumped all right. Stumped as to why they called it that. The other jokers had suggested it and he had just gone along with it like a blind jackass being pulled along by its bridle, the bit an unnatural hardness chaffing the corners of its mule mouth and covered with spit.

But they went around and got gigs at the bars and clubs and he sang the covers, just like he had done with Vinifera.

And it turned out he had groupies! Girls who hung by the stage and stared at him with dreamy eyes and flirty smiles. They must have been hanging around when he was with Vinifera too but he had never noticed them nor paid a bit of attention to them. Because he had been with Dixie. But now here they were giggling and jiggling with their skinny jeans and skimpy tops, practically throwing themselves at him, hotter to get into his pants then he was to get into theirs!

He went out with a few of them a couple of times. There was Evelyn who laughed too loud, couldn't stand Bruce Springsteen and didn't even know who David Bowie was! And Fatimah who always smelled like cigarettes and who could switch from laughing to crying to laughing again and then crying again as if she had a switch on her someplace that Greg kept bumping by mistake.

They were all tramps, not worth the feeling that he was losing his dignity and values every time he was with them, not even worth wasting his boner on. And not a one of them was as fluffy as his little Dixie Chickie.

So now here he sat, outside her apartment. He glanced at the folder on the seat next to him. It was full of songs. Original songs. His songs. He thought they were good but how did he know if they really were? This question had dogged him for months now. He had been afraid to sing them on stage, afraid even to show them to his brothers and erstwhile band members. The songs were personal and intimate, exposing him like a naked infant through the glass eye of a projector onto a huge screen above his head.

Dixie was the only one he felt he could trust with his bare naked soul. She would know if his songs were worthy. She was the smart one, the creative one, the one with the education and the degree. The one with the curls he used to run his hands through and the blue/green eyes that used to sparkle and shine when she looked at him. She was the one he still hadn't gotten over. The one he still loved.

Poetic License

WITHOUT (Lyrics)

Had the morning started out
Any different from another?
Life's dreams, all shattered
Lay surrounding me and laughing
At my innocence and naivety

Morning sky opens pink
On a worthless day
All days are worthless days
Since you went away
I am without

Sun
Tries to bore a hole into my ice cold heart
Tries to push through the pain and the sorrow
Tries to bring a smile to my lips
If only for a little while

Worthless efforts
On a worthless day
I am without

Without happiness
Without purpose
Without love
Without you

Where is the hand to pull me from these depths?
My own hand has grown weak
Will no one come and rescue me?
Help me glue back the shards of my dreams

What is it that I said?
What is it that I didn't say?
What is it that I did
Or didn't do
That made you go away?

Now I am without you

Chapter 13

REALIZATION LICENSE

D ixie's little blurb for the nightly newscast about take-out food had sky rocketed into a full-fledged fun filled high jinx of a competition! Every restaurant in town wanted in on the game. It was a chance to gain recognition for their establishment and carve out a name for themselves as "Best Take-Out in Town".

Hundreds of places had called to make sure they were on the list and Dixie quickly realized she could not handle this project all on her own. They would have to cart her out in a wagon like a heifer if she did! So she had enlisted the help of several of her co-workers - Mike, Hilary, Dee Dee and the very handsome Jay. Jay reminded her in many ways of Greg – the way he laughed, the way he walked, the way he brushed his hair out of his eyes – but Dixie tried not to think about that.

The five of them sampled take-out foods running the gambit from airy pastries, scrambled eggs, chopped salad with warm beets and goat cheese and Kansas City burgers to French fried zucchini.

They all got together every morning, over take-out breakfasts, of course, to go over their notes and judge the foods based on accessibility, transportability, value and, most importantly, flavor. Dixie always tried to either sit next to Jay, so she could 'accidentally' brush against him, or across from Jay, so she could snatch glimpses of his hunky visage and give him coy, flirtatious looks. Nothing seemed to draw his attention to her any more than to anyone else though. And she was starting to think that maybe, just maybe, the handsome Jay was gay.

Every Friday Dixie would present their findings to an ever-growing, anxious audience and the gavel would descend to elect the winner of the week. The plan was for all the weekly winners to then be entered into the grand finale race to the finish when the king of the take-out food empire would be declared.

Most nights, on her way home from work, Dixie would stop at one restaurant or another to pick up her test subjects. Tonight, she had gotten a falafel filled pita with cucumber and yogurt sauce from Sinbad's, a chicken fajita from Texas Mexas, and edamame from Asia House. Now, here she sat at her little table with the internationally eclectic smorgasbord spread out before her. So far, the edamame was her favorite. She loved the way the beans popped into her mouth as she ran her lips over the warm, salty pod.

As she ate, Dixie gazed out the window, letting her mind wander. The sky was streaked pink, yellow, and orange with the approach of the setting sun, casting a golden glow that seemed to accentuate the colors of the landscaping, propelling them into vivid brilliance.

Her eyes rested, as they always did, on the petunias across from her window. Their vibrant colors always seemed to relax and refresh her after a long day at work. They were like little evangelists, preaching renewal, resetting her creative juices and opening doors in her brain so new ideas could flow in.

Memories flowed in too - memories of the petunias at home that had been one of her chores to weed. Sure, she loved to look at the flowers, but weeding? How she had hated doing it! Sinking her fingers into the damp, grimy dirt was not something she considered a pleasant experience. And having horribly awful millipedes, grotesquely slimy slugs or gruesomely hairy spiders come crawling by would completely gross her out, sending shivers through her spine, and making her jump up and down screaming. She had been ecstatic knowing that, once she moved into her own apartment, her weeding days would be over.

And now that she didn't have to weed, what do you think she did? She weeded! It was like a compulsion! Unfortunate was the weed that Dixie might spot poking its offensive head out from between the lovely petunias. She would run over, stick her fingers into the dirt, grab that sucker as close to the base as she could, jiggle it around a little to loosen its grip and pull it out, roots and all! Seeing that weed dangling limply from her hand gave her such a sense of satisfaction. Victory!

Well, isn't that just the way of it though? Sometimes what you think you want and what you really want are not always the same thing! You think you want a salad but what you really want is a hamburger. You think you want the blue dress but it turns out you really wanted the green one. You think you hate to weed but then you can't wait to rid the garden of the invading nutrient stealers and set the flowers free.

The garden back home was not the only thing those petunias brought memories of. They also reminded her of Greg. It was the purple and white striped ones that did it. They had reminded her of Greg the first time she saw them. They reminded her of Greg every day. She had actually contemplated sneaking over to the garden like a vandal in the night and pulling the purple striped petunias right out of the ground. But how could she possibly? They were her favorites.

It was funny how many things reminded her of Greg. Why was that? She had been the one who broke up with him, not the other way around. But now she found she missed him.

She missed his laugh and his crooked smile, the way he chewed and the way he wolfed down his food. She missed seeing him on stage, belting out a song, tilting his head and swaying his hips. She missed the way he had guided her through a crowd, protecting her from being bumped into or trampled on by jerks that weren't paying attention. She missed the way he burped after having a beer and the way he nibbled on the lobe of her ear.

Even that car parked out there next to the petunias reminded her of Greg. He used to have a car just like it. A Chevy Malibu.

Hey! That Malibu was the same mutated dark red color that Greg's used to be, all faded and oxidized and covered with rust spots.

Imagine that! An almost exact duplicate of Greg's car sitting right here in her parking lot.

Could it actually be Greg's car? No. Why would Greg drive all the way here? They hadn't had any contact since she called him on the day she first moved in. That was months ago! She had told him, she hoped in a nice way, that basically, she thought he was a loser.

Dixie peered through her window at the doppelganger Malibu. The waning light made it hard to see but she was pretty sure someone was sitting inside! Could it really be Greg? Whoever it was didn't seem to have Greg's trademark purple hair, but....

Now, what was it that he used to call his car? The Aardvark! Dixie peered again, trying to read the license plate on the Malibu – ADV 754. ADV = Aardvark.

It was Greg!

She jumped up and ran to her door. She flung it open and ran outside just in time to see the Malibu faltering away, hesitating, as if it was unsure whether it was staying or going. Finally it picked up speed and shot out of the parking lot like it was on fire.

A cerulean sadness filled her. Dixie knew her leaving had destroyed Greg. What she hadn't realized until now was that she had broken her own heart as well.

It had been cracked, held together only by a flimsy membrane of stubbornness and denial. As Dixie watched Greg's car disappear into the distance, that membrane dissolved and the fractured fragments of her heart began to fall apart, leaving her standing there empty, aching and alone.

How could she have been so clueless? So immature? So damn stupid?

Oh yes, sometimes what you thought you wanted and what you really wanted were most definitely not the same thing.

Chapter 14

LICENSE TO BE TOUCHED

It was a mistake. He shouldn't have come. Brain dead moron! Greg's fingers found the keys. He started the car and sped away.

Moments later he pulled into a shopping plaza a mile down the road and parked, right outside The Dollar Store.

Driving for four hours and then immediately turning around and going back? Now that was really being a freaking, jackass, brain dead moron!

Anxiety, frustration and exhaustion clouded Greg's face. He dropped his head, rested it on the steering wheel, and tried to think, to organize the partially constructed, hazy thoughts that hovered in his head like ghosts, waiting to be sucked up by a brain that seemed to have evaporated right out of his skull.

He had to take charge! No losers allowed! He had come to see Dixie and that is what he was going to do.

Again he started the car. Again he parked across from the green door with the number fifty-three on it.

It's now or never, Dude. Now or never.

Dixie stood, arms hanging limply by her side as Greg drove away, her usually bright face dull with regret. She walked slowly back inside and started to clear the table of the Styrofoam boxes containing the remnants of her dinner, food she no longer had any appetite for. A few tears trickled from the corners of her eyes and she wiped them away with the tips of her fingers.

Then she stopped in mid stride, dropping a fork that clattered to the floor, flinging bits of chicken fajita as it fell. Was that a knock on her door? She grabbed a tissue to wipe her teary eyes and blow her nose and listened. Yes, someone was knocking. Maybe it was Dee Dee or Hilary wanting to compare "Take-Out or Leave It" notes. But it was not either one of them.

"Greg!?" Dixie was so surprised that his name tripped all over itself as it burst from her mouth, trying to be an exclamation and a question at the same time. Hadn't she just watched Greg drive away only moments ago? He must have turned around and come back!

"Hi, Dixie. I hope I didn't come at a bad time or anything. I…um…I wanted to see you. I probably should have called first but it was kind of a spur of the moment thing." Greg brushed his hair out of his eyes and waited for some kind of response from Dixie but she just stood there staring at him.

Dixie's heart was racing in her chest. Should she tell him that she had seen his car in the parking lot earlier? Should she tell him how happy and excited she felt when she realized that it was him and of the incredible sadness she had felt watching him drive away? Should she tell him that she missed him? That she was as raw and broken as he was? That she had been a fool and that she loved him still?

She was not that brave.

"So, can I come in?"

"Oh! Yeah! I'm sorry! Sure! Come on in. I'm just so surprised to see you! And I kind of got caught by your hair. No more purple!"

"Yeah, Vinifera broke up so purple just didn't fit anymore. I'm with a new band now." Greg hesitated and shrugged his shoulders. "Stump."

"Stump. Is that the name?"

"Yeah." Greg rolled his eyes and shrugged his shoulders again.

"Covers?" Dixie tried to stop the word from forming, tried to suck it back after it escaped her mouth but it was too late. Cover songs - the topic that had led to the argument that had led to their break-up. How could she have asked that now?

But Greg only nodded, unfazed. He shoved his hands in his pockets, took a deep breath and then let it out slowly. "That's really why I'm here, Dixie. I actually wrote some songs. And I... I wanted you to be the first one to hear them. I wanted to know if you thought they were any good."

"Really? Okay! Sure! I'll listen to them!" And Dixie was surprised again. Greg had written some songs? Unmotivated Greg? The Greg that had assured her, and himself, that he had absolutely no song writing ability? The Greg that had talked endlessly of becoming 'big', 'famous', 'a star' but whose attempts to make that happen added up to a total and complete zero?

"My guitar's out in the car. I'll be right back."

Dixie took several slow deep breaths. She splashed some water on her face and ran her fingers through her hair. Then she went to the window and watched Greg as he walked back to her apartment with his guitar swinging by his side - his jeans showing off his flat stomach and straight hips, sandy brown hair tousled, hazel eyes squinting in the final rays of the setting sun, a stubble just starting to show itself on his chin.

"So, do you want a chair or are you going play standing up?" Dixie asked when Greg returned.

"I'll stand."

Greg strapped on the guitar and looked at Dixie. "Now, I want you to pretend like you don't know me, like you don't know about us." His voice was soft, almost a whisper. "Pretend I'm just some guy you never saw before in your whole life standing on a stage in some no name club or at a little hometown festival, singing some songs. Can you do that Dixie?"

Dixie closed her eyes and shook her head yes, afraid that if she spoke she would reveal all of the confused emotions tumbling about inside her.

And Greg started to sing.

He had been hesitant and unsure when he had first knocked on her door. No longer. With the guitar in his hands, Greg was strong, confident and in control. His voice cried out, powerful, wrapping emotion around his words. Sadness, longing and regret danced naked in the air, swirling with the rise and fall of the notes and laying bare his fragile soul. Tenderness, at once both soft and sharp, broke through the lyrics and sat as on the edge of Excalibur's shining blade, piercing her heart again and again. Dixie sat, mesmerized.

When the last song was done and the last note had reverberated and faded away, Dixie and Greg gazed at each other silently, all that they had been, all that they no longer were keeping time with the beating of their hearts. A tear or two squeezed from their eyes each time they blinked and swam like minnows down their cheeks.

"So," Greg finally asked, his voice quiet, a little half smile flitting across his lips, the crooked smile that Dixie had missed so much, "What does the girl who never saw me before in her whole entire life think?"

"She thinks," Dixie answered, her own voice hushed and quiet, a little half smile of her own flitting across her lips, "that they were completely, totally, insanely, awesome."

Poetic License

ABOUT YOU (Lyrics)

Elusive
Elusive song
Jumbled words float like feathers in the air

You said I should write about
Something that I know about
But the only thing I know about
Is you

I could write about the moon and stars above
I could write about the sun up in the sky
The sun as warm and bright as your face
The stars like sparkles in your eyes

I could write about walking on a summer's day
I walked with you, our fingers were entwined
I could write about morning grasses tipped with glistening dew
Dewy drops like tear drops if I made you cry

I could write about the time
A dog pissed on my shoe
But the dog was yours
And the song was really about you

You said I should write about
Something that I know about
But the only thing I know about
Is you

Read between the lines, you'll see
Every song's the same, you'll see
Every song is really about you

Everything I write about
The only thing I know about
Every song is really about you

Elusive
Elusive song
Jumbled words float like feathers in the air
The poet in my heart tries to catch them as they float there
The poet in my heart
Released by losing you

Chapter 15

ARGUMENTATIVE LICENSE

This was not one of the good times. Somehow the bond between them had been fractured. Terms of endearment, if they were said at all, were said out of habit with no feelings behind them to back them up. Kisses, if they were given at all, were meaningless pecks on the check. There was no passion, no spark.

Joe and Lainey tried to put on a good show as if nothing was wrong, as if they didn't want to brawl with each other just at the sight of each other's face, to at least be civil with one another, for the boys.

But Owen and Gabriel weren't blind. They weren't immune to the exodus of warmth in the house. They could see the stony faces and the cold stares. And they could see the barbs that seemed to shoot out of those cold stares. It was obvious they knew something was up. They came home with haunted looks on their faces as if they were entering a crypt and then had to climb over a craggy, briar covered and hilly terrain in order to escape the glowering monsters that used to be their parents. They had to be bribed to come down to dinner.

Yes, somehow the bond had fractured, but it was not really an enigmatic 'somehow'. Joe knew how it had happened. It all started with that photo album, 'Our Honeymoon'.

Lainey had left it sitting out on the coffee table, left it sitting out so he could look at it. But he hadn't looked at it. Honestly, it aggravated him. Their actual honeymoon was in the beginning of the album but the rest of the album was filled with pictures of their anniversaries – all twenty-five of them. Somehow Lainey had gotten the sappy idea to call each anniversary another honeymoon. And it wasn't a private joke just between the two of them either. Lainey was fond of telling other people, especially after she'd had a glass or two of wine, that she and Joe were, after all these years, still on their honeymoon.

Joe would roll his eyes, embarrassed, and the other guys would all roll their eyes too. And the women would get all smiley and giggly, as if Lainey were hinting at the intimate and juicy details of their sex life.

Joe had ignored the album sitting there in all its leather bound glory and tromped up the stairs where he found Lainey folding laundry, laying his boxer shorts in a neat stack on the corner of the bed.

"Hi, Joe! Did you look at the Honeymoon Album I left out on the table? I put the new pictures in there today! Honeymoon Number Twenty-Five!" She had been so enthused.

"I just got home from work, Lainey! Do you think the first thing I'm gonna do is look at a photo album?" he had replied. But he had not said it nicely. Irritation was in his voice and the word 'stupid' was implied in front of the word 'photo album'. He saw Lainey's green eyes flash at him and he knew if he didn't smooth things over fast, a brouhaha was going to break out, but he had not been in the mood for smoothing.

"Honeymoon number four and Honeymoon number eight and Honeymoon number twenty," Joe tried to mimic Lainey in a high pitched, sing song voice. "I think you've been hanging around with fifth graders too long. I think somehow one of their eleven year old brains got sucked into your forty-five year old skull. They're anniversaries, Lainey, not honeymoons! Anniversaries!"

"What the hell are you talking about? What's the matter with you?" Lainey's arm lashed out as she spoke, colliding with the neat stack of underwear, sending boxer shorts flying, like wildly colored and patterned birds, across the room.

And so it had begun. An argument over nothing really - the name on a photo album. It was the proverbial 'who left the cap off the toothpaste?' argument, which they had done before. Or the 'which way to hang the toilet paper, over or under?' argument, which they had done before too.

Mean and hurtful things roiled up and spewed out of their mouths in and around the things about nothing. They flung past slights and personal dislikes at each other like rotten fruit. They said things that they didn't really believe, that they never should have said, that they regretted saying as soon as they'd said them. But what can you do when the words have already gushed out? You can't catch smoke, no matter how hard you try.

Chapter 16

LICENSE TO MAKE UP

From a small spark to a hot burn to a slow simmer and now cold nothingness. A bad mood igniting, spreading, and deforming reason. A week of living in its charred remains. He felt like dice without spots, a cone that had lost its ice cream, a book with no pages, a deed left undone. Almost nonexistent even, like a shadow or a ghost.

She that meant the most to him lay on her side of the bed, as close to the edge as she could manage without falling off, which translated to as far away from Joe as she could get. An invisible fissure filled with frigid air cleaved the bed in two, assuring that Joe stayed on his side and Lainey stayed on hers.

Joe couldn't blame Lainey. He'd started the whole thing. He'd been a complete jerk. He was just in a really bad mood that day. Maybe he'd had problems at work. Maybe the popcorn he'd had for a snack had been stale and chewy instead of light and airy. Maybe some moronic jackass had cut him off in traffic and almost caused an accident. Maybe, maybe, maybe. He could make up excuses all day. But none of them were any reason to have said what he'd said and started the huge blowup with his Lainey.

He couldn't sleep. He hadn't slept well the whole week. Not since the stupid argument. How could he sleep when he was cold even if he was warm, when he had a hollow ache in the pit of his stomach that had nothing to do with hunger?

Joe got out of the bed and went to the window. The night sky was clear, dark and full of stars. He stared up, entranced, searching, as if the solution to his heartache might be written like Morse code in the tiny specks of starry light. But no divine advice ensued.

With the soft light of the moon and stars to guide him, he wandered quietly through the house - up and down the hall, in and out of rooms. He peaked into the twins room to see them both sprawled out on their bunks, peaceful and quiet in their sleep. Dixie's old room seemed a barren place now, just a bed and an empty dresser, awaiting a visit from its former occupant when she came home for the holidays.

In the family room, he found himself looking at the books on the bookshelf. Lainey's favorite, Stephen King, occupied two entire shelves. There was the Harry Potter series and the Hunger Games series. There were biographies of John Lennon, Townes Van Zandt, Marilyn Monroe and Arnold Palmer. There were books about history, photography, baseball and how to play the guitar. And then, there is was, the infamous 'Our Honeymoon'.

Joe took it down off the shelf, sat on a chair and began flipping the pages. He smiled and chuckled and he cried as the past twenty-five years flew before his eyes with wistful nostalgia.

Why had he made such a fuss? So what if she called each anniversary another honeymoon? Honeymoons were good things. How would he feel if instead she chose to call each anniversary another day in Hell? How would he feel if there were no anniversaries at all? No Honeymoon #26?

With the album in his lap and visions of wedding rings and cruise ships, candlelight and champagne, and Lainey and the three kids dancing around in his head like sugarplums, Joe fell asleep.

"Joe?" A soft voice whispered in his ear, a gentle hand touched his shoulder.

Still half asleep, Joe was sure this was a dream. He had left Lainey sleeping, her back to him, trying to ignore him, to pretend he didn't exist, cold as an Eskimo in an arctic wasteland.

But the gentle pressure the dream hand applied to his shoulder remained. He could feel warm breath on his cheek. He opened his eyes and there was Lainey's face, almost touching his own.

"You weren't in the bed and I got kind of worried. I do love you, you know. It's just that... Well, you know, we're both so.... Oh Joe, I'm just sorry. I'm sorry for everything. I don't want to fight anymore."

"You don't have to be sorry. It was all my fault, Lainey. I'm the one who's sorry. Sorry for being such a stupid jerk. Sorry for letting my stubborn streak get the best of me. I love you, Lainey! I don't want to fight anymore either."

"Well, I'm stubborn too and I said such horrible things, and... "

"OK, so now are we going to argue about who's the most stubborn and who said the most horrible things?"

"No but..."

Joe placed his finger lightly against Lainey's lips, stopping any further conversation. He pulled her onto his lap and they kissed. It was a long, slow kiss that spoke of apologies, forgiveness, and love.

It was something how a bad mood could switch things around, taking the things that you loved the most about someone and transforming them for a moment into something that you disliked instead. The tinkling laugh that was like sun-kissed drops of cool rain on a parched soul became a sound that grated your eardrums and scraped on your nerves. The innocent and childlike spirit that made you feel like every day was a holiday, instead seemed silly and childish – irritating and annoying you to your core.

Joe and Lainey cuddled on that chair for a long time, till the early morning light peeked through the curtains and shone like a beacon on their faces. Then they hurried back upstairs, lest the twins should come down and find them there, inseparable, melded together as one.

Chapter 17

LICENSE TO BE TORN

F ool. Wasn't it only a few hours ago that Dixie had realized that's what she had been - a fool? Even after Greg sang his songs and it was like a magnetic tractor beam had drawn their hearts and souls closer and closer together until they were fused into one, even after she had felt closer to Greg in that moment than she had ever felt to anyone in her whole life, the lesson went unlearned. Fool stuck to her like glue.

The fool in her told her she should not give in to her heart. Greg was finally on his way. He had always had the voice, the moves, the looks and now with the remarkable songs he had written his dream could actually become a reality. The fool told her that revealing her heart would make him lose sight of his dream, dead end his momentum, derail his plans.

Another little voice deep down inside her yelled and screamed to be heard. 'Tell him, Dixie, tell him! Everything he does is for you! His spirit will fly! His momentum will not be lost. It will soar! Tell him, Dixie!' But Dixie pretended she did not hear the little voice. The fool's pull was stronger.

She should have run into Greg's arms. She should have kissed his cheeks, his eyes, his lips.

But instead Dixie, foolish Dixie, went into the kitchen and started opening cupboards and running water.

She said, "I'll make tea."

Instead of, "I love you, Greg."

She asked, "I've got some left over take out. Want some?"

Instead of, "I was so stupid. I made such a terrible mistake. Will you take me back?"

She said, "The songs were great! I'm so proud of you!" like she was his mother patting him on the head for getting an A on his report card.

Instead of, "Oh Greg. Your songs. They're brilliant. Touching and marvelous. I can't stop crying. I'm so sorry for everything I put you through. Can you ever forgive me?"

And later she said, "You must be tired. The couch is pretty comfortable. I've fallen asleep on it lots of times."

Instead of, "Stay with me tonight, Greg. Please. Stay."

"So, do you want to sleep on the couch?"

"Dixie, I….." Greg faltered, a shaky sigh escaping his lips. His eyes looked into hers - searching, pleading and then he quickly looked away. "I... I can't, Dixie. I better just go. Thanks for your help."

He leaned in and kissed her softly on the cheek, a kiss so tender it almost stopped her heart. It was a final kiss, a kiss releasing the last bit of hope he had clung to that Dixie might be his again, a kiss letting her go, setting her free.

And then he was gone.

For the second time that day, Dixie watched the dark red Malibu pull out of the parking lot and drive away. She watched until the tail lights were nothing more than red tinged specks on the dark canvas of the night, until her straining eyes could no longer see them at all.

Like the walking dead she stumbled back inside and closed the green door with the gold fifty-three on it. She covered her eyes with her hands, sobbing, filling her palms with pools of salty tears.

For the second time that day, Greg pulled into the little shopping plaza a mile down the road and parked outside The Dollar Store.

He was wiped out – completely exhausted, completely drained, completely empty.

He had sang Dixie his songs, songs like a delicate water craft carrying a cargo of anguish and heartache, sadness and despair, love found and love lost over a warm and misty bay. He had laid himself spread-eagled before her - vulnerable, unprotected, unguarded.

They had both looked at each other, eyes glistening with tears, and Greg had felt that they were one and the same person, connected by their hearts and souls, their minds feeling each other's pain and sorrow, their longing and regret. And love. Hadn't he seen love in Dixie's eyes?

"Awesome," she had breathed, the word full of emotion and wonder.

Now what? What happens next?

Greg closed his eyes. He heard Dixie stir in her chair and rise and he anticipated her approach. He could feel her arms wrapping around his neck, her lips soft and warm as she kissed him. He could feel her breath tickling his ear as she whispered 'I'm so sorry, Greg. I made such a mistake. I love you, Greg. Will you take me back?' But there was no touch, no words of love.

Instead he heard her in the little galley kitchen, opening cupboards, running water, putting something in the microwave.

"I'll make some tea," was what she said.

"Got any beer?" he had asked.

Dixie fumbled around in her fridge, moving bottles of ketchup and orange juice and containers of yogurt to see if a stray beer might be hiding in there somewhere but unfortunately there was none to be found.

So Greg sat across the table from her sipping the bland tea, his face showing an odd combination of pumped up excitement and sadness, psyched energy and longing, determination and despair.

She told him his songs were great. She told him that with her connections at the television station where she worked, she could hook him up with some time at a recording studio. She could probably even get him some airtime. She could get him lists of clubs, restaurants, coffee houses, bars and festivals all over the state that were looking for singers and bands.

This was what he had come for, wasn't it? Dixie's opinion? Dixie's help?

And Greg knew then that he had been fooling himself all along. What he really wanted, what he had really come for was not Dixie's opinion but Dixie herself.

But he wasn't going to beg. He wasn't going to grovel. He had laid it all out there for her. She would have to be blind not to know how he felt. He searched her face, willing her to say the words she would not say, the words he longed to hear. Those words never came.

She offered him to sleep on the couch. How could he lay on her couch knowing she was right in the next room? He'd never sleep. He would toss and turn, imagining running his hands through her golden curls and over her warm soft body, imagining the feel of her silky smooth skin pressed against him and her sweet gentle breath on his neck, imagining her face inches from his own, her soft lips on his.

"I can't Dixie," he had said and he kissed her softly on the cheek, a kiss he wished could have been so much more than good bye.

And here he was again, parked outside The Dollar Store. The shopping plaza was deserted now. No cars waiting patiently for their owners to return, no people scurrying in and out of the stores, the stores all dozing under a dim half-light.

Greg put his head on the steering wheel and closed his eyes, tears squeezing out from under his lids. They fell one by one through the steering wheel and splashed onto his heart which lay, beating frantically, on the floor at his feet.

His heart had crumbled. It had splintered, fractured, and cracked. It had shattered into hundreds of tiny, sharp pieces that cut him and poked him over and over again.

Could it possibly break any more than that? Apparently the answer was yes.

He was so tired of feeling this way. So god damned, fucking tired.

Poetic License

TORN

I feel torn in two by emotions
Not knowing which is true
And which is false

I feel like two separate people
Both of them scrambling for answers
Both of them lost

One is yellow and green
Bright as a summer's day
One is gray and violet
Like clouds before the rain

Questions swirl and whirl
They bash into my heart
I know the answers I scramble for
But I will not let them out

Gray rain will fall like tears
Yellow sun bores through the sorrow
Coaxing, calling, foretelling
The bursting forth of flowers

Those flowers,
So bright the purple and the pink
So bright against the brown earth
Like jewels to pierce your soul

I must let the jewels pierce me
The answers I have hidden
Will flow out bright and red

To love or not to love?
Soul mate or weight to hold me down?
I know these answers
Why am I so afraid?

Answering
Will make my torn self
Whole again

Chapter 18

OFFICIAL LICENSE

Someone that was supposed to be him but didn't look like him at all was standing on a hilltop tossing pea sized gravel at the trunk of a downed evergreen tree. Tap, tap, tap went the gravel as it hit. Tap, tap, tap. Tap, tap, tap. With each hit, a geyser of brown gunk shot up and then fell back down, spreading like thick, melted wax over the knobby bark.

Tap, tap, tap. The tapping got ever more insistent until part of Greg's brain began to realize that he was dreaming, but the tapping sound was not a dream. It was reality.

Greg lifted his head and groggily opened his eyes, peering through his windshield at the faint hint of morning light that was just beginning to appear as the sun made its way over the horizon.

Peering through the windshield? I'm in my car! Sleeping in my car? What the...?

And then it all came back to him, crashing into his brain, shoving itself like an undigestible lump into his stomach. He had gone to see Dixie. And now he was here, not there. Here, sleeping in his damn car, feeling like some huge beast had spent the night sitting on his chest.

He dropped his head back on the steering wheel but a dull pain made him raise it up again. Tentative fingers felt a dent, a gift from the steering wheel to his forehead after hours of lying pressed against it.

Tap, Tap, Tap. Greg turned his head to the sound of the tapping. The dark blue of a police officer's uniform met his eyes, the officer tapping at his window.

Great. Just great.

"Sir, I need you to exit the car. Slowly. Don't make any sudden movements. Keep your hands where I can see them."

Greg did as he was ordered.

"I'll need to see your license," the officer demanded as Greg stood before him.

"Yes, officer." And Greg began to reach behind him.

"Slowly!" The officer barked.

"Yes, officer."

Greg raised his left hand in the air and then moved his right arm as if in slow motion to retrieve his wallet from his back pocket. He removed his license and handed it to the officer.

"State your purpose for being here, young man."

"Sleeping, sir."

The officer raised his eyebrows and looked at Greg quizzically.

"I had a fight with my girlfriend last night and she kicked me out. I didn't have anywhere else to go so I pulled in here and I must have fallen asleep. Sir."

It wasn't the complete truth but close enough. The real truth would have been too hard and too painful for Greg to explain.

The police officer's demeanor softened. His blunt, authoritative questioning gave way to a more sympathetic tone. "Well, that explanation is very believable, young man. You look like crap."

Greg gave a halfhearted chuckle and rolled his eyes. "Thanks."

"Listen, I can't let you stay here. The plaza's closed and the lot is not meant for overnight parking. I suggest you stop into Betty's Pantry just down the way there. You look like you could use a good strong cup of coffee. She serves a nice little breakfast too. Get yourself some coffee and something to eat and think about getting that girl of yours back."

"I don't think there's much chance of that, Sir."

"Why not? Did you do something so bad that you don't deserve to be taken back?"

"No."

"Is there another guy?"

"Not that I know of."

"Is there another girl?"

"No."

"Do you still love her? Do you want her back?"

"Yeah. I do. More than anything, I do."

"Well then son, there's a chance. There's always a chance."

Chapter 19

DESPONDENT LICENSE

How long does it take to drain the lizard? Wasn't it ever going to stop? He just kept going and going and going. Finally, Niagara Falls finished its run.

Greg stared at his reflection in the mirror above the restroom sink as he washed his hands. What the cop had said was true. He did look like crap. Like a real douche. His face was blotchy, his eyes were red, puffy, and lifeless, his hair was sticking out in all directions and he had a red line imbedded in his forehead from the steering wheel like freaking Harry Potter.

Maybe he should splash some water on his face, try to neaten his hair? Nah, what the hell for? And he walked out of the restroom and into the diner.

Betty's Pantry was empty except for one burly guy in the furthest booth with his head stuck in the newspaper, and the waitress, who was busy filling salt and pepper shakers, preparing for her busy day.

She smiled at Greg as he took a seat at the counter, put a mug in front of him and filled it with coffee. "If anyone ever looked like they needed a cup of coffee, it's you!" she said as she poured. "Don't usually get young guys like you in here this early in the morning. The kids your age that I know think morning is two in the afternoon!"

"Yeah, well…." Greg let his voice trail off. What else was there to say?

"Today's breakfast special is two poached eggs over biscuits 'n sausage gravy with hash browns, and coffee for $5.25."

"Yeah, sure. I'll have that." He didn't really care. Eating nothing would have been just as good.

Greg cradled the mug in his hands, letting his face linger over the cup as he sipped. Steam rose into his face, heat seeped into his hands. The warmth soothed and comforted him. The hot coffee traveled down his throat and into his stomach and he started to feel a glimmer of life returning to his stone cold soul. Then the gurglings and grumblings started, so loud that Greg was sure even the trucker dude in the far corner could hear what Greg's stomach had to say.

By the time the waitress came out of the kitchen and headed towards him with a heaping plate, it was all Greg could do not to jump up and grab the food right out of her hands so he could get to it faster.

"Enjoy!" she said as she set the plate in front of him and topped off his coffee.

"Looks good!" Greg said with what sounded like some actual enthusiasm, and started to chow down.

And it was good! Really good. After a few mouthfuls he began to feel more human than he had all morning.

"Are you Betty?" he asked conversationally.

"No, I'm Sheila. Just a simple worker bee. Betty doesn't come in till the lunch crowd starts knocking at the door," she replied as she checked all the napkin holders on the counter to make sure they were full. "I see the biscuits and sausage gravy's going down good! Want a little more? It's on the house!"

"Thanks for the offer but I'm totally stuffed. It was awesome though."

"Everyone loves it! It's our most popular item. Especially after it won us week four of the Take Out or Leave it contest. Folks just flock in here hankering for a taste!"

"The what contest?"

"Take Out or Leave it. It's sponsored by Channel Twenty News. They go around getting take-out food from local restaurants and then they judge which one's best. It really drums up business if you win. They even give you a gold colored take-out box and run a story in the paper!"

Sheila topped off his coffee again and left to take care of a few new customers who had just walked in. Greg spotted the golden take-out box on the wall behind the cash register, 'BETTY'S PANTRY – WEEK 4 WINNER' emblazoned on it in royal blue. A laminated newspaper clipping was displayed below it.

When Sheila passed by the register on her way back to the counter, she untacked the newspaper clipping and brought it over to Greg. "See! Here's the article that ran in the paper. That's Betty right there." And she poked the article with her finger. "And there's me and Coop, one of the cooks, right behind her."

Greg set his cup down with a thump and stared at the picture, eyes wide with surprise. The smiling blond girl presenting Betty with the golden box looked very familiar.

"Dixie!"

"That's right! That's Dixie Andrews, the darling of the local news! She's the star of the show, you know. Quite the celebrity around here. Betty was so proud!"

Greg closed his eyes and started chuckling softly, shaking his head and running his hands through his hair. He blew out his breath in a quiet sigh.

Dixie was a celebrity! A star! Famous! And he didn't even know.

Sadness filled him again. Sadness and shame. Dixie had moved to a new city away from her family and friends. She had gotten her own apartment, started a new job. And he had been so stuck on his own poor, sorry, loser ass he hadn't even thought to ask her about it. He hadn't even wondered about it at all. And here he had thought everything was about her. He was wrong about that now wasn't he? It was really all about him - his pain, his sorrow, his anguish, his loss, his life, his future, his pathetic worthless soul.

"Everything all right?" Sheila asked.

"No, not really."

"Do you know Dixie Andrews?"

Greg didn't answer. His face was hovering over the coffee cup again, waiting for the steam to warm and comfort him. But the coffee had gone cold.

Chapter 20

LICENSE FOR KINDNESS

It broke her heart just to look at him. He couldn't have been any more than twenty-two, twenty-three years old. What had fate thrown him that had made him so dejected and joyless, as if the last flower on earth had just been trampled by a heavy, uncaring boot, the red and the yellow mashed beyond recognition into the brown dirt?

A few sips of her strong, hot coffee had brought a bit of life back into his eyes. And, why, once he had gotten some of Betty's sausage gravy in him it was like some invisible cable holding down his spirit lost its grip and his soul was set free.

He had smiled and chatted with her. That is until she showed him the newspaper clipping of Betty's Pantry winning the contest, with the photo of Dixie Andrews handing Betty the golden award. 'Dixie!' he had blurted out. There had been happiness and surprise and wonder in his voice. And then it was like someone had punched him in the gut. Pain crossed his face. The light went out of his eyes. The cable renewed its grip on his soul.

Sheila tried to ask him what was wrong but he just sat hunched over his cup, no longer interested in conversation. She wanted to try to help him, offer some friendly support, some kind words but the morning rush was starting and the customers were pouring in. She had a job to do, people to serve.

She laid her hand briefly, gently on his shoulder to let him know she cared and put his breakfast check on the counter in front of him.

Total Due - $0. Inside the zero, a smiley face. It was the least she could do. She hoped it would help.

The next time Sheila rushed past the counter, the young man was gone, a ten dollar bill left sitting under his cup.

She lifted up her eyeglasses to wipe a stray tear. She hoped he was going to be okay. Whoever he was, whatever his story, she prayed he would find an ending that made him happy.

Something in Sheila's nature drew her to lost souls. She believed that the kindness of strangers could make a difference. A kind word, a listening ear, a gentle touch - just to let them know that someone cared, that they were not as alone as maybe they thought they were, that someone was willing to help them find what they had lost. And in her fifty plus years, she liked to think she had helped her fair share of the lost and lonely.

She knew for a fact that she had helped her Gordy. Of all the lost souls that had ever called out to her, his soul had cried the loudest. She'd been waiting tables at The Ayrault Tavern then - a feisty young thing she was, buxom, slender and fine with waves of ginger hair flowing around her head. Nothing like the slightly plump, wrinkling and graying women she was now.

Gordy had been a fine young thing too, with short fuzzy hair, piercing blue eyes and a strong, square jaw. But his mouth did not know how to smile, his blue eyes were haunted, and the aching of his heart was like a heavy cross he wore around his neck, visible for anyone to see. At least it was visible to Sheila. He started coming in every Thursday night, a stranger to her, just like all the others. He always sat in the last booth on the left, had himself a couple of beers and ordered a bowl of the Cajun Gumbo but he never ate more than half of it. Sheila longed to reach out to him and hold him close, to ease his pain, to pull it from his depths and banish it from his being.

She was kind and patient and over the weeks he opened up to her, letting her know his story, word by painful word, line by agonizing line. It was Vietnam that had done it to him. The horrors he had seen, the lives torn asunder, the sins he had committed. It was more than he could bear.

Sheila let him know that she understood, that she was there for him, that she would help him carry his pain. And he had started smiling, had started eating his whole bowl of gumbo, had come alive again, she felt because of her.

The pungent fragrance of spilled beer and sweaty bodies had always hung heavy at The Ayrault. Amorous fools who thought they were God's gift to women ogled Sheila's cleavage and tried to proposition her. Sometimes they even got up the nerve to put their arms around her shoulders or slap her slender behind. She'd smile and put them in their place gently but firmly. Most of them were decent guys underneath the drink. No need to embarrass them. They knew the meaning of the word no.

One Thursday night though, one of the drunks did more than stare at her cleavage. He tried to put his groping hands inside her shirt. He grabbed her by the hair with his grease smeared fingers and tried to put his stinking mouth on hers. He did not know the meaning of the word no.

Gordy was at her side in an instant. "Things seem to be getting out of hand here. I heard the lady say 'no'." Gordy's voice was steady and calm. He was giving the drunkard a chance to redeem himself.

But the drunkard did not hear the danger playing at the edges of Gordy's words. "I think things are getting in hand!" he had chortled, still fumbling around under Sheila's shirt against her struggles and actually grabbing one of her breasts with his filthy, lecherous hand.

"Ooo haa!" he shouted as he squeezed her breast, smirking and winking at his drinking buddies with perverse glee.

And then, bam, Gordy had decked the S.O.B.

A look of complete bewilderment exploded on the drunk's face along with Gordy's fist. And then he was out cold, sprawled flat on the floor, thick red blood oozing from his nose and trickling from the corners of his ugly, gaping mouth.

Gordy was her hero that day. He was her hero every day after that too. And he was still her hero today.

Her and Gordy. They had rescued each other. Where would they be now without the kindness of strangers?

Chapter 21

LICENSE IN BLUE POSITIVE

Once they had decided to do it, they got started right away. Why wait? Sometimes this kind of thing could take a while! They worked on it every day too, sometimes even several times a day, and although you couldn't exactly call it hard work, they still ended up sweaty and out of breath sometimes. But it was a good kind of sweaty, a satisfying out of breath.

Their diligence and attention to detail really paid off because four weeks later, the little stick turned blue! Blue!!!!!

They stared at the stick in disbelief! They stared at each other in astonishment! They stared at Pam's stomach in wonder! And Boyd tried to imagine the tiny pin prick of a life that must be living in there now. The tiny pin prick that would change and develop and grow, like a miracle, into a baby! Their first child!

They had exploded then like fireworks on the fourth of July, jumping wildly up and down, round and round and whooping like a couple of nutcases. When their excitement finally let up a bit, Pam went online to google pregnancy, babies and the reliability of at home pregnancy tests. And Boyd went out to do some shopping.

This miraculous event merited a celebration! He got two bottles of sparkling white grape juice. At least it looked like champagne! He knew Pam wouldn't want the real bubbly now. Alcoholic beverages were off limits when you were preggers. And he got a lovely bouquet of blue, pink and white carnations surrounded by clouds of airy baby's breath.

Next stop was the department store. He wanted to scout out the baby section, just to get a feel of what it was going to be like to have a baby in the house. There were tiny clothes, bibs and blankets, baby bottles and sippy cups, brightly colored rattles and teething toys, high chairs and cribs, strollers and car seats. Were they really going to need all this junk? He didn't have a clue what half of this stuff was for! His brain started to feel like it was in a gridlock. He was overwhelmed.

Then Boyd spotted the big, soft, yellow pillow shaped like a rubber ducky. His breathing slowed. The gridlock straightened out. His heart melted. He just had to get it.

"My wife's going to have a baby!" he had announced to the cashier, his face as sunny and bright as the yellow ducky pillow.

"Well, congratulations! When's the big day?"

"Oh, probably not until April or something like that but I am just so pumped!"

Pam couldn't get enough of that rubber ducky pillow. She hugged it and she hugged Boyd and she kissed him all over. "Oh, Boyd! It's the cutest thing ever! You are the best, sweetest, most wonderful husband in the entire world. You're going to be such a good father." Her eyes sparkled with tears. Her face was soft with love.

'Ducky' took up residence on their bed, like a yellow sentinel ensuring that only happy thoughts would be allowed into the room or into their dreams as they slept. Pam hugged it to her chest every night, just before she started what had become the evening ritual - the spouting off of possible baby names that had been gestating in their heads throughout the day.

"You know, Boyd, if it's a boy we could name it after you – Andrew Vincent Boyd II."

"No, I don't want to do that. But I would like the middle name to be Andrew though, if it's a boy."

"That works for me. What do you think of Chester? Chester's a nice name. Chester Andrew Boyd."

"Don't like it. I used to have a gerbil named Chester when I was a kid! Besides, that's so old fashioned."

"Well, you know, lots of the old fashioned names are coming back again."

Pam had always been one to keep everything neat and orderly but now magazines and books galore about everything baby lay scattered in every room of the house. They supplied a feast of information that Pam delved into with gusto. She had so many questions! If the answer couldn't be found in the books and magazines, she went online. And every bit of information that she deemed important or interesting was relayed in a deluge to Boyd.

What are Braxton-Hicks contractions?
False Labor.

Did babies yawn in utero?
Yes!

What did it feel like to have feet pressing on your belly from the inside?
Out of this worldly, unbelievably, amazing!

When did babies usually start to smile, to crawl, to walk, to talk?
Two months, eight months, twelve months, fifteen months.

Were zesty, spicy foods okay to eat when you were breast feeding?
No.

Boyd hoped Pam wasn't going to quiz him on this stuff! There was no way his memory could hold onto all this material!

"You know what name I like, Boyd? Kate! Or Emily! What do you think of Kate or Emily if it's a girl?"

"Not bad. What about Robin? Or Deidre?"

"Deidre? Where in the world did you come up with that name?"

"I saw it on a license plate! And I used to know a Deidre. In second grade. I had a crush on her!"

The spare room was to become the nursery. They painted it green, a light moss green. It was a fresh, hopeful color; relaxing and soothing for sleep times but also pleasant and happy for awake times or playtimes. Baby monkeys and elephants, lions and giraffes in varying shades of yellows, browns and greens frolicked on the curtains. Other than that, the room was empty. After all, it was only September and the due date wasn't until mid-April. It was way too early for cribs and dressers, changing tables and diaper pails.

"If it's a boy, what do you think of Daryl or maybe Benjamin?"

"Daryl I like but not Benjamin. Ben Boyd. That just doesn't flow. I think if it's a boy we should name it something really masculine like Jaguar or Tiger."

"Yeah, right! And if it's twins, a girl and a boy, we could name them Mink and Fox!"

They had agreed not to find out the baby's gender ahead of time. It was more natural, the way they used to do it before technology had even made it a possibility. And not knowing was more exciting too. What a fun surprise it would be discovering if it was a boy or a girl right at the moment the baby was born. And besides all that, the baby name game just wouldn't be as much fun if there were only one name to decide on instead of two.

"If it's a girl, we could name her Lyre! The sweet sound of music!"

"Come on, Pam! Seriously? No way! Kids would change that to Liar. Liar, Liar, Pants on Fire. What do you think of Jasmine? The sweet scent of flowers?"

"I think that's it Boyd! I really do!"

So it was settled. It would be Jasmine Kate if it was a girl and Daryl Andrew if it was a boy.

Maybe. April was still far, far away.

In October, Pam would probably start to show. A baby bump! Visible proof that the little bugger was really in there! In November, the sex could be determined, if they wanted to know, which of course, they didn't. In December, Pam might actually be able to feel the baby kick. And if Boyd put his hand on her belly at the right time, he'd be able to feel it too! How much more amazing could things possibly get?

"Hey Boyd, you know what name popped into my head today? Dixie! What do you think of Dixie?"

"Dixie. Dixie Boyd. You know, that has a nice ring to it. Yeah! I really like it!"

Scratch Jasmine. They were on the baby highway alright. It was going to be an awesome ride.

Chapter 22

LICENSE TO TREASURE

E rika Boyd had started boxing up the books first. Already read, some several times over, they certainly weren't anything that she had to have. Clothes that she and Andy hadn't worn in years and the kitchen drawer full of useless spatulas that were too wide or too flat, melon ballers, citrus peelers and bottle openers galore would be the next things to go. Decisions to make. To leave or to take? The harder choices would come soon enough.

They had lived in this house for thirty-five years – 3108 Crosby Avenue. The address was imbedded in her brain like her birthday or her social security number. Could she possibly remember a new one?

"Address?" Someone would ask.

"Three one o…. No, no, sorry. Address is ……." And there would be a long pause as her brain scrambled to remember the new one.

"Four Twenty Five Bellwood Court! Apartment J."

An apartment. It was going to take some getting used to. No dining room, one bedroom instead of three. What did they need all those bedrooms for anyway? The boys, Andy Jr. (somewhere along the line they had started calling him Boyd, of all things!) and Tom, hadn't lived home in fifteen years! The big house, the big yard – it was just getting to be too much for them. She and Andy weren't spring chickens anymore. They had stiff joints, stiff backs, high blood pressure, and arthritis. They moved much slower than they used to and they weren't that flexible. Downsizing. That was the name of the game now. At least there would be a nice patio out back where she could still put pots full of flowers.

The little bookcase was light as a cloud without the books on it. Erika lifted it up and let out a tiny "Eek!!!" Was that a mouse nest under there? A huge pile of dust? She wasn't that bad of a house-keeper, was she? She set the bookcase off to the side and gingerly poked at the mystery pile with the toe of her shoe.

It was soft and faded yellow, with bits of green and blue. This was no pile of dust! It was a baby blanket! Or rather, the tattered remnants of the baby blanket that had been Boyd's constant com-panion. Whether he was on the couch watching TV, in his car seat going for a drive, or listening to a bedtime story, 'Blanky' was always by his side. He used to rub its silky edge between his fingers while he sucked his thumb.

As he grew, he had carried it around less and less. He must have stuffed it under the bookcase when he decided he was much too old to be carrying around a baby thing like that. She had never even noticed when it had disappeared from sight. Had completely forgot-ten that it had even existed. Now, here it was.

She should give it to Boyd! Put it in a box and wrap it up like a surprise mystery gift! He'd probably get the biggest kick out of it! Especially now that he and her wonderful daughter-in-law, Pam, were going to have a little one of their own. Ten years they'd been married. Erika had thought it was never going to happen.

On second thought, he'd probably wonder why she would even think he'd want this disgusting, threadbare, faded rag of a thing. It had been his, and he had loved it then, but he wouldn't want it now.

Once, many years ago, Andy's mother had sent them a box of Andy's old stuffed animals. She had probably been imagining the same thing that Erika was musing about now; the happy, surprised look on her grown child's face as they gazed with nostalgic bliss on the beloved objects from their childhood. But the stuffed animals had been dirty, bedraggled things; all worn out and missing parts. Into the trash the box had gone, without a second thought.

And that's what she should do with Boyd's old blanket too, toss it. But she found that it was her own face gazing at the blanket with nostalgic bliss. She could still feel Boyd's sleepy little head lying soft and warm on her shoulder as she carried him off to bed. She could still remember the smell of the baby shampoo and how fine and silky his hair was after a bath. She could still see him sitting in his high chair, grinning and giggling, with spaghetti sauce all over his face and in his hair.

This blanket was a jewel, a delicate memento of a time long past, a time when she and Andy had been no older than their children were now and the boys had been innocent angels entrusted to their care.

No, instead Erika would wash the blanket and she would keep it. Surely they could find room in the new apartment for one tiny blanket. It was a treasure, something to keep forever, close to her heart.

Chapter 23

LICENSE TO GET IT RIGHT

How could he have missed Dixie so bad for all these months and not wondered what she was up to?

How could he have gone to see her and not even have asked her how she was doing?

How could he have sung her his songs and sat at her table and talked about himself and let her talk about him too and not have had hardly anything in the conversation about her?

Was he really that much of an egomaniac? Such a self-centered, egotistical jerk?

The cop had said there was always a chance to get back together, so long as he hadn't done anything that didn't deserve forgiveness. Had he done anything that didn't deserve forgiveness? He had told the cop no. But maybe he had. Maybe he had never given Dixie the consideration and thoughtfulness that she deserved. Maybe he had always been a selfish jackass.

Greg left the diner and walked over to his car. He paused for a moment and then kept right on going. He couldn't go home. Not yet. He had to think, to try and get his head straightened out. He had gone about things all wrong. Somehow he had to make it right.

The plaza where he had spent the night sleeping in his car was still closed, all the shops locked up tight. He walked up and down, looking in all the windows. Fashion jewelry glinted in the early morning sun at Dawson Jewelers. Cheese wheels, loaves of Italian bread and jugs of wine beckoned at Vino E Formaggio. Cheap scarecrows and plastic pumpkins heralded the coming of autumn at The

Dollar Store. Dance! Dance! Dance! had notices posted in their windows advertising classes in Ballet, Tap, Jazz, Zumba, Ballroom and Zydeco.

Greg looked but he didn't really see. His mind was fastened on how to apologize to Dixie, how to ask her forgiveness, how to tell her that he loved her and missed her and would like another chance, how to make himself into a better man.

He headed north out of the plaza and walked the mile to Dixie's apartment complex. Her blue Jetta was there in the parking lot so she must still be home. Should he go and knock on her door? Should he call? Should he text? He kept on walking.

He could knock on her door and when she answered he could say, "Hi Dixie! I'm still here! I want to say I'm sorry for being a jerk." Lame.

He could knock, and when Dixie answered, he could grab her in his arms, sweep her off her feet, give her a big, deep, passionate kiss, and tell her she was the love of his life. Too Disneyland.

When he came to a bus stop with a bench, he sat down, still thinking. Vehicles rushed by, a monotony of nondescript gray, black, white and tan broken up by an occasional blue, or green or red. The gleam of a garnet red Infiniti caught Greg's eye. It was smooth and sleek, a real beauty. A shimmering black Malibu made Greg take note. The same as his own piece of junk only shiny and new. A police car hurried past and Greg wondered if it was the same officer that had stopped him that morning. A loud rumbling made him turn his head to see a military Humvee approaching. A caravan of six of them zipped by, sand colored, their vibrations echoing in Greg's ears and pounding in his chest.

He stood and headed back.

He could call and say, "I'm still in town, Dixie. We need to talk. Can I come over?" Straight crap.

He could text – 'still in town forgot to ask how r u.' Like a real douche.

He passed by her complex again and paused as he glanced into the parking lot. He was relieved to see the Jetta still there. He was nervous to see the Jetta still there. He still wasn't ready. He kept walking; back down towards the plaza, towards the restaurant where he had parked his car.

He could take her hand in his, look her right in the eye and say "Dixie, I couldn't leave without telling you I love you. Things didn't go the way I meant them to yesterday. I'm so sorry." Yeah! Now that was going somewhere!

He'd tell her that he heard about the Take out or Leave it Contest and how proud he was of her. He'd tell her how ashamed he was for not asking her how she was doing. Did she like her job? Did she miss her family?

And he'd let her talk. He'd just stand there and listen. And then he'd tell her that he was ready to put everything he had into a career in music but, without her in his life, he hardly even cared about that. Making it big was not the most important thing to him. The most important thing to him was her. Could she forgive him? Would she take him back?

He was ready now. He knew what he wanted to say and how he wanted to say it. He would drive over to Dixie's again and take his last chance at getting her back, at filling in all the empty holes that his life had without her. Maybe he'd get her some flowers! Hadn't he seen a florist shop in the plaza?

Always be aware of your surroundings. His father had repeated that advice to Greg many, many times. It was good advice; advice that Greg wasn't remembering now. He was busy making plans, thinking about Dixie; completely lost in thought, completely unaware.

Greg spotted the three guys in the parking lot by Betty's Pantry but he paid them no mind. It didn't register that most of the cars at the diner were parked in the front of the restaurant but these guys were standing in the side lot and the only car there was his.

He didn't notice that one of the guys was facing Greg's car, bent slightly, hands fumbling in the vicinity of the door handle and the door lock. Or that the other two guys were trying to act nonchalant but doing a pretty poor job of it. They appeared nervous, taking their hands in and out of their pockets and casting furtive glances in every direction.

When he did finally notice that things were not as they should be, he rushed over, heedless – an inexperienced suburban dweller unfamiliar with thugs, robberies, or the seedy side of humanity.

"Hey! Dude! That's my car! What the hell are you doing?"

Greg saw a flash of silver and felt a cold prick, like ice, in his stomach. The ice turned to fire and a searing pain began to tear through his body. He clutched his stomach, a hot wetness gushing red through his fingers, as he doubled over and collapsed onto the pavement, his face pressed to the rough, pebbly surface.

A partially flattened French fry lay inches from his face, bits of ketchup stuck to it like eyes and a nose, or like blood. He stared at it and it stared back, its little ketchup eyes mournful and hopeless.

"Tough luck, Dude," it seemed to say. "Brothers in arms we are, brothers in arms."

The sound of his blood rushing through his veins throbbed in his ears. He heard screams and yelling, scuffling and running, sirens. He saw flashing lights and flashing colors. But his ears felt stuffed with cotton. His eyes would not stay focused. Everything he was seeing and hearing seemed to decompose in his mind before his brain could make sense of them.

Someone turned him over onto his back; wads of paper or cloth were being pressed to his stomach, darkening quickly as they became soaked with blood.

He had to go get those flowers for Dixie! He had to go see her and say he was sorry. He had to ask her how she was doing, ask her about her hopes and her dreams. Maybe she could hold him. Rub his head with her cool hands. Maybe she could stop this terrible, terrible pain.

Someone was kneeling by his side, one hand on his shoulder, their other hand squeezing his hand.

"Stay with me. Stay with me now." They repeated over and over.

Why were they saying that? Where was he going? He couldn't even move.

Greg turned his head to the side, looking for his little French fry buddy but it was gone, mashed into oblivion, its little ketchup face destroyed, plastered perhaps to the bottom of someone's shoe.

He closed his eyes. Everything got quiet then.

Quiet, peaceful and black.

Chapter 24

LICENSE TO BE SAVED

Dixie was washing her face, splashing the cold water, trying to get some relief into her hot, red, puffy eyes. Eyes that felt like sandpaper. She had hardly slept, had spent most of the night crying. Greg had sung to her and she had let him leave. Let him leave, when all she really wanted was for him to stay.

When her cell phone rang, she almost didn't answer. It was her mother's ringtone. She didn't know if she could handle talking to her mother right now. But maybe her mother was exactly who she did need to talk to. Advice was what Dixie needed, someone to help her figure out how to fix what she had messed up so badly.

"Hi, Mom."

"Dixie?" Her mother's voice didn't sound right. There was a catch in it, a sound almost like fear.

"Mom? Mom, what's wrong?" There was fear in Dixie's voice now too.

"There's been an accident, Dixie. It's Greg. He's in the hospital."

Greg?! No! No! He must have gotten in a car accident on the way home from her place. It was so late when he left and he had such a long drive ahead of him. She should never have let him leave. She should have made him stay!

"I'm coming down! I'll grab some things and leave right now!"

"No, Dixie. He's not in the hospital here. He's at Falcon Ridge Hospital, by you. The hospital just called Greg's parents and then his parents called us. Something about a robbery, a knife. Greg was stabbed! He's in surgery right now. Dixie, it's not good." Lainey was trying to keep her voice calm but Dixie could hear the almost hysterical worry her mother was trying to control.

"What? What do you mean? Mom! I'm going there right now!" Dixie shoved the phone in her pocket, grabbed her purse and ran out the door. Ran to her Jetta, threw it in gear, sped out of the parking lot, tires squealing. Her heart was in her throat, thumping so hard and so fast she could barely breathe.

Tubes and wires were everywhere - attached to bags of IV fluids that hung from hooks and flowed slowly, drip by drip, into Greg's arm - attached to a machine that made sucking sounds as it drew bloody red liquid from the surgical site - attached to a monitor that recorded Greg's vital signs, squiggly lines shifting on the screen, as they indicated his heart rate, blood pressure, body temperature, respiratory rate. Every few seconds the monitor beeped.

Greg was so pale. He'd been in surgery for hours. The attacker's knife had penetrated deep, slicing through tissue and muscle, damaging organs. Lots of blood had been lost. The doctor had said it was touch and go. But Greg was young, strong. His chances were good.

Dixie stood next to the bed, holding Greg's limp but warm hand, staring at his face, praying silently for him to wake up, to be ok, to be Greg. Finally, she saw his eyes moving underneath his lids and then they opened. Greg saw her and smiled. It was a weak little smile but a smile just the same.

"Hi," he said, almost too quiet to hear.

"Hi," Dixie replied, her voice as fragile as his.

Greg's lips moved again but no sound came out. He seemed to struggle, trying to speak, but he didn't have the energy to form the words.

"Shhh. Don't try to talk, Greg. Just rest. You've been through a lot. You just rest and you listen. I'll talk."

Greg closed his eyes, as if relieved, and shook his head slightly. Yes, he would listen. That's all he wanted to do. He wanted to listen to his Dixie.

"I love you, Greg. I never stopped loving you. I should have told you yesterday. Told you after you sang to me. I don't know why I ever broke up with you. I was a stupid fool. A stubborn child throwing a temper tantrum. It's like I had a case of temporary insanity or something! A brain freeze! Or a heart freeze! I'm so sorry. So sorry for everything I put you through. I love you so much."

A serene happiness washed over Greg's face as Dixie spoke. He smiled again and squeezed her hand.

"Love you too," he whispered.

Sudden, unexpected pain shot across Greg's features then, stealing the happiness from his face. He took a quick, shaky breath and let it out slowly in a soft moan. He clenched Dixie's hand tightly. And then his hand went limp.

"Greg!" Dixie screamed in panic, just as the machine monitoring his life forces began to emit a loud, steady beep, the squiggly lines running flat across the screen.

"Code Blue, Code Blue. Recovery 205. Code Blue, Code Blue, Recovery 205." Blared through the halls.

Doctors and nurses came rushing in and Dixie fled to the corner of the room to give them space. Chest compressions, paddles, syringes. She watched, wild eyed, as they tried to save Greg's life for the second time that day.

But Dixie knew their efforts would fail. She had seen the spark leave Greg's eyes. And it seemed there was a shimmering, a barely perceptible folding of iridescent air and light, that had hovered over him.

It had trembled and swayed as it drifted across the room and she felt a softness brush against her cheek and whisper in her ear. The whisper was a note, the note a melody, and the melody a song. Greg was singing to her again, of life and love, like before, but now also of sad passings and final goodbyes.

And the song was a melody, and the melody a note, and the note a whispered sigh that grew quieter and quieter and faded slowly away.

Greg was gone. A life - taken for a beat up old car, a folder full of songs, and a Gibson guitar.

Greg's parents came rushing into the room then. And her parents too. Their looks of concern and hope exploded and flew off their faces. Incomprehensible, uncontrollable sobs and unbearable grief filled the room.

Never ending love. Sad passings and final goodbyes. And a message in a whispered sigh.

'Life goes on, Dixie. Life goes on.'

Chapter 25

LICENSE TO REMEMBER

Lainey couldn't deny, she was kind of leery the first time she met Greg Grapensteter. He had purple hair for god's sake! And he played in a cover band in bars every weekend. Was this the right kind of guy for her sweet, darling daughter?

Dixie had to get special permission to be able to be in the bar from Joe and herself and from the various bar owners where the band played since she was underage (only sixteen!) with the express understanding that she not drink any alcohol.

Lainey and Joe had gone with Dixie several times to watch the band. Lainey had been very impressed! The band was tight, well-practiced. And Greg! He could sing all right! He put everything he had into every song. And with his good looks, his moves, his smile, his great audience interaction - He had all the girls in the crowd swooning.

Lainey wouldn't admit it to anyone, tried not to admit it even to herself, but she had felt a few twinges in her own nether regions at the sight of Greg on that stage.

And this really worried Lainey, the sex appeal Greg had. She was afraid Dixie was setting herself up for a fall. To be cheated on and betrayed by this handsome young man that had girls throwing themselves at his feet.

But those other girls might as well have been lampposts or bar stools for all the attention Greg paid them. He only had eyes for her daughter, only for Dixie.

When Owen and Gabriel first saw him, they stared and stared at Greg's purple hair. Greg had put a maniacal grimace on his face and lurched towards the twins, dragging one leg, arms outstretched, growling menacingly.

The boys had run, screaming at the top of their lungs, like Greg was the devil himself. Then Greg had laughed, went and got his guitar, sat the boys down and let them strum it. He took their hands and tried to show them some chords but their little arms could barely reach the frets. The guitar was almost as big as they were. They were only seven years old, after all.

After that the twins thought Greg was the coolest person on the face of the Earth, that the word awesome was invented for the sole purpose of describing Greg Grapensteter.

Lainey was hooked. This was some great guy her Dixie had fallen in love with. Kind, loyal, friendly, fun, respectful.

Lainey was sure Dixie and Greg would get married someday. They'd been together for four years! But then they'd had that big argument and broken up. Lainey could never really understand what the argument was all about. And then Dixie had gotten a real job, the kind of job she deserved, and moved out of town. Lainey hadn't seen Greg since. She had actually missed him.

And now this.

How could something so terrible have happened?

How could .....

Can't believe.......

Oh God.

Dear Lord.

Oh Greg.

Joe had thought that Greg was a buffoon with his purple hair. What kind of guy was this that his little girl had hooked up with? At least he didn't wear sag pants! But Joe didn't like him.

He started calling Greg 'Grapehead' behind his back. It was a little private joke between him and Lainey. He'd never call Greg that to his face, though.

But the kid had been respectful and friendly. He was always attentive, thoughtful and caring around Dixie, and Joe started to like Greg in spite of himself.

And he seemed to know everything there was to know about music. Joe was impressed! He'd quiz Greg with different questions every time he saw him. Greg always knew the answers.

What song put Bruce Springsteen on the charts?

When did Les Paul invent his namesake guitar?

What was the name of David Bowie's alter ego in the early 1970's?

Who are the members, both past and present, of the Drive-By Truckers?

How many CD's has Radiohead put out?

Who is the lead singer for The Decemberists?

The only question that tripped him up was – Is The Fifth Dimension still together and putting out albums?

"The Fifth who?" He had asked.

That was ok. Joe didn't know the answer either.

Joe never did like it that Greg sang in bars though. He didn't like his little golden nugget spending so much time around booze and drunks. He told Greg he'd better keep his little girl safe. If anything ever happened to her, he'd hold Greg responsible; he'd punch him out cold. Dixie always came home safe and sound. Within her curfew too! And happy. After she'd been out with Greg, she always came home happy.

Until that one night, when she came home all upset after an argument with Greg. Joe had completely sided with Dixie. He had pretty much encouraged her to drop him and to put more effort into her job search. Why had he done that? It wasn't like it was one or the other – job or Greg. She could have had both. And Greg really was a terrific, wonderful young man. He should have urged her to calm down and work things out. Everybody had arguments. Look at him and Lainey. They argued sometimes. And about the dumbest things, too! But they always made up. They loved each other. Dixie and Greg had loved each other, as well.

And now Greg was dead.

His parent's must be going through a living hell! Dixie was inconsolable.

How could.......

Why didn't.......

Damn it.

Son of a bitch.

Son of a god damn bitch.

Poetic License

STAR

I have your folder full of songs
And I have your guitar
They were given to me by your family
When you became a star
Shining down from above

You sang those songs to me
Your voice so clear and true
Words of heartache, love and loss
Echoed around the room

You could have been a star
And now you really are
Shining down from above

Your voice remains in my head
Your words remain in my heart
Remain in the corners of my room
Covered with cobwebs and dust

If my heart ever heals
I'll pick them up
I'll wipe them off
With a soft velvet cloth

I'll toss them up to the sky
So you can catch them
They will hang by your side
Like faceted diamonds
Like colorful gems
Shining down from above

You could have been a star
And now you really are
Shining down from above

Chapter 26

FRAZZLED LICENSE

Frazzled. That was how she felt – frazzled! Lisa doubted she'd had a good night's sleep in ages. There were toys strewn about in every room of the house, a trail of Fig Newtons was imbedded in the living room carpet from the kitchen to the stairway, the sink was filled with dirty dishes, and now one of the kids had doodled with berry juice all over the apricot colored couch. How the heck was she going to clean that off?

'Be forewarned', she had emailed Tony at work, 'I will NOT be in a good mood tonight!'

She knew Tony didn't understand how she could be home all day and not seem to get anything done. He got upset with her sometimes. But it's not like she could just leave Daisy and Bower to their own devises while she cleaned and straightened the house all day! Daisy was only five and Bower was still a toddler in diapers! She had to get them dressed and cleaned up, get them breakfast, lunch and snacks, entertain them and keep them happy and safe. And besides all that, there was the crazy knucklehead of a dog to deal with!

When she did try to squeeze in some housework, she still had to keep her eye on the kids. And even though she had them with her nearly every moment of the day, with her eye stuck on them like epoxy glue, they still managed to get into things they shouldn't be getting into – like that berry juice!

And what made it even worse, they had company coming for dinner on Saturday. A couple they had never had over before. One of the guys Tony worked with, Andy Boyd. But Tony said nobody called him Andy. Everyone called him Boyd, even his wife! And his wife's name was Pam. She couldn't have the house looking like a bunch of wild chimpanzee's had rampaged through it. Oh man, Tony was going to kill her!

Except for worrying about how she was going to make the house presentable, Lisa was actually looking forward to having this new couple over. Tony had said Pam was pregnant with the couple's first child. Lisa could regale her with pregnancy stories!

Like how horribly bad her back had ached one night when she was almost due with Daisy and how that turned out to be the early signs of labor because at three a.m. that morning, she started having full blown contractions. At six a.m. she was off to the hospital with contractions five minutes apart and at nine a.m. Daisy was finally born! For a total of about eighteen hours of labor!

Or how the labor pains were so bad and she was doing her who who who, hee hee hee Lamaze breathing like she had been taught, to help her deal with the pain, and also rubbing Tony's butt because, for some reason, that seemed to help keep her mind off the pain too. And the OB/GYN came in to check on how she was doing and both Tony and the OB/GYN were standing next to her bed and a contraction came and she started who-ing and hee-ing and rubbing Tony's butt, except it turned out that this time she was really rubbing the doctor's butt! She was absolutely mortified! She must have turned every shade of red in the book except that no one could tell because her face was already red from her childbirth exertions!

Or, her favorite, about the day Bower was born. The contractions were five minutes apart that morning and they went to the hospital but she was only three centimeters dilated and still had a long way to go so the doctor sent them home. And that afternoon, she was out in the yard. And what was she doing out there? Picking up dog poops! Well, she had to do something to keep herself occupied, didn't she! And the neighbor had spotted her out there on poop patrol and asked 'You must be about due, aren't you?' And she had answered 'Yes! I'm going to have the baby later today. I'm in labor right now!' The neighbor's jaw had dropped right along with the watering can they were holding.

But first, what about the house? What about the couch? Maybe she should try lemon juice!

Just then, the Knucklehead Explosion came prancing in, his terrier nose raised in the air detecting the smells of possible food acquisition. His first stop was the cookie trail. He started pawing the rug, trying to pry loose the Newtons. Lisa was afraid he'd dig a hole in the carpet!

"Knucklehead! No, No! Stop!" she scolded, yanking him away from his quest.

He did as he was told and then he charged over to the couch, sniffed its life story out of it and started to lick at the sweet juice dribbles and smeared finger shapes.

"Not to head! Not to head!" Bower squealed, clapping his hands and bobbing up and down on his little chubby legs.

"Look at silly Harley! He's trying to eat the couch!" Daisy giggled, using the dog's proper name, as she always did, instead of his more personality correct Knucklehead nickname that everyone else called him by.

Daisy tried to grab his crazily wagging tail but it kept swishing away from her. She kept trying though, giggling the whole time.

Lisa started to push the dog away from the couch but then changed her mind. Maybe a hardworking dog tongue covered in slimy spit would actually work! "Go for it, Knucklehead! Go for it!" she laughed, clapping her hands along with Bower and thinking she surely must be nuts.

But, wait! What's this? It actually seemed to be working! The stains were really disappearing! Well, if the dog could help by cleaning the couch, maybe the kids could help too! Why not?

"Listen up, boys and girls!" Lisa exclaimed enthusiastically, "Do you know what we are? We're a team. And teams work together! Right?"

"Right!" Daisy and Bower screamed. "A team!" they yelled.

"We're going to show Daddy what a good team we are! He's going to be so proud of us!"

"Yeah! Yeah!" they agreed. "Proud!" they cried.

And Lisa put them to work.

She gave Bower a soft toothbrush, sat him on the floor by the embedded cookies and had him rub the brush over the Fig Newton trail. Knucklehead Harley abandoned couch licking for the more lucrative position of crumb snatcher and stood next to Bower at alert attention. Bower laughed with glee as the dog scarfed up the cookie crumbs as soon as they were loosened from the carpet fibers by his determined brushing.

She got out the matching mother/daughter aprons with the pink and brown polka dots and frilly lace that Tony had gotten her for Mother's Day and tied them around her own and Daisy's waists. Lisa washed and Daisy helped dry - the unbreakable stuff, like plastic cups and plates, pots and pans, and forks, spoons and non-sharp butter knives.

Lisa got out the stop watch that Tony used years ago when he ran track in high school and made a game of how fast the kids could run around, collect all the toys and put them in the toy box.

It was so much fun! They were all having the greatest time, even Knucklehead, and the house was really shaping up too. Why hadn't she ever thought of this before?

She took another look at the couch to see how the dog's valiant efforts with his miraculous tongue had fared out in the end. Pretty darn good but not perfect. Lisa could still see faint bluish stains showing through.

She set the kids up at the kitchen table with crayons and sheets of paper and then sprayed the spots with some upholstery cleaner she found way at the back of the closet behind the laundry soap, fabric softener and toilet bowl cleaner. It cleaned up the remaining berry juice evidence like a charm.

Bower came running out then with a sheet of paper held out in front of him.

"Mommy, look what I draw!" he said proudly.

Lisa took the sheet from his little hands, prepared as always to compliment his scribbles but then her eyes opened wide in astonishment. This was no undefined scribble or simple stick figure. It was an obvious clown with a round red blob nose, blue oval eyes, wild streaks of orange hair, a red grin and a blue beret like hat. There were even crinkle laugh lines at the corners of the clown's eyes. Lisa was awe struck!

"You drew this, Bower?" Lisa asked with amazement.

"I did! A cwown!"

"Bower! This is really good, Honey! You're an artist!"

"I am ardis!" he crowed and ran back to the table to begin a new masterpiece, his little tongue sticking out the side of his mouth in concentration.

Tony came home from work that night to the smell of meatloaf baking in the oven. He saw the refrigerator covered with a whole new group of crayoned drawings. He saw the table set, haphazardly, with the napkins and silverware on top of the plates. There was not a single dirty dish in the sink. There was not a single toy scattered on the floor.

He found Lisa sitting in the big overstuffed arm chair in the corner, her arms encircling the children, Daisy on one side of her and Bower on the other. 'Green Eggs and Ham' lay open on her lap. And all three of them were fast asleep. Even Knucklehead Harley was asleep, sprawled carefree on the floor at Lisa's feet.

He walked quietly over to his wonderful family and kissed them, one by one, on the tops of their heads. Lisa opened her eyes and smiled.

"Hi, Tony! Welcome home! Guess what we did today!"

Poetic License

THREADS

Something round and something white
Bothers you both day and night
Pitter pat of little feet
Nothing ever seems to stay neat
Laughing, crying, tears and smiles
Love rolling around all the while

Threads intertwining, intermingling, getting tangled
Sometimes you think you're going to get strangled
Always the threads get straightened out
And words of love are the ones you want to shout

Something round and something white
The threads that kept it together weren't right
But now everything is all better
I re-sewed the button on your sweater!

Chapter 27

LICENSE FOR A KNUCKLEHEAD

Pam could hear a dog barking the moment they pulled into the driveway. And by the time they stood ready to knock at the front door, the dog sounded like some half crazed beast, ready to lunge for their throats as soon as the door opened.

"Somebody's here! I think they're here!" a child's voice called out from the land of commotion behind the door.

"Knucklehead! Shut up!!" a women's voice yelled.

"Get ahold of that dog!" a man's voice shouted.

"Lisa! Grab him! Can't you shut that dog up?"

"Mommy? Mommy!"

"Knucklehead! Darn you! Knucklehead!

Yelling and shouting, ferocious barking - the sounds of complete confusion and chaos. Was this the right place? More than that, was this someplace they really wanted to be? Pam was ready to high tail it and run!

Suddenly the door opened and a little girl, with short dark hair and the bluest eyes Pam had ever seen, was staring up at them. "Hi! My name's Daisy and that's my dog," she said proudly as she pointed down the hall.

There it was alright, not as big as it sounded from its bark but not a little dog either, probably about sixty pounds. It had the coloration of a German shepherd but with a wild crop of stiff wiry fur at its neck. It reminded Pam of something – A goat!!!

A man, presumably their host, Tony, was crouching down, holding the dog by the collar in a death grip. And the dog was squirming and whining, its paws running madly in place, desperately trying to escape from his captor and get to these strangers that had entered its domain. And if it did escape, what would it do? Jump on them? Knock them down? Lick them? Tear them limb from limb? At least it had stopped barking.

"Hey, Boyd! Dude! And you must be Pam. The dog's okay. He's just overly rambunctious. He thinks everyone's his new best friend. Just come on over and pet him and then he'll be ok. He'll calm right down. I just don't want him to knock you over. You're not afraid of dogs I hope!"

Pam didn't say a word. She just stood there, trying to smile. But was she afraid? Oh, yes! She was definitely afraid. She most assuredly was not a dog person. Especially not when they acted like a deranged lunatic. Boyd, on the other hand, had no fear.

"Tony! Hey! Afraid? Not me! I love dogs. What's his name?" And Boyd ambled over, hand outstretched.

"Knucklehead." Tony laughed, grinning.

"Daddy! You know his name's not Knucklehead! It's Harley. His real name is Harley!" Daisy piped up, chastising her father.

"Yes, Daisy. You're right. His name is Harley," Tony agreed with his daughter. "But I call him Knucklehead!"

"Hi, Harley. Hi, Boy. Take it easy now." Boyd greeted the dog, letting it smell his hand and then trying to pet the top of its head.

Once the dog got to smell Boyd's hand, he did seem to settle down a little and Tony let him loose. He bolted then, like a thoroughbred at the sound of the starting gun, down the hall to Pam. Impending collision! Get ready for impact! Pam braced herself, hoping she didn't end up flat on her ass. But he only smelled her, madly wagging his tail and then he dashed, back and forth, up and down the hallway, over and over again.

"Look at my dog! Crazy, crazy dog Harley!" Little Daisy laughed and screamed with delight at sight of such doggie shenanigans.

Pam laughed too. Crazy? Crazy was an understatement. No wonder Tony called him Knucklehead!

Finally the dog came to a stop, panting for a moment before he flew to his water bowl and started feverishly lapping water. When he was done drinking, he stood there, grinning a doggie grin, water dripping off his chin like it was an open faucet that somebody had forgotten to turn off.

A lady came down the stairs then, holding a little tow headed boy in her arms. He looked at Pam shyly and then looked away as soon as she looked at him. He kept trying to look at her without her knowing, turning his head each time she caught his gaze. He was so adorable that Pam wanted to scoop him out of his mother's arms and smother his little cherub face with kisses.

"What a way to greet guests, huh?" The women laughed as she shook her head "We've got the knucklehead explosion going here and as soon as you knock at the door, Bower springs a leak. I'm so sorry. You must be Boyd and Pam! I'm Lisa. Would you like something to drink?"

And the ice was broken.

Lisa got beers for herself and the two men and a sparkling water for Pam. All four of them sat chatting together and nibbling on cubes of havarti, muenster and cheddar cheeses and assorted crackers.

The knuckleheaded dog sat with his eyes glued to the snacks, watching each piece of cheese and each cracker on its journey from the tray to someone's mouth, hoping against hope that the delectable morsel's intended destination would change as it traveled, and end up in his mouth instead of theirs.

"So, what kind of a dog is Harley, anyway?" Boyd asked curiously.

"He's a Terrier/Shepherd mix. And am I glad he's got that shepherd in him! It's the terrier half that makes him a lunatic," Tony explained. "And the shepherd half that calms him down."

They all stared at each other in disbelief at that statement. Did Tony really say what they thought he said?

"Eventually!" he added.

And they all burst out laughing.

Daisy and Bower ran back and forth between their toy box, where they went digging on a quest for their favorite toys, and the appetizer tray. They stuffed cheese cubes into their mouths with wild spontaneity.

"One at a time, boys and girls, one at a time! We don't want anyone choking on cheese chunks!" Lisa admonished the kids. "Or poop out bricks later," she whispered under her breath in an aside to the adults, winking.

It was obvious Daisy had a thing for Boyd. Even little girls could tell a handsome guy when they saw one. Even little girls could get crushes. And when Boyd had called the dog Harley instead of Knucklehead, siding with her and using the dog's proper name, that had cemented the deal for Daisy. She was totally smitten.

She had to show Boyd how she could dance and she had to show him her stuffed animals. She had to tell him what her favorite colors were and show him how good she could color and draw.

Pam could tell Boyd was a little befuddled by all this attention from a five year old. But he feigned awe and wonder at her dancing skills and told her she was a real ballerina. He shook the floppy arms of each one of her stuffed animals and said 'How do you do.' He told her green and orange were his favorite colors too! He asked if he could keep one of her drawings since it was 'true brilliance'. And he folded it carefully and put it in his pocket for safe keeping.

Pam smiled as she watched her husband interact with the little girl. "Your kids are the cutest things I've ever seen. And I just love their names! Daisy and Bower. Names of the field and the forest. That's so creative!" Pam gushed.

"Well, you know, both Tony and I are nature lovers. That's how we met! In a hiker's club – The Dulaney Park Hikers! There's miles of trails in that park - just gorgeous – through meadows and woods, around ponds and streams. Anyway, we wanted to pick names that meant something to us, that reflected the beauty we saw all around us. Daisy and Bower just flowed right into our heads one day. And here we are!"

They talked about kids in general and about Pam being pregnant, and then Lisa started telling stories about her pregnancy and labor experiences with the timing of a comedian. She was hilarious, demonstrating her stories with facial expressions, sound effects and hand motions that had them all nearly rolling on the floor with laughter. Pam almost peed her pants she laughed so hard. Being pregnant didn't help. She had to pee all the time anyway. Her bladder always felt full!

They talked about how Boyd and Tony had known each other for years. They both worked at Lymekiln Extrusions and ate lunch together almost every day. A few times a year they got together with several of the other guys from Lymekiln and went bowling or to a baseball game or out for drinks. But for some reason they had never thought about getting together as couples until now. And they all declared how glad they were that they had finally done it.

"Oh no!" Lisa suddenly exclaimed as she jumped up and ran into the kitchen. "I'm having such a good time, I almost forgot I'm supposed to be cooking dinner!"

"Let me help!" And Pam jumped up too.

While Lisa put the finishing touches on the dinner, Pam set the table, Boyd sliced the Italian bread and Tony put Bower in his high chair, Daisy on her booster seat and tied bibs around their necks.

"I want Boyd to sit next to me! You sit right here, Boyd! Right next to me!" Daisy implored, looking at Boyd with her bluer than blue eyes and batting her long lashes at him.

Boyd looked at Pam helplessly, shrugged his shoulders and sat in the chair next to Daisy. "Okay, little princess, your wish is my command," he said as Daisy giggled.

When they were all sitting, Lisa came out of the kitchen with a sly, playful look on her face, her hands behind her back. "We're having the messiest of messy dinners tonight folks. Spaghetti and meatballs! It's bibs for everyone!" And she whipped out from behind her back four adult size bibs and proceeded to tie one around everyone's necks.

That Lisa really cracked Pam up.

At dinner, Daisy kept up a constant conversation with Boyd until her parents told her she needed to be quiet and eat her dinner and let Boyd eat his. People could not chew and swallow and talk at the same time!

Pam saw Boyd looking at her with relief flashing through his eyes now. As much as he liked the little girl, he needed a break. All Daisy's attention had been on him since they arrived!

Dinner was excellent. Lisa had made the sauce herself and it was thick and rich. It had been simmering for hours and was chock full of meatballs, Italian sausage, chunks of beef and even hardboiled eggs. For dessert, they had hazelnut coffee and a chocolate marble cheesecake that Pam and Boyd had brought. By the time dinner was over, everyone was so stuffed they could hardly move. And Pam was very glad she'd had the bib!

Eventually, Lisa rounded the kids up and announced it was their bedtime.

"Say goodnight to everyone," Lisa instructed her little munchkins.

The duo ran to their daddy and it was big hugs and kisses all around. They politely bid Pam goodnight, little Bower still kind of shy. And then over to Boyd for another goodnight.

"Good night, Boyd." Daisy said and then she unexpectedly threw her arms around his neck and kissed him. "I'm glad you came over. I had fun. I like you!"

"Well, I like you too, sweetheart! It was very nice to meet you. Good night, Daisy. You sleep tight now." He gave her a gentle hug and kissed the top of her head.

The soft smile that had been blooming in Pam's eyes all evening as she watched Boyd with little Daisy spread to her insides now.

Glittering lights detonated in her head, and fluttered like fireflies in her stomach, sending out glowing tendrils of radiance that warmed and melted her heart.

And Pam found herself falling in love with Boyd all over again.

Poetic License

THE FIRST TIME I FELL IN LOVE

The first time I fell in love
I was only seventeen
His hair was brown
So were his eyes
And his face was the handsomest I had ever seen

I knew that it was really love
Because I felt a flutter
In my stomach
And in my heart
The place where it really matters

The second time I fell in love
I was twenty three
His hair was brown
So were his eyes
And his face was the handsomest I had ever seen

He supported me through times of pain
And in joy he shared with me
He put up with my many moods
And knew no greater love could ever be

The third time I fell in love
I was thirty three
His hair was brown
So were his eyes
And his face was the handsomest I had ever seen

He was tender, sweet and loving
Honest, thoughtful and kind
And I was glad in times of trouble
I had never changed my mind.

Because even though the brown hair
May have changed from long to short
And some wrinkles may have been added
To that handsomest of faces
Those brown eyes still sparkle
With a shine that time cannot erase

The boy that I had fallen in love with
When I was only seventeen
Is still the man that I adore
When I am thirty three

Chapter 28

RETURN LICENSE

Dixie followed Arizona all the way down to North Creek and got on the highway. Wild asters bloomed purple on the sides of the road, in the meadows and on the edges of the cornfields, corn all picked, cornstalks dry and brown.

She tried not to look, kept her eyes straight ahead, on the highway. Purple was not a color she wanted to see anymore. Nor light brown, the color of Greg's eyes. Nor green, the color of Greg's favorite T-shirt, the one he had worn the night he sang her his songs, the night that was his last night. Nor red, the color of his car, or of his blood.

Dixie thought she knew now why people used to wear black when someone died. It was because colors reminded them too much of the loved ones they had lost. Colors became harbingers of sadness and grief.

She had taken a leave of absence but it had been three weeks now. Three weeks and she really needed to get back. Back to work. Back into the swing of things. Back to whatever else there was - life?

So now here she was, driving back along the same route she had taken in June, when the sweet excitement and exhilaration of a new beginning had shot through her like the scintillating lights of a disco ball. The only thing that shot through her now was sorrow; Sorrow, supported by a crutch of never ending tears.

Her concerned parents really hadn't wanted her to go yet. They kept asking her - Was she sure she was alright? Was she sure she could handle being alone? And Dixie had assured them that, yes, everything was good. She was ok. She was fine.

But it was a lie. She was not fine. Every time she took a shower and ran her soapy hands over her stomach, she pictured Greg's perfect, flat stomach, innocent and unsuspecting, just before it was pierced by the knife. She pictured his hot blood running over his skin just like the hot water was running over her skin now, only thick and red. And then gushing, hot and red, between his fingers as he tried to hold it in. She imagined him doubling over in pain and she would double over in pain too, only her pain was in her heart, and she'd cry delirious tears that swirled down the drain along with the soapy bathwater.

Dixie turned on the radio as a distraction, something to draw her mind away from her loss. She should have known what a mistake that would be. Too many songs had been sung from his lips. His lips, that used to smile at her along with his eyes. His lips, that used to talk to her and kiss her softly.

'Look at the stars, look how they shine for you' came floating out of the speakers. It was the beautiful 'Yellow' by Coldplay, one of the covers Greg used to sing. He would catch her eye out in the audience and grin and wink at her as he sang, letting her know he meant the song for her.

And Dixie was sobbing again, her vision blurred by an orgy of fresh, dastardly tears running in rivers down her cheeks. She pulled her Jetta over to the side of the road, waiting for the tears to diminish so she could see again, disgusted and angry with herself for being a spineless cry baby. And angry at herself as well, for a long list of other transgressions that she whipped herself for every day, number one on the list being - All My Fault.

The rooster flag still hung outside Fitzpatrick's, beckoning, welcoming hungry diners into its folds. The place was empty except for Dixie. It was one of those lulls that happen at restaurants sometimes, when people are done thinking about lunch and have not yet moved on to thoughts of dinner.

She sat down in the same booth she had sat in before, when she had been on her way to her new beginning. It was comforting to experience the familiar, the tried and true, these days. Change was what she had sought then. Comfort was what she sought now.

Before she barely had time to settle into her seat, a waitress came out of the kitchen with a rolled paper napkin full of silverware and a menu. A tiny hint of a smile flitted across Dixie's face when she saw that it was the same bubbly young waitress she'd had before. And she seemed even bubblier today, like she had wings to fly with and had to keep reminding herself to stay anchored to the ground.

Dixie wondered for a moment if the waitress would recognize her as someone she had waited on before. But why should she? Dixie was certainly not a regular. She had only been in Fitzpatrick's that one other time, month's ago. Hundreds of people must have come and gone since then, hundreds of people whose day had been brightened by service with a smile.

"Hi there! Gorgeous day isn't it?" the waitress beamed as she placed the menu in front of Dixie. "My name's Pam and I'll be your server. We've got two nice soups today – chicken escarole or butternut squash bisque. Soup always goes good on a cool fall day! It warms you, body and soul."

"Soup does sound good. I'll try the bisque." Dixie tried to smile back at Pam, tried to match Pam's enthusiasm for the beautiful day (Was it beautiful? She hadn't noticed.), but her voice was flat.

"Cup or bowl?"

"Cup."

"And what else would you like?"

"Just the soup. I guess I'm not really that hungry."

"Well, if you change your mind, you just let me know, Honey."
And Pam started to move away from the table. But then she stopped,
as if she had just realized something. "I just noticed the rooster pin
on your purse! You've been in here before, haven't you? I thought
you looked familiar! It was summertime, right?"

"Yes. It was June." Dixie kept her reply short and to the point.
Too much talking and something was bound to trigger more tears.

"Do you live around here or just passing through?"

"Passing through." And then something about Pam's happy
mood made her say more. "I live about an hour and a half north of
here. My name's Dixie."

"Dixie! You know, I love that name! Well, here I am talking your
ear off. I better go get your soup!" And Pam hurried off.

The bisque was very good - savory, smooth, comforting. It came
with a nice warm wholegrain roll too. And Dixie ate it all. It was so
good she thought maybe she should get more. To go. She could eat
it when she got back to her apartment.

Soup to go. Take out or Leave it. Channel Twenty News. Her
job. She had hardly thought about her job since... Well since....
And there were tears threatening to fall again.

Pam came back to the table then, just when a few of those tears
began to trickle down Dixie's cheek.

"How'd you like the soup?" Pam asked, but then she noticed the
tears. "Honey? What's wrong?"

And the whole devastating tale spilled from Dixie's mouth along
with the tears that spilled from her eyes and rolled, like crystalline
drops, down her cheeks.

Poetic License

THE DREAM

She must run, she must hide
She is frantic to get away
But her jacket is bright pink
And on her feet are heavy weights forcing her to stay

Like a goose she waddles with her heavy weights
A goose with no wings to fly
Except for the bright pink jacket
Which flaps and billows by her side

They are everywhere she goes
Those from whom she tries to flee
They are in the next room
She turns her face so as not to be seen
They are around the next corner
She slips behind a person or behind a tree

Now she is standing in line
With her bright pink jacket
With the weights upon her feet
Waiting to order an ice cream cone
Cool, creamy and sweet

She anticipates the freshness
The cold melting smoothness
Her tongue is poised to lick the dulcet cream
But instead she holds a spicy burrito
Filled with salty meat and pasty refried beans

Now she is in the restroom
Her feet are bare
Nothing to protect them from what has been left
Wet and slick, tacky and smeared
On the filthy tile floor

Her mind cringes and screams
Pictures grotesque things
That will attach to her skin, absorb through her pores
Soak into her blood and into her soul

And they are there, always there
They see everything she does
She can't run, she can't escape, she can't hide
They stare at her, she stares at them
Her face reflected
In her own haunted eyes

Chapter 29

LICENSE TO COMFORT

P am snuggled against Boyd and spooned his warm body. She kissed the smooth valley between his shoulder blades and glanced at the alarm clock on the nightstand by his head. Fifteen more minutes until the incessant beep would jar him from his sleep. Fifteen more minutes for her to perhaps doze off again herself, snug and cozy, rocked by Boyd's gentle breathing.

Boyd was an automation mechanic at Lymekiln Extrusions. His job was to ensure that all the lines ran smoothly and to repair them if they went down. One of the good things about his job was that his hours were always the same; seven a.m. to three thirty p.m. Monday through Friday. It made it easy to plan things in advance when you always knew what your hours were going to be.

On the other hand, Pam's hours at Fitzpatrick's were all over the place. There was the breakfast shift, the lunch shift and the dinner shift. There were overlapping shifts, underlapping shifts and shifty shifts. And she didn't always have the same days off either. Every Saturday, the hours for the coming week were posted in the back room. And if you didn't like what you saw, you tried to switch with another waitress.

It didn't really bother her that much. She had gotten used to the unpredictable hours over the years. But now that she was pregnant, it would be nice to have a little more stability. She'd definitely need more stability after the baby was born. How else would she be able to arrange daycare? Maybe she'd approach her boss and ask him if he could give her a steady, consistent schedule. After all, she'd worked at Fitzpatrick's for six years, been one of their most reliable, dependable waitresses. Pam didn't see any reason why he should balk at her request. Maybe she could even get seven to three thirty, just like Boyd. That would really be great!

Today was one of the days that Pam didn't have to be at work till ten, but she planned to get up at six with Boyd anyway. She liked to get him his coffee and kiss him goodbye before he left. She hated it if he left for the day without a kiss.

The buzz of the alarm clock woke Pam up. She had dozed off again! But the digital read out said eight o'clock, not six. This was the secondary alarm that had gone off. Pam had done more than just doze off, she had fallen sound asleep. So sound asleep that she had missed the six o'clock alarm. And Boyd was already gone.

Could there be a day more gorgeous than this? The mellow, hushed sunlight of autumn, filtered through trees adorned with burnished colors of yellow, orange, red and gold, followed Pam into work. She glowed golden along with the golden trees.

The restaurant was hopping! A steady stream of people, out and about on the beautiful fall day, kept pouring in. Pam was a smiling whirlwind, carrying plates of the usual stuff like burgers and fries, hot turkey sandwiches smothered with gravy, and bowls of chili, along with plenty of the daily special too - cheese, spinach and arugula blintz's with a creamy hollandaise sauce. The soup special, butternut squash bisque, was also a hot item, inviting the abundance of the harvest into hungry bellies and warming their souls.

Fitzpatrick's prided themselves on offering several fancy, high-end restaurant selections at reasonable diner prices, every day.

Finally the stream became a trickle and the restaurant actually emptied out. Pam got herself a little cup of the butternut bisque and went to sit in the backroom to relax after the lunch time torrent. Her taste buds popped! The bisque was that good!

Eva and Nikki, a couple of the other waitresses, came in with little cups of soup too and they all chatted about which kind of apple made the best pie, how her pregnancy was progressing, and if anyone was planning to go to the upcoming Bumpkin Pumpkin Fall Festival in nearby Circleton.

When the little bell over the door tinkled merrily announcing the entrance of another hungry customer, Pam bounced up before the others could even make a move. "I've got it!" she bubbled.

She grabbed silverware and a menu and hurried out to greet the new arrival. It was a young woman who looked to be in her early twenties. A cute girl, but her face was somber and expressionless. Something about her looked familiar but Pam couldn't place her.

Pam hated to see anyone so dejected and unhappy. She gave the girl one of her happiest, friendliest smiles and made cheerful small talk as she took her order, trying to perhaps lift her spirits and draw her mind away from her all too apparent sorrow.

The girl tried to smile back at Pam but it was more of a grimace. Not a hint of the light that usually accompanied a smile shone from her eyes. She said very little, giving short, simple responses to anything Pam said. And all she wanted was soup! Not even a bowl, just a cup! The poor kid.

As Pam started to move away to get the soup, she noticed that there was a rooster pin on the girl's purse. One of the pins they sold at Fitzpatrick's! And then it struck her. Honey blond hair, blue/green eyes, a little spit of a thing. This was the girl that had stopped in during the summer, the one that Pam hadn't been able to get out of her mind! She had been so lively and full of life then, like she'd had electricity running through her veins, like a sunbeam had taken up permanent residency in her smile. Her eyes had danced with vibrancy.

But a haunted sorrow dulled those blue/green eyes now, eyes that were puffy and shot through with red. The electricity had been unplugged. The sunbeam had vacated. Sadness covered her face like a mask. The same girl, but barely recognizable.

"You've been in here before, haven't you?" Pam asked brightly, almost hoping that the girl would say no.

But the answer was yes. And it turned out the girl's name was Dixie! Imagine that! One of the names she was considering for her own tiny baby to be!

Pam kept her eye on Dixie as she ate, and when it appeared that the soup was gone, she headed back to the table. Maybe the delicious warmth had livened Dixie up a bit! Maybe she might like a little something more to eat after all! What she saw instead were tears trickling slowly down pale cheeks. The sight broke Pam's heart.

"Honey, what's wrong?" Pam asked tenderly, with honest concern.

She didn't really expect much of an answer. Even people she knew never answered a question like this truthfully. They kept things bottled up, somehow feeling that they were admitting a shortcoming or a weakness if they revealed the source of their sadness, or even admitted to being sad at all. So she was surprised when Dixie actually opened her mouth. And it was tragedy that came tumbling out.

It was the story of Dixie Andrews - a smart, bright girl, but stubborn, headstrong and naïve. A girl who thought she knew where she was going, what she wanted and how to get it but who found out she really didn't know anything at all. A girl that had denied and rejected that which she valued most. And when she finally realized her mistake, finally understood what she really wanted, it was too late.

It was the story of the man she loved, how she had hurt him in so many ways, and all he had ever done to her was love her.

Of how he had died, gripping her hand - pain, mixed with a sad acceptance of finality, and love, shining from his eyes.

Of the devastating emptiness that dwelt in her now. Emptiness that was as heavy as lead, crushing her heart, squeezing wet tears from eyes that felt as dry as hot sand.

And of the terrible guilt that dwelt within that emptiness. Guilt, because she felt she was to blame, because the disastrous ending to the story was all because of her.

Silent tears fell from her blue/green eyes with every word, her sorrow so great it was like a living thing.

And Pam took this girl that she didn't even know in her arms, held her like a mother would hold a child, and tried to comfort her as best she could.

Chapter 30

LICENSE FOR RELEASE

Pam got her a little pot of hot tea, told her to just sit for a while, told her she was in no condition to drive right now. And Dixie did as she was told because she knew Pam was right. She felt withered inside, as dry and brown as the corn stalks in the fields she had passed as she drove, as lifeless as the brown leaves skittering along the sidewalk outside, blown by the October winds and crushed into tiny crumbs under people's feet.

The restaurant was starting to get busy again and Dixie watched with depressed, glossless eyes as Pam and the other servers bustled about. She slowly sipped at her tea but it did nothing to comfort or warm her. The ability to be comforted did not seem to exist for her anymore. It was just something to do while she tried to compose herself enough to be able to leave.

The tea was gone. It must be time to go. Dixie stood, fumbling in her purse for her wallet. Pam hadn't given her the bill yet and she glanced around Fitzpatrick's trying to locate her. She was nowhere to be seen. Well, she'd just leave a ten dollar bill on the table. That should be more than enough to cover a cup of soup, some tea and a tip.

Suddenly Pam was at her side, placing her hand gently on Dixie's shoulder, taking the ten dollar bill out of Dixie's hand and stuffing it back into Dixie's purse. "Hey, Honey. You know what? My shift's over and I really don't think you should be alone right now. How about we spend the rest of the afternoon together? I could take you to my house, put on a pot of coffee or something. We could sit and chat. What do you think?"

Dixie hesitated for a moment, but the look on Pam's face was so kind, so thoughtful and concerned, so honest. And Dixie didn't want to be alone. Didn't want to get in her car and drive with despair as her only companion for more than an hour. Only to arrive at the apartment that she hadn't been to in three weeks, still alone. And she would remember that the last person that had been in the apartment with her had been Greg. Greg, with his guitar and his green t-shirt and his songs. Greg .....

"Okay. That sounds nice. I'll go." The words popped out of Dixie's mouth quickly, interrupting her thoughts, trying to prevent them from going in a direction she did not want them to go.

"Good. Come on, I'll drive. It won't hurt anything to leave your car here at Fitzpatrick's for a while." And Pam led Dixie over to a shiny black Firebird with red leather seats.

It was a sleek beauty and if sorrow hadn't been squeezing Dixie's heart in a vise, she would have thought the car was really something, totally awesome.

Pam lived in a dove grey house with white shutters and a goldenrod yellow door on Elm Street. The first thing she did was show Dixie around her yard. Flowers were everywhere. Pam said they were winding down for fall but to Dixie they were more beautiful than anything she had ever seen.

Pam pointed and named them all. There were marigolds, zinnias, yarrow, twinspur, hydrangea, lavender, goldenrod, monkshood, dahlias, asters and every color of chrysanthemum you could think of. Dixie surprised herself, and Pam, by being able to rattle off the names of at least half of this dazzling assortment right along with Pam. She must have learned more by weeding her mother's flowers than she realized.

Then Pam took Dixie inside and showed her the moss green room with the baby animal curtains. Pam was pregnant! Although, you couldn't tell from looking at her yet. She was due in April! And this was to be the baby's room. She showed Dixie the yellow rubber ducky pillow that her husband, Boyd, thought he had gotten for the baby but that Pam had commandeered for herself instead.

She dragged out some photo albums and showed Dixie pictures of what a dump her now beautiful house had been before she and her husband had fixed it up. Dixie couldn't believe the difference. It was an amazing transformation.

While they were sitting on the couch looking at the pictures, the front door opened, and Pam's husband walked in. Dixie could tell he was surprised to see her there. He gave Pam a quizzical look out of the corner of his eye and the look on his face said 'Who is this stranger?' He reminded Dixie of her father for some reason although she couldn't say exactly why. He had to be ten years younger than her dad. Maybe it was his smile.

Pam seemed to glow at the sight of him. "Hi, Boyd! How was work? This is my friend Dixie. I'm showing her pictures of our house, before and after!"

"Hi! Nice to meet you." And he extended his hand to Dixie. "I didn't even know Pam had a friend named Dixie!"

"Well, I'm not really Pam's friend," Dixie tried to explain as she shook Boyd's hand. "I've eaten in Fitzpatrick's a couple times so we kind of know each other from there. But I'm here because... Well, Pam's just so nice and I guess I kind of needed help because I was.... Well, I was crying and ...." And then, there she was, crying again.

She tried to continue, to let Boyd know the reason his wife had felt it necessary to bring home a teary faced stranger. But the words got wrapped in her tears and tangled in her tongue. She couldn't do it. Not twice in one day.

"Dixie's having a tough time right now, Boyd," Pam explained as she handed Dixie a tissue and hugged her shoulders. "Life has not been kind to her lately. Is it ok for me to tell him about it, Honey?"

And Dixie nodded yes.

It seemed odd to hear her story out of someone else's mouth, from someone else's perspective. She dried her tears and listened along with Boyd as if she didn't already know what the outcome would be. And for some reason it gave Dixie a catharsis she desperately needed.

No one knew quite what to say when Pam finished talking. They just sat, looking at each other with sad eyes, lost in their own thoughts. Then Pam hopped up, got a pot of coffee going and insisted that Dixie stay for dinner.

Boyd did most of the cooking. He grilled chicken breasts and roasted potatoes. He made popovers. 'Pam's favorite!' he said. And Pam made a salad with avocadoes, tomatoes and fresh mozzarella.

While they ate, they talked about Dixie and they talked about Greg. They talked about life and love and mistakes that people make. They talked about death and about grief.

"Death is so final!" Dixie brought the fork to her lips and then set it back down, the piece of chicken still speared in the tines. "I miss Greg so much but I can't call him. Greg's not here with me, but he's not back home getting ready for a gig either. He's not sleeping, or eating pizza, or practicing his guitar. He's not taking a shower or reading a magazine. He's not laughing or crying or sitting at the Laundromat waiting for his clothes to come out of the dryer. He's nowhere! There is no longer a being on the face of this earth that is Greg."

"I know what you mean. It's hard loosing someone. I felt hollow and empty when my father died. It's not like I thought about him all the time when he was alive, not consciously anyway. But after he died, I realized that the fact that he existed was always in the back of my mind. He was a part of me, woven into my being. And when he didn't exist anymore, some of my being came unraveled." Pam nibbled on a popover, contemplating her next words.

"But death is part of life. You have to accept it. And then the pieces that unraveled start to weave back together. They form a different pattern, weaving around a memory instead of an existence. And you realize that they are still a part of you. It's just a different part, that's all."

"The thing is, I don't think my life will ever weave back together. And I don't even deserve it to. Because I'm the one responsible! Greg was stabbed to death! And it was all because of me."

"You didn't hold the knife in your hand. You weren't even there. It wasn't your fault, Dixie. Greg was just in the wrong place at the wrong time!" Boyd tried to reason with her.

Dixie stood up and paced around the kitchen, she grabbed a tissue and wiped her eyes, she sat back down and pushed the food around on her plate with her fork. Facts. She didn't hold the knife. She wasn't there. Facts didn't necessarily add up to the truth.

"But that's just it! He wouldn't have had any reason to be in the perfectly wrong place at the perfectly wrong time if it wasn't for me! I broke up with Greg, leaving him missing me and wondering why. I didn't tell him I loved him, when I really did. I let him leave that night instead of making him stay. I should have made him stay!" Dixie's voice was thick with frenzied despair.

Pam and Boyd kept their voices steady and calm, a counterpoint to Dixie's turmoil. They empathized with her, sympathized with her, but they held their own ground as well. They played out different scenarios, illustrating how different beginnings could have still resulted in the same tragic ending.

And over the course of the evening, as the conversation waxed and waned, Dixie began to see that they were right. Greg's death was horrible, heartbreaking, devastating, one of the most terrible things that could ever have happened. But it was not her fault.

The truth of this finally opened itself into Dixie's mind and etched itself into her soul and Dixie felt at peace.

Dixie slept over at Pam and Boyd's that night. They dragged a blow up mattress out of the closet and put it in the green baby-to-be's room. And Dixie slept as if she was a baby herself, at ease, comfortable, safe and secure. No dreams screamed at her as she slept, waking her up in the middle of the night, frantic, with her heart racing, her face pressed to her pillow to muffle her sobs and catch her tears.

The morning found her feeling refreshed and more alive than she had in weeks. She felt like Dixie Andrews again, still with a sad ache of longing in her heart for what had been lost, but no longer destroyed.

It was a Saturday, and as luck would have it, it was one of the rare Saturday's that Pam had off. And Boyd had off too because he always had off on Saturdays. Dixie cooked breakfast. She had to do something to show her appreciation for Pam and Boyd's kindness and generosity. She made scrambled eggs and pancakes. And then it was time to leave.

Pam and Boyd drove her back to Fitzpatrick's for her car.

"I don't know what to say. Thank you just doesn't seem good enough. You guys... I mean, who else would have done all that you did for some stranger they hardly knew? You helped me so much. Thank you for everything. Thank you so much." There were tears in Dixie's eyes again but this time they were tears of gratitude instead of sorrow.

"Be good to yourself, Dixie. And we're friends! Not strangers! You call me. Anytime. And I'll call you. I'll let you know when the baby's born!" There were tears in Pam's eyes too.

"Always remember, Dixie," Pam called out, smiling and waving, as Dixie started to drive away, "Life goes on!"

Life goes on. Soft words carried on transparent butterfly wings. A message in a whispered sigh. Dixie had not forgotten. Greg had whispered this to her as his shimmering spirit had diffused and faded slowly away.

Life goes on.

And it did.

Chapter 31

TORMENTED LICENSE

L ainey hurried into the kitchen and shut the door quickly against the brisk autumn night. Joe was sitting at the kitchen table, his feet resting on the chair opposite him, a coffee cup in his hand.

"Hi Honey! Brrrrr, it's getting chilly outside. Sorry I'm so late. The meeting ran over," she said as she hung her coat on the hook by the door.

"No worries," Joe replied simply, taking a sip from his cup.

Lainey looked at Joe quizzically for a moment. Something about his voice seemed a little off - kind of... fuzzy. She shrugged to herself. Maybe it was a pressure change thing; her ears hadn't caught up from going from the cold outside into the warmth of the kitchen. She shook her head, swallowed, jiggled her fingers around in her ears.

"I thought we'd all go out for pizza! Maybe to Scalise's! Where's Owen and Gabriel? Upstairs?" And Lainey went to the bottom of the stairs to call them down.

"Not here. Asked if they could sleep over at their friend's house. You know, that kid with the funny name - Mustache? Useless? Eustace! That's it. Eustace. Told em sure. Go for it. It's Friday night. Go have some fun. Why the hell not." And Joe took another big sip from his coffee cup.

It was not Lainey's ears. Joe's voice was definitely fuzzy. "What is it you're drinking there, Joe? Coffee?" Lainey asked with a hint of suspicion.

"Irish coffee. Irish coffee, without the coffee." And another big swig made its way down his gullet.

Lainey sat down at the table next to Joe and took his hand in hers. "What's wrong, Joe?" she asked with concerned tenderness. "This isn't like you, Honey. You haven't been yourself in months, not since… Not since what happened to Greg."

"What kind of person stabs someone?" Joe cried out with such sudden intensity that Lainey jumped in her seat. "Stabs someone over a guitar on the back seat of a beat up Chevy Malibu? What kind of fucking bastard shoves the knife in and keeps on pushing till it almost comes out the other side? What kind of a person does that, Lainey? It's me! I'm afraid it's me. You really don't even know me, Lainey. It's fucking me and you just don't know it."

Joe's anguish and despair was so deep that Lainey could almost see the air around him shimmer, like heat waves rising from hot pavement. His eyes filled with tears. One escaped and started to crawl slowly down his cheek until Lainey reached over and wiped it gently away. "I'm here, Joe. Talk to me. Please. Talk to me."

Joe had grown up on Bizmark Street, right in the center of the city. It was on the wrong side of the tracks, the bad part of town, the dodgy end, and was nothing like the little suburban town of Newel, where Lainey had grown up.

Newel had tree lined streets, well-kept houses with neatly mowed lawns and flower gardens. You could walk down the street at any time of the day or night without having to worry about being mugged or raped.

Not so the neighborhood around Bizmark. Greasy paper plates, dirty Styrofoam cups, crumpled cigarette packs and broken beer bottles sprouted up in the yards and gardens there. Old newspapers blew down the street and used condoms could sometimes be found discarded under untrimmed bushes or in the narrow alleyways between the shops on Main Street. Bums could be found in those narrow alleyways too, trying to sleep it off under fly away sheets of newspaper or under a cardboard box, if they were lucky.

Joe told Lainey it wasn't a good neighborhood. He had even taken her there once so she could see what it was like. He pointed out the graying white house with the sagging front porch and the broken shutters that his parents had rented the downstairs of, the rusty swing set encircled by cigarette butts and crushed beer cans in the weed infested little park across the way and drove past Saint Lawrence's Church where, at his mother's insistence, he had been an altar boy.

But he knew Lainey didn't get it. Even though it looked nothing like Newel, Joe knew Lainey still imagined his childhood to be the same blissful fairyland that hers was. Where she could walk down to the creek and watch the minnows slide through the water or catch tadpoles in a bucket. Where all the kids were in the house after dark, doing their homework or watching TV with their folks. Where she could play Clue or Scrabble or Mystery Date on the front porch with her little girlfriends and giggle over what color their mood rings were that day or what color the rings changed to when a cute boy walked by.

She probably got that fairyland impression because Joe mostly only told her the good things about his early life. He told her about his friends, Larry and Bobby and Freddy, and how they used to ride their bikes up to Al's Market on the corner of Saratoga and Clark for candy or popsicles. Or sometimes, if they could scrounge up enough cash, they went to Veltri Bakery and got a small pizza to share.

He told her about Larry being so lucky because his family actually had a swimming pool in their back yard. It was a four foot deep, above ground pool and it felt like paradise on a hot summer day. They would play in that pool all afternoon and then come out shivering and wrinkly and they'd eat whole sleeves of saltine crackers, they were so hungry.

He told her about how he had a crush on Bobby's older sister, Sophia, and about the time she had convinced him to let her look down his swim trucks and touch his privates. And then she had let him do the same to her. She probably would have let him do more than that too, if he had been capable of it or had the guts to try it at eleven years old.

He had even told her about how Freddy's mom would send young Freddy to Dinky's Joint on the corner with an empty tumbler glass. And Freddy would return the glass to her nearly full of vodka, a few sips having been stolen along the way by Freddy and his traveling companion, Joe. She never sent Freddy with any money, though. She had already paid the sleazeball bartender in advance, many times over, with the used goods that resided between her legs.

But there were other things that he had never told her and it was these things that he told her now.

He told her about the street gang that used to hang out by the abandoned, boarded up house next door to his. They called themselves The Fiends. The Fiends banged whores every night by the light of the moon right under Joe's bedroom window. Their moans and sighs and panting breaths as they went at it seeped into Joe's brain no matter how many pillows he shoved over his ears.

He told her how one night, The Fiends ambushed Joe and his friends, dragged them to a vacant lot, and held them with their arms pinned to their sides. The Fiends had tied a German Shepherd to a tree and they made the boys watch. Watch as they cracked the bullwhip. Listen as the dog's screams ripped open the night, just as the whip they wielded ripped open its flesh. Over and over again they cracked that whip. Over and over again the dog screamed. How The Fiends had laughed. And Joe, tears streaming down his face, had died inside, bit by bit, just as the dog had died, bit by bit, each scream of pain weaker than the one before until finally there were no more screams, just a merciful stillness.

Joe shut down his mind after that. He shut down his heart and his soul. He had to. It was the only way he could survive. It became do or get done, give it or get it.

There were new kinds of games that he and Freddy and Bobby and Larry started to play then.

They made spears by adhering nails to the end of sticks with twine and duct tape and tried to see how many rats they could skewer. They held the rats suspended in the air and watched, heartless, as the rats squealed and squirmed, struggled and bled, and died.

They snuck into the alleyways with baseball bats at their sides. They snuck up on the bums as they slept huddled under their newspapers or boxes. And they swung the bats. And the bashes and whacks and thumps echoed off the alley walls along with the bum's cries, and sometimes the sickening crack of bat breaking bone.

Joe was thirteen when he was rescued from Bizmark Street. His parents came into some money and were able to buy a house of their own. They moved to Cypress Lane in the town of Newel and Joe made new friends, friends whose parents invited his family for picnics in their backyards, where they grilled hot dogs and ate potato salad and played lawn darts or bocce ball.

People in his new neighborhood were friendly! They waved and said hello when you passed them by on the street and Joe soon realized that he didn't have to watch his back constantly or peer at strangers out of the corners of his eyes for the signs of someone ready to pick a fight.

By the time Joe met Lainey, he'd been living in Newel for five years. He had reopened his heart, reopened his soul; had become human again.

He had tried to forget his wretched past and the horrible things he had done, burying the memories so deep he thought they would never find him.

He tried to become a good man, a good husband, a good father.

It was the knife that did it, made all those memories surface and come out hacking and tearing at Joe's soul. He had seen the police report. It was a four inch long stiletto switchblade that had ripped into Greg's gut, leaving him writhing and bleeding on the pavement in a restaurant parking lot.

Joe had owned a knife just like it - razor sharp, dangerous. Kept it in the back pocket of his jeans. And he told Lainey about that too. About how he had stolen it from one of The Fiends, the one that had pinned back his arms so tight Joe thought they would break, the one that had laughed the loudest, that had hissed between tortured screams into Joe's ear things that no child should ever hear, the one he hated most.

Joe had slipped that knife right out of the bastard's pocket while the son of a bitch was preoccupied slipping himself into yet another skanky whore. And Joe had thought about how easy it would be to reach over and slit that fucker's throat. Just flick open the blade and draw it right across his Adams apple and watch the blood come flowing out. He almost did it too. Had his thumb poised over the button. Instead he had turned and faded into the night like a ghost, the knife a cold, hard security held tight in the palm of his hand.

The knife, all the memories, the sins he had committed. They were tearing Joe apart now. Because, of all the things that he had done since leaving Bizmark Street, the one thing he had never done was forgive himself.

Poetic License

MEMORIES

Memories, like shadows
Sleepwalk deep within our minds
The past
For good or bad
Inhabiting their vague outlines

A sight, a sound, jogs them from their sleep
They become a pinprick of light
Dim hint of dawn on the horizon
Then spreading and morphing to bright

How things were!
Perhaps you smile
Who you knew!
Bittersweet
What you did!
Fond nostalgia
And what was done.
Buried terror, guilt, shame, defeat

The present calls you away from your reflection
Memories fade back to the shadowlands
Some leave you with a kiss
A smile upon your lips
Some leave you with trembling hands

Chapter 32

LICENSE TO BE FORGIVEN

"**A**nd now you know who I really am, Lainey. A fucking bastard. The same kind of fucking bastard that killed the man our daughter loved." Joe gulped the last of the whiskey, slammed the cup down and shoved it across the table. He slumped over, elbows on the table, hands over his eyes, shoulders shaking slightly with deep sighs and silent sobs.

Lainey took him in her arms and held him, her own quiet sobs matching his, her tears wetting the back of his shirt.

When the tick of the clock and the hum of the refrigerator were the only sounds to be heard, Joe pushed away from Lainey's embrace, went to the cupboard for the bottle of Bushmill's, uncorked it and started to pour more into his cup.

"Joe, stop. I really don't think you need any more whiskey. You've had enough, Joe!" And Lainey grabbed his arm to stop his pour, covering the cup with her other hand.

"I'll tell you when I've had enough to god damn drink!" Joe's eyes flashed anger, his arm tensed, ready to pull away from her grasp.

They stared at each other, both their eyes flashing, neither one willing to give in. Finally Joe relaxed his arm. He let Lainey take the bottle away from him and put it back in the cupboard. He let her take the cup and rinse it at the sink. He sat back down at the table and watched her in silence as she started a pot of coffee, buttered bread, got out the cheese to make grilled cheese sandwiches, opened a can of cream of mushroom soup and poured it into a pan to warm on the stove.

Suddenly, Lainey banged the soup ladle down on the counter, breaking the pensive hush that had fallen over the kitchen.

"Damn it, Joe!" she cried out. "How can you think for one single moment that you are anything like the cold-blooded, inhuman monster that stabbed Greg? You are nothing like that! Nothing! How can you think that I don't know who you are? I know who you are! You are a wonderful, kind, thoughtful, sensitive, compassionate man. You don't even like to kill a spider or an ant! If you see any kind of bug in the house you don't try to smash it. Oh, no. You try to save it! You try to scoop it up in a tissue and carry it outside. And you help people. When Eric next door slipped on the ice and broke his arm, you took him to the hospital. And then, you even shoveled his driveway all winter! You spend lots of time with your kids, playing with them, showing them things, teaching them and helping them. You bring me flowers for no reason except that you love me! I know who you are! The best husband I could have ever had. The man I would marry again a thousand times!"

Lainey briskly stirred the soup around with the ladle and flipped the sandwiches. She walked over to Joe and put her hands on his shoulders, kissed the top of his head, leaned over and kissed his mouth.

"I understand now," she said quietly. "You had a horrible childhood. Bizmark Street was a wretched place. You did bad things. But that was more than thirty years ago. You were just a kid! Forced by your surroundings, molded by a hell hole. Why do you think those things are bothering you so much now? Because it's not you! It was never you. You're a good man!"

She kissed his mouth again and stared into his eyes. "And now you're disrespecting the man I love. You're putting words in his mouth and thoughts in his head that don't belong there. Stop dissing the man I love, Joe. Because the man I love is you."

And then Lainey dashed to the stove to rescue the cheese sandwiches that were starting to get an alarming shade of blackish brown and to turn off the soup that was bubbling fiercely.

She brought their dinner, such as it was, to the table along with two steaming coffee cups.

"Here," she said as she set one of the cups in front of Joe, "this is what you need. A good, strong cup of Irish coffee. Irish coffee, without the Irish."

Joe closed his eyes, shaking his head and chuckling softly. He took Lainey's hand in his and looked at her with such love shining from his eyes that her eyes filled with tears.

After they ate, they went for a walk around the neighborhood, like they used to do every night when they had a dog to walk but only did occasionally now. Neighbors they encountered smiled and waved as they passed, inquired as to how they were all holding up after the tragedy, urged them to stop over sometime for a couple of drinks and maybe to play some cards.

When they passed the Bigelow household where their boys were spending the night with their friend, Eustace, they paused and smiled at each other as Owen and Gabe's unmistakably fun-loving and rowdy laughter escaped through the brick walls and sailed out into the dark night.

Joe and Lainey walked around the whole neighborhood twice, just because. Because the air was cool and crisp, because the sky was so clear and full of stars, because the crickets were singing their starry night songs, because it felt good to walk together, hands clasped, fingers entwined.

Chapter 33

LICENSE FOR AN EPITAPH

The afternoon sun shone brightly down on Dixie as she stood next to Betty's Pantry. The parking lot was empty. The restaurant was closed. It was Sunday and on Sundays Betty's Pantry was only open till noon, for the breakfast crowd. Sunday was their well-deserved day of rest. Well-deserved indeed. Every other day they were open sixteen long hours, from five a.m. to nine p.m.

Dixie had gone to Betty and gotten her permission first, explained exactly what it was she intended to do. She didn't want to be accused of being a vandal. Didn't want her labors be to whitewashed over and eliminated from view.

Betty had looked at Dixie with tears in her eyes. She had patted Dixie's hand, hugged her, kissed her cheek and given Dixie her blessing.

Dixie had gotten a sheet of heavy plastic, had cut the inch and a half high letters into it carefully, with an X-Acto knife. And now she held the sheet up to the side of the building, at the base of the wall, just above the pavement.

The pavement was smooth and dark. After it happened, a fresh coat of blacktop had been applied, to cover up all evidence of the warm blood that had spilled there, had turned cold there.

Inch and a half high words at the bottom of a building wall would hardly be noticeable. But they were bound to catch a few eyes. Someone would see the purple words. And they would wonder for a moment what it was all about, why they were there, what they meant.

And then they'd shrug their shoulders and go on their merry way. It wouldn't be of any importance to them. But it was important to Dixie.

Dixie adhered the plastic sheet to the wall with duct tape. With a stiff brush she spread thick glossy purple paint over the template. She waited for a few minutes for the paint to set. She didn't want the paint to run and make the words illegible.

Slowly, carefully she lifted the plastic template away from the wall. And there it was. Perfect purple letters forming perfect purple words.

A STAR WAS BORN HERE
FOREVER LOVED
FOREVER DEAR
GREG GRAPENSTETER
SEPTEMBER 2013

"I love you, Greg," Dixie whispered.

And then she turned and walked away.

Chapter 34

LICENSE FOR A FIGHT

The cell phone vibrating in Boyd's pocket grabbed his attention and he pulled it out. Cell phones were off limits during work hours at Lymekiln Extrusions but Pam was well into her sixth month and if there was an emergency, Boyd had to be available. Sometimes, rules had to be broken.

It was a text message, but it was not from Pam. It was from his brother, Tom! Tom? He hadn't heard a thing from him in years and that was just fine with Boyd. What did they say - 'You can choose your friends but you can't choose your family'? Yeah, unfortunately you were stuck with family whether you liked them or not. And that really sucked because if he could choose, Tom would never make the cut.

He was about to ignore the text, delete it without even reading it, but something - Obligation? Responsibility? Family ties? - stopped him.

'Bro! Am in town. Meet 4 lunch?'

'Where?'

'Bigwigs. Know it?'

Boyd had heard of it alright. It was a dump of a bar with a bad rep several blocks from Lymekiln Extrusions. In the sleazy part of town. Of course his brother would pick a dive like that. And did they even serve food there?

'Thumbs down! Another place?'

'No. Already here. Not leaving.'

Damn it. He should just say forget it. Tell Tom to try again in another few years. But he couldn't do it.

'Fine. B there 11:30'

'OK C U'

                        ⁓

Boyd stamped the snow off his shoes and brushed the hair out of his eyes as he entered Bigwigs. The bar seemed almost completely dark after the bright white of the snowy day outside and Boyd peered into its dimly lit interior trying to see. As his eyes adjusted, he could see that it was an even dumpier dump than he had imagined it would be. And there was Tom, sitting at the bar, a pint of beer in one hand and four shot glasses, filled with varying shades of liquids ranging from golden amber to dark brown, arranged in a row before him.

Boyd walked over, hung his coat on the back of a barstool and sat down next to his brother.

"Ah! Here he is. The famous Boyd Boyd! Hero of all his mother's hopes and dreams!"

A lot of come backs to Tom's sarcasm came to Boyd then. What he wanted to say was 'And if it isn't the family loser, come home to spread more shit.' But he had more class than that.

"Hey Tom," Boyd said simply.

"Did you know that there are four different growing regions in Scotland? There's the Lowlands and the Highlands. And there's Speyside and Islay. And did you know that each one those regions produces barley malt with a flavor unique to its area and from which they make distinctly different scotch whiskeys?" Tom's words were slurred. Eleven thirty in the morning and he was already drunk.

"And I really wanted to try those four different scotches. But this shit hole don't carry top shelf stuff. So I'm pretending!" He waved his arm with a flourish in front of the four shot glasses. "What I've got here is a mystery! One of these might be scotch. Or maybe not!

Maybe one is bourbon or rye! It's a taste test, Boyd! And you are my rotgut tasting guinea pig."

"What the hell are you doing, Tom? I haven't seen you in years and you're sitting here blabbering about scotch whiskey. I can't do shots right now! I've got to get back to work. This is supposed to be lunch we're having here!"

"Marko!" Tom called out, motioning to the bartender, "Bring us out a basket of fries! And a beer for my Bro!

"There! Lunch will be coming right out! No need to get all hopped up! Now, on to the taste test! All you need to do is take a little sip out of each one." And he picked up one of the shot glasses and shoved it up to Boyd's lips.

"Tom! Get that freakin' glass out of my face!" Boyd started to say but as he opened his mouth to get the words out, Tom poured the whiskey in, squeezing Boyd's mouth closed and forcing him to swallow before he loosened his grip.

"You asshole!" Boyd sputtered, coughing and gagging. He felt like he had inhaled more of the whiskey than he had swallowed.

Tom just laughed and started whacking Boyd on the back, presumably to help him get the booze out of his windpipe.

"That's it. I'm out of here. Next time you're in town, be sure NOT to call me." And Boyd started to get out of his seat.

"Come on, Boyd! I'm just trying to have some fun. Loosen up. We used to have fun all the time when we were kids. Remember when...."

And Tom began talking about their childhood, when things had been good between them, and Boyd sat back down. They started having an agreeable conversation, chuckling and laughing, as memories of their boyhood days surfaced and were shared.

Once upon a time, Tom had been Boyd's best friend. He had always been a little on the wild side, someone that had a hard time knowing when enough was enough, but he had still been a good kid. And then, inexplicably, he had changed. He became surly, disrespectful and remote. Calls came in the middle of the night. Tom was in jail. Come bail him out. Fighting, vandalism, robbery. Drugs and alcohol entered the picture and they would find their wallets thinner and their credit cards missing as Tom pilfered from his own family to support his habits.

Their parents went to the ends of the earth trying to figure out what had gone wrong and find ways to try and help Tom. There were counselors and rehab programs. Nothing worked. You can't help someone that won't help themselves. You can't save someone that doesn't want to be saved.

Tom hurt and betrayed his family for their efforts. Boyd would hear his mother, and even his father, crying in the middle of the night, devastated at what their youngest son had become. And Boyd wondered how it could have happened. How could the brother that had been his best friend morph into something that barely bore any kind of resemblance at all to a decent human being?

Right now though, at this moment, he seemed like the old Tom again, the good Tom. And Boyd was glad.

"Hey, you know, I actually talked to Mom the other day. She says you finally knocked your wife up! I guess all your screwing with that little prick of yours finally paid off. Took you long enough. And now, a little rug rat on the way. Well, congratulations Boyd. How is Pam anyway?"

"Good! Excited about the baby! She's getting pretty big now," Boyd said cheerfully, trying to ignore his brother's derogatory tone and all indications that the old Tom he had been enjoying had left the premises and that the jackass Tom had returned. "She..."

"Must be big as a cow!" Tom interrupted, "Maybe big as that big black cow and her mulanyans over there, huh?" And he pointed at a group of imbibers at the other end of the bar. Imbibers that came in varying shades of brown much like the varying shades of whiskeys that had been in the row of shot glasses earlier. Whiskeys that Tom had ended up downing along with pint after pint of Bigwigs' finest swill.

After Tom had started in with the racial slurs, he couldn't seem to stop. He kept pointing and whispering under his breath to Boyd, but when you're wasted, your perceptions are off. Tom's whispers reverberated off the wall of Bigwigs as if he was talking through a loud speaker. Boyd could see the hate filled glances and warning stares coming from the group at the end of the bar.

"Shut your damn mouth, Tom! What the hell's wrong with you? Are you crazy? Come on, let's get out here." Boyd said tensely, trying to pull Tom off the barstool and get him out the door.

It was too late. Suddenly, Tom and Boyd were flanked on both sides and fists started flying. Boyd took a couple in the gut before he even had time to react and then he defended himself as best he could. He was not prepared for this, had not been in an actual fight since he was a kid. And fine establishments such as this, where fights were perhaps more likely to occur, were not the types of places he frequented. But now, here he was, and it was two, Boyd and his brother, against five.

He managed a look to his left to see how Tom was faring against the barrage of blows but Tom was nowhere to be seen. Somehow he had managed to slip away, an expert at starting a fight and then disappearing from the consequences. He had deserted, leaving Boyd to take the blame, to take the punishment that should have been Tom's. Not two against five. It was only him.

Out of the corner of his eye, Boyd saw the fist come sailing through the air at his face. Too late to duck, too late to intercept, it slugged him hard. He fell backwards, hitting his head on the edge of a table, and then lay sprawled on his back, spilled beer soaking into his shirt.

A laughing sneer on a face hovering over him and the swift approach of the bottom of a boot was the last thing he saw.

And then, it was lights out for Boyd.

Chapter 35

LICENSE IN PAIN AND ANGER

B oyd opened his eyes slowly. He was dazed and confused, unsure of his whereabouts. His entire body was an aching mass
of agony. Each intake of breathe yielded misery. A fuzzy dream
kept nibbling at his fragile consciousness. His brother. Bar fight.
Abandonment.

A dream? But his pain was real. And there was an officer of the
law standing at his side, staring down at him. His brother Tom. Bar
fight at Bigwigs. Betrayal and Desertion. Fists and feet tearing into
his body like a reciprocating saw, again and again. His heart plum-
meted in his chest. This was no dream. It was reality.

"Okay, buddy, on your feet," the officer said curtly,
un-compassionately.

Boyd struggled to rise on shaky legs. No sooner had he gotten to
his feet, than he started to pass out again. The officer caught him
under the arms, dragged him to a chair and plopped him down in
it. He slapped on a pair of handcuffs, one end on Boyd's left wrist,
the other end connected to the chair.

"We're going to need an ambulance for this one," he called out
to one of the other officers.

Boyd sat slumped back in the chair, willing himself to stay focused, trying to determine the sorry state of his affairs. He had
never been in a bar fight before, had never been knocked out before,
had never had a black eye before either, but he was pretty sure he
had one now. His right eye throbbed dully and he could only open
it half way.

He thought he probably had a broken nose too. It throbbed more than his eye did and when he touched it gingerly with his fingers, his fingers came away sticky and red.

And now, since he was sitting here with handcuffs on, another thing he was pretty sure he was going to be doing for the first time was going to jail. After they took care of him at the hospital, that is. A day that had started out like any other had gone completely awry. And Boyd felt like shit.

Boyd could see the bartender, Marko, over by the bar, waving his arms and gesturing as he gave an incident report to one of the police officers. He pointed several times in Boyd's direction and Boyd wondered what he was saying. That Boyd had been the instigator? That Boyd should be thrown in a cell and the key flushed down the toilet?

Then the officer was pointing at him too, but instead of the key being flushed down the toilet, they were unlocking the cuffs.

"You're off the hook, buddy. Bartender says you had nothing to do with it really. Says you're just some poor sucker in the wrong place at the wrong time. An innocent bystander, more or less. Just hang tight. I've got an ambulance on the way."

Luckily, there would be no trip to jail for Boyd; only a trip to emergency with a swollen face, a bruised and battered body, and maybe, a concussion.

"Who do you want me to notify of your condition? They can meet you at the hospital."

Pam. She would be at Fitzpatrick's now, in the middle of the lunchtime rush, scurrying about serving a flurry of sandwiches and soups to the hungry multitudes, her pregnant belly leading the way.

"My wife. But I don't want her to see me looking like this." Boyd had to pause. His voice was cloggy and he was having a hard time pronouncing his words, the result of his broken, bloodied nose and a split lip. "She's six months pregnant. I don't want to upset her more than I have to. And besides, she's at work, really busy. Can't she be notified later, after I'm cleaned up and they figure out what the damage is?"

"It's our policy to notify someone immediately when an innocent is accosted or injured at the scene of a crime, sir. What's your wife's number?"

"Can't you break with policy this time? Rules are made to be broken, aren't they?"

The officer's eyes opened wide in surprise, not believing what he had just heard Boyd say. "You do know you're talking to a cop, don't you? We're supposed to uphold the rules, not break them," he said sternly.

He took real note then of the pathetic sight that was Boyd and his tone softened. "As you wish. Here's the ambulance now. Let's get you to the hospital."

It was not as bad as it could have been.

In addition to the numerous cuts and bruises, the black eye, the broken nose, and the split lip, he had five cracked ribs, a fractured clavicle and minor bruising on his kidneys.

But, he did not have a concussion. And, he was still alive.

They wanted to keep him overnight for observation but as long as there were no new developments or complications, he would able to go home in the morning.

So now, here he was, lying on the narrow hospital bed, stitched and bandaged and loaded up on pain killers, waiting for Pam to come visit his sorry ass.

He was just starting to drift off to sleep when he felt a gentle pressure on his hand. It was Pam, still wearing the black pants and sage green shirt she wore at Fitzpatrick's. Even the burgundy apron was still tied around her waist, barely covering her growing baby bump. A look of intense worry covered her face.

"Boyd? Are you all right? Oh my god. Look at you! They said you got beat up in a bar! What were you doing in a bar on your lunch hour, Boyd? What the hell happened?" And she started to cry.

She tried to put her arms around him, to hug him. But there was no place she could put her arms without hurting him. There was not even a place where she could put her lips to kiss him. She started to cry even harder.

"Pam, don't cry. I'll be all right. It's not as bad as it looks. Really. I'm going to be okay." And he tried to move to comfort her but pain shot through him. He stifled his cry and tried to keep the pain from showing on his face.

"What happened, Boyd? Tell me what happened!"

Anger hot as fire radiated off Pam as Boyd told her of his encounter with his brother. By the time he reached the climax with Tom's desertion and his own beating, Pam was a volcano ready to erupt. She exhaled smoke. Flames leapt from her eyes.

"I'm going to kill that son of a bitch! How could he do that to you? You could have been killed! Give me your phone!" And she stormed through the remains of Boyd's blood splattered, bar stinking clothing and other belongings that had been stuffed into a plastic bag and left in the closet across from his bed, searching for his cell. She stabbed the call back button, practically foaming at the mouth.

Of course there was no answer. They both knew Tom would never pick up. And they both knew he would never call back either. He was too much of a coward to own up to what he had done, too gutless to apologize or offer help, too spineless to even beg forgiveness.

Pam left a message for the piece of shit, though. It was full of words Boyd never expected to hear spewing from the mouth of his sweet, darling, kind hearted wife who rarely had a bad word to say about anyone or anything, words that even the lowest dregs of humanity would be ashamed to say or would blush to hear.

And his brother deserved every one of those words. Boyd hoped they punched, kicked, gouged, cut and broke him, like the merciless fists and heavy boots had broken Boyd today. He hoped they wedged themselves into his ears and embedded themselves into his worthless soul so he would never forget what he had done.

Once, a long time ago, Boyd's brother Tom had been his best friend. He was not Boyd's best friend now. He was not his brother anymore, either.

Chapter 36

SCUM BAG LICENSE

Tom saw them all glance at each other, their eyes flickering in the dim bar light, saw them all nod slightly and blink. Tom knew this look, had seen it many times aimed in his direction. This was the signal, affirmation between cohorts that they'd had enough, that now was the time.

Tom lived for this. He had a fixation with causing trouble, riling people up and seeing how long it took before they reacted. His heart raced as adrenalin coursed through his body. Excitement excreted like sweat right through his pores.

His dumb ass brother was getting nervous as hell. He kept trying to get Tom off his barstool and pull him towards the door. He had no clue it was already too late. But Tom knew and he was prepared. Before the first punch was thrown, he had his escape plan already in motion. A right hook here, a duck there and he had slipped under an arm and was headed for the door, hardly the worse for wear. One little love tap to the chin was all he got.

But what about his brother? He hadn't even considered what his actions might mean for Boyd. He turned briefly just in time to see a fist connect with Boyd's face. He saw the ruby red drops fly. For half a second he considered turning back, helping Boyd survive the odds that were stacked so high against him. For just half a second, and then he turned and ran even faster, out the door and into the glare of sun on snow.

Snow melt blackened by car exhaust and mixed with salt, ash and cigarette butts kicked up and splattered filth on the bottom of his pant legs as he hurried down the street. Sirens began to scream in the distance, getting louder by the second, probably called by the bartender to break up the fight.

He turned the corner and paused, fished around in an inside coat pocket and pulled out a flask from which he took a big swig. Fished around in another pocket and threw something small and round down his gullet, followed by another long swig.

He started chuckling softly to himself with perverse pride, as he pictured the fight that must be going on in Bigwigs right now. Fists flying, chairs and tables flying, bottles and glasses flying, probably bodies flying too. Flying and breaking. And all the crashes and the cries, the grunts and groans, the hissing, spitting rage, and the moans of pain. And it was all because of him. He was getting a hard on just thinking about it!

Dumb shits. Assholes. Fucking morons.

He froze in his spot when the word 'brother' entered his head. He had already forgotten. His brother was still in there. One of the flying, breaking bodies would be Boyd's.

The magnitude of his sin hit him then. Waves of guilt and remorse washed over him with such force that his stomach lurched, sending hot, acrid bile shooting up into his throat till he thought he might puke. His blood seemed to thicken and curdle in his veins, threatening to cease flowing all together, stopping his vicious, traitor's heart.

But it was only for an instant. He shook the feeling off, or at least he thought he did, took another swig from the flask, and hurried away again, stumbling over icy chunks and slipping in mucky slush as he went.

"Collateral damage. That's all it is. Collateral damage," he kept mumbling to himself, over and over, until he no longer knew what it meant or why he was even saying it.

He tried to shake off those words too. 'Collateral damage.' He didn't want to say them anymore! But collateral damage was part of him now. It was his soul that he had paid with, given up in exchange for a festering void that would ooze shame and weep guilt. A nagging wound that would never scab over, never heal.

Chapter 37

LICENSE FOR LOST LOVE

"Hey, Mom! You've got to see this new round house kick we learned today!" Owen was tugging at his coat and trying to show her the kick before he was even through the door."

"Cool! Very impressive!" Lainey complimented, winking at Joe who came through the door right behind Owen.

Joe winked back, ducking as Owens' flying foot went sailing over his head.

"Hey! Flea brain! Remember to gauge your distance! You almost nailed Dad in the head!" Gabriel admonished his twin as he followed his father into the kitchen.

Owen and Gabriel were growing so fast. Since they had turned twelve last August, they were like April grasses after the spring application of lawn fertilizer. At eleven, they had still looked like boys. Now, at twelve and a half, Lainey could see the men that they would become starting to emerge.

Owen was getting tall, lean and muscular, with a faint shadow of soft fuzzy stubble showing on his upper lip. His curly mop of caramel colored hair framed his face, accentuating his bright green eyes.

Gabriel was tall and muscular too, his fuzzy stubble more pronounced than Owen's. His voice had even started to change already, cracking, especially when he was excited, and sending an embarrassed blush across his cheeks. He was like a younger version of his father, dark and smoldering.

Maybe she was prejudiced, but she thought they were both handsome beyond belief.

"Master Amos says we're going to have our brown belt tests in two weeks! We've got a new kata to learn and all the old ones to practice up on," Gabriel announced excitedly as he kicked and punched his way across the kitchen floor and over to the refrigerator.

He stuck his sweaty head in the fridge, looking for something to eat and came out with a slice of left over pizza in his hand. "Aw yeah! This is what I want!" He smacked his lips in anticipation.

"Pizza! That's not the only piece is it?" And Owen headed for the fridge too.

Lainey grabbed the slice from Gabriel's grasp before he could even start to unwrap it and headed Owen off at the pass.

"Hold it right there, you two. Before you start stuffing your faces or doing anything else, you've got to go get cleaned up. You're gross! Sweaty, stinky messes! Throw those gi's in the wash and jump in the shower. I'll make some sandwiches for you to eat when you get back down here. How about ham and cheese?"

"And the pizza too? I'm a starving bottomless pit of hunger!"

"You're bottomless all right! Now get up those stairs!"

"Yes Ma'am Sir!" The twins shouted out in unison, saluting her and laughing like loons before they turned and bounded up the stairs, throwing punches and kicks at each other as they went.

"Gotta love em!" Joe chuckled as he hung his coat on the rack.

"Dixie called while you were out!" Lainey sounded happy and excited, like she had beans to spill and couldn't wait to fill Joe in on the news.

"Did she! How's she doing?"

"Really well! She said things were great at work. She's got a snowman contest going at the station right now. And then, by coincidence, they got a foot of snow yesterday! Can you believe that? A foot! Great for the contest but bad for anything else. Took her sixty five minutes to get to work instead of twenty but the roads are all cleared up now.

"And you know what else?" Lainey continued eagerly, "I think she might have a boyfriend! She talked a lot about one of the guys she works with. It was 'Mike did this and Mike said that'. I asked her if Mike was her boyfriend and she said 'no', that he was just a 'regular friend'. But I don't know! I think something else is going on there!

"But anyway, she sounded good, Joe. Happy and full of life!" Just a touch of somberness crept into Lainey's joy then. There was a reason her daughter's happiness was something to celebrate instead of simply being the norm, and she added, "Like our old Dixie."

"That is so good to hear. My little golden nugget deserves to be happy. I still worry about her, you know. After everything that happened with Greg and all......." Joe was quiet, contemplative for a moment, then he sighed and shook his head, dismissing thoughts he didn't want to entertain, and a sadness over events he had no power to change.

Lainey caught Joe's eye and shook her own head, a sad, understanding little smile appearing and then disappearing from her lips, heading off a tear that threatened to form in the corner of her eye.

"You'll never guess who I ran into at the grocery store this morning," Lainey said, changing the subject, "Brenda Akerman!"

"Brenda! I was just thinking about her and Clay the other day and all the good times we used to have together. What's going on with them?"

"Nothing good. They're separated, going to get a divorce! Bren was almost in tears."

"So they're really going to do it, huh? Well, I guess I shouldn't be surprised. All they did was argue with each other and put each other down anyway."

"Kind of like us, huh?" Lainey teased.

Joe grabbed Lainey from behind and folded her into his arms at that statement, leaning around and kissing her playfully, almost making her drop the packages of ham and cheese slices she had just pulled out of the fridge for the twins' lunch.

"Come on Lainey, we don't argue that much! You know I love you. And when we do argue, we always make up. Arguing's just a ploy, you know. For the makeup sex!" He grinned and kissed her again, his fingers inching mischievously down her stomach towards what lay below.

Lainey slapped his hand and wriggled out of his grasp, but she was smiling, a flirty, coy smile, and her eyes were shining. 'Later' her smile and her eyes promised. 'Later'.

Brenda and Clay Akerman. Their dog walk friends! Lainey and Joe had met them years ago, when they used to walk Astrid around the neighborhood every day, pushing the twins in the stroller with little Dixie skipping ahead of them. Astrid's fluffy tail would be waving like a flag over her back, her four white doggie paws prancing merrily along.

And when they came to the white ranch on the corner of Burlwood and Dragonfly Lane, there would be the Akermans - Brenda puttering about in the garden or getting ready to go out for a bike ride, and Clay mowing the lawn, practicing his golf swing or flipping hamburgers or steaks on the grill, the mouthwatering aroma wafting in the breeze, making their stomachs rumble.

First it was just a friendly wave, then they'd stop and strike up a bit of conversation, about the dog or the kids or the weather or about how the vegetable garden was doing and the pros and cons of going organic. Before you know it, they were inviting each other over for dinner. They were going out to see a movie or ringing in the New Year and dancing the night away at Godiva Party House's Year End Bash.

And then something changed. Brenda and Clay didn't seem happy anymore. Their smiles were forced and artificial, stuck on their faces to hide the glares they shot at each other when they thought nobody was looking. Tension lay between them like a swamp of fetid water and sucking mud that they couldn't seem to wade through.

Lainey tried to uncover the reason for their discord. Both she and Joe gently prodded Brenda and Clay and snuck casually disguised questions into the conversation. They slipped in hints on ways that they themselves handled arguments or misunderstandings. But none of their attempts at amateur marriage counseling had any affect. The Akerman's relationship continued to deteriorate.

One of the last times they had all gotten together had been over a year ago. Lainey would never forget it. They had been at The Burger Emporium, laughing away, when Brenda had made a jab at Clay about something. Maybe it was that his T-shirt was on backwards or a bit of lettuce was stuck in his teeth or that she thought he was laughing too loud, but she had made him feel like a gauche fool. Poof! The smile had vanished from his face like someone had flipped a switch. And there came the tension, settling over the whole group like odorous swamp gasses.

Lainey and Joe had tried to bring the joviality back to the evening. They recounted Owen and Gabriel's' stunt of the week – filling the egg carton with hard-boiled eggs and then convincing Lainey to make a cake! They revealed Lainey's recent cooking disaster when she had mistakenly grabbed baking soda instead of cornstarch, creating a cauldron of foaming stench instead of beef stew! They even tried telling dirty jokes – liquor in the front, poker in the rear! But joviality's return would not be had. Clay had not smiled, had barely even spoken another word, for the rest of the night. And Brenda had sat there cold and stiff, a feeling almost like hatred emanating off of her and oozing over to Clay.

Lainey called Brenda a few times after that with invitations for drinks or dinner but lame excuses were given as to why they couldn't make it. Return invitations on Brenda's part were never made. Then Astrid died and Lainey and Joe's daily walks ended too. The friendly wave and bit of conversation as they passed the white ranch on the corner of Burlwood and Dragonfly became a thing of the past, and their friendship with the Akermans drifted away, just as Brenda and Clay's relationship with each other left completely the realm of love and togetherness and vanished into nothingness.

How could love be lost? How could it disappear entirely from someone's heart? How could its vacant spot be claimed by indifference or even hate?

These were questions Lainey couldn't answer. In a language she didn't understand. And never planned to learn.

Poetic License

LOVE'S LOSS

There must have been a reason
For the bended knee
The ring and the vows
There must have been that feeling of completeness
Eyes soft and glistening
Two hearts brimming over with love

Did they forget that first glimpse
How their eyes caught
How their hearts pounded in their chests
Did they forget the court and the spark
Did they forget what they gave each other
Both fierce and tender
In the dark

Did they know their love was lost
Did they search for it
Did they fight to get it back
Did they struggle with the thief that stole it
And try to wrench it from his grasp

Or did they just sit, watching it fade
Waving goodbye
As it evaporated and floated away
Only realizing too late
The brutal tragedy
Of their mistake
And how much they would miss it
When love was gone

Chapter 38

LICENSE FOR A PUNCHING BAG

Day four and he still scared himself every time he glanced in the hallway mirror or looked in the mirror over the bathroom sink. The swollen, battered face of a nightmare looking back at him was not something he had gotten used to seeing yet. And he could swear that each time he looked, the deep fuchsias, dark purples and bluish blacks around his eye were spreading, migrating down his cheek till they blended with the same brazen colors that bloomed across his nose.

He had scared the floral delivery lady too when she rang the bell with a Get Well Bouquet from Dixie Andrews and he had come to the door looking like some sinister, evil clown right out of a Stephen King horror movie.

Somewhere they had a box with funny hats, wigs and fake noses that they had collected from Halloweens past. He could put on the big red puffy clown wig. That would draw attention away from his face! Make people laugh before they screamed!

But that box was probably in the crawl space. No way was he going to try to go crawling around on his knees with one arm in a sling under a four foot high ceiling looking for a box of costume paraphernalia.

Maybe what he should do is make up a sign to hang on the front door, to warn people that they were bound to get an eyeful

175

of something unpleasant when the door opened and they saw what used to be, was supposed to be, Boyd standing there.

Beware Of Hideous Monster!
Prepare For The Worst!
Knock At Your Own Risk!

A bunch of the guys were going to be stopping over after work for a visit. He had already warned them that he was not a pretty sight. They still weren't prepared.

"Boyd, is that you? Shit!" Josh blurted out, his eyes so wide they covered half his face.

"Whoa!" Brad cried, almost losing his grip on the bouquet of 'Get Well Soon' Mylar balloons he was holding. He regained his grasp on their black and blue ribbons just in time to prevent their take off into the waning light of dusk.

Tony stared in disbelief with his mouth hanging open, speechless. The gift bag he was carrying fell to the floor and clouds of tissue paper came puffing out, like rainbow colored smoke.

PJ was the only one that was able to keep his cool. "Hey, Boyd. How you doing?"

"Well, except for every part of me looking and feeling like I was trampled by a herd of rampaging zebras, I'm doing just great!"

Everyone chuckled, but just a little bit. Just a little bit, because they knew Boyd really wasn't joking. He was telling it like it was. He felt like hell and they all knew it.

"Just throw your coats over there," Boyd said, motioning to a chair in the hallway.

Tony handed Boyd the gift bag, and they all sat down to watch him open it.

There was a card, addressed to Andrew "Punching Bag" Boyd, and signed by everyone at Lymekiln.

'Take my advice. If you see a fist headed towards you, run!'

'Don't let anyone use you for a punching bag ever again!'

'Hurry back! We miss you!'

'Avoid bar fights at all costs!'

'You win some, you lose some. Next time, don't lose!'

'Keep your head down and your dukes up! Get well soon!'

There was also a book, *How to Protect Yourself for Dummies*, a gift certificate for three months' worth of self-defense lessons at Hilton Davis Karate Studios, and a bag of chocolates wrapped in black and blue foils, each piece shaped like a tiny boxing glove.

"So when do you think you might be back to work, Boyd?"

"The doctor said ten to twelve weeks, but I'm shooting for four or five. I've been checking stuff out online. My face should be back to normal in about three weeks and the ribs should heal in about four or five weeks. I can't get a handle on how long it's going to take before my kidneys stop bleeding into my urine, though. And the collar bone might take three months, but it doesn't have to be completely better before I can start to do things. I'm going nuts around here already and it's only been four days. The life of boredom is not for me."

"You gotta take it easy, Boyd. It doesn't pay to rush this stuff."

"Don't worry about me, boys. I'm not rushing anything. I'm doing exactly what my doctor says. I just think he's exaggerating my downtime."

"What's he got you on for pain?"

"Vicodin. It makes me loopy, though, so I'm trying to tolerate the pain without the meds during the day and only take the pill at night, so I can sleep."

"I'd go for loopy if I was you, dude! What's wrong with loopy? What have you got to lose?"

What indeed. The jokes started flying then. The guys were really cracking him up but he was already cracked so the tears of laughter that appeared in his eyes became tears of pain. Boyd hoped the guys couldn't tell the difference.

They had only been there for forty minutes or so, but Boyd was fading fast. His chest ached, his shoulder ached, his back ached. It was all he could do not to start moaning right in front of them. So he was glad when his four visitors all stood up in unison and said they should be leaving.

"Thanks for coming. I really appreciate it. Tell everyone thanks for the gifts. Maybe I'll try to stop in to say 'hi' in a couple more weeks." And Boyd ushered them to the door, about ready to collapse.

But Tony didn't go out the door. He hung back. "Looks like you could use a little help there, dude." And he helped Boyd back over to a chair, got the bottle of pain meds from the bathroom and a big glass of water and made Boyd take one.

"You know, you could have told us we needed to leave earlier. You didn't have to play Mr. He-Man for us."

"But everyone went out of their way to come over here. I didn't want to make anyone feel bad or think they wasted their time on some ungrateful jerk."

"We were here for you Boyd, not for ourselves. Everyone knows your situation. We would have understood."

Tony started to head for the door again but then he paused, and instead of leaving, he sat on the couch across from Boyd, a pensive look on his face, as if he was trying to figure something out. And whatever that something was, he must have settled on it because the look that crossed his face next was 'I'm gonna go for it'.

"So, have you heard anything from that cock sucking, ass wipe brother of yours?"

"Yeah, right." Boyd answered with sarcasm. "Did you really think I would?"

"You know, Boyd, I know someone who can take care of that piece a shit for you."

"What are you talking about, Tony?"

"Come on, Boyd! Maybe you did get a concussion. Do I have to spell it out for you? I'm talking about having your brother whacked! My last name's not Luccio for nothing."

Boyd stared at Tony, trying to absorb all that this implied.

"How much would that set me back?"

"Not as much as you might think. Five grand could get the job done."

"That's it? Five thousand to have someone killed? Are you kidding me?"

"I'm serious." Tony paused, letting this sink in. "Are you serious, Boyd?"

Boyd sighed, slowly, deeply and then winced with the painful expansion of his ribs. He ran his good, right hand through his hair and sighed again. "What do you think, Tony? Do you think I'm serious?"

"I think you should be. I think you should be damn serious. I think your brother deserves to get whacked and then sent to hell to rot in his own stinking stomach acid. But I know you're not."

The two men just sat staring at each other for a moment and then Tony stood. "Listen, I'd better go. Is Pam going to be home soon? Is there anything you need me to do for you?"

"Pam'll be home in about an hour. I'll be fine. Thanks for everything, Tony."

"Sure, no problem. Take care of yourself, Boyd. Just think about what I said."

"I don't have to think about it. It's a flat out no. If I ever see the bastard again, I might strangle him with my own two hands but, having him whacked? No way."

"You're a better man than me, Boyd. Listen, I'll give you a call tomorrow. Tell Pam I said hello." And Tony put on his coat and walked out into the twilight.

Boyd sat there. The pain killer was starting to work, taking the edge off his pain. Anger at Tom boiled up inside him again; for making him suffer, for making him think thoughts that made him feel reduced to something less than human for just thinking them.

He grabbed one of the chocolate boxing gloves, ripped off the foil and flung the candy into his mouth. He forced himself to hold it on his tongue, to not chomp down on it, to not obliterate it in one crushing bite. It started to soften and melt, spreading like smooth, creamy silk, over his tongue.

Boyd closed his eyes, savoring the warm chocolatyness, and then he fell asleep.

Chapter 39

LICENSE IN MOONLIGHT AND SNOW

The soft nighttime light spilling through the curtains had a brightness to it tonight - moonlight reflecting off falling snow. Maybe she should go to the window and see how much snow had fallen? But why? There was no reason really. No reason to get out of the warm bed, to leave Boyd's side and perhaps disturb his already less than perfect slumber.

The service would take care of it. The plow showed up faithfully between the hours of 6:30 and 7:00 every morning that there was over three inches of snow. It had already come three times this week and Pam had the feeling that today would be the fourth.

It was hard to get used to, having someone other than Boyd or herself take care of the snow. Boyd was her hardworking man. But he couldn't do it now. And they threatened to tie Pam to a chair if she even thought about doing it herself. Pregnant women were not allowed to shovel snow! Boyd's parents had hired the service for them, paying in advance for the rest of the winter season.

Pam studied Boyd's sleeping face in the dim, hushed light. The thought that she could have lost him was stuck in her mind these days. Lost him! The man that she loved! To a vicious depravity that she never wanted to believe could really exist in this world in which she lived.

The reassuring heat of his body radiated out to her. She drank in the essence of his being. Life was fragile, the future uncertain.

These were truths that everyone knew but no one believed. No one believed, until cruel proof rammed into them head on, throwing them from their path, gripping them with boney, ice cold fingers and changing the rhythm of their beating heart. These truths had been proven to her before but never with the force that they were proven to her now. That Boyd was here beside her, warm and alive, was a precious gift she would never take for granted.

It had been nearly two weeks since his assault and most of the swelling was gone. The ominous blues and blacks that had circled his right eye and traveled down his cheek, that covered his nose and appeared in blotches around his mouth and on his chin, were fading to sickly shades of yellows and greens now.

As she watched him, his eyes squeezed together in a wince and he shuddered slightly, a barely audible moan creeping from his lips. His breathing was quick and shallow, not the quiet, peaceful breathing that usually accompanied someone at rest.

Suddenly his eyes opened and he was staring back at her, not really seeing at first, and then surprised to see her face lying so close to his own.

"Boyd, are you ok?" she asked quietly, her voice as soft as the moonlight. "Do you need more pain meds? I can go get them for you."

"That's ok, Pam. You stay in bed. I gotta take a leak anyway." But he made no attempt to actually move or to get out of the bed.

"Let me get them, Boyd." And Pam started to rise.

"No. I can do it. I'm gonna do it. I'm just trying to gather my courage. Steal myself against the pain. And against seeing blood every time I take a piss." His words were heavy with bitterness and anger.

Bitterness and anger, frustration and despair. Pam was surprised to hear Boyd revealing these despondent emotions to her. He usually tried to conceal them, to protect her from feeling them herself, to prevent her from worrying about him too much. But she still knew they were there. They haunted his eyes every day; hiding behind the screen of hopefulness and cheerfulness he erected to shield her from his misery.

He took a determined breath and slowly rose, low moans and groans escaping with each movement, despite his attempts to hold them in. He usually tried to keep his pain from her too.

Pam's heart broke with anguish. Was there nothing she could do to help him? No superhuman ability lying dormant within her that she could call forth to absorb his pain and heal his wounds? Some misplaced magical incantation she could recite that would whisk the attack at Bigwigs from his life as if it had never happened and make him strong and whole again? She searched her being for these things but they did not exist. She was powerless.

When Boyd returned from the bathroom, he sat on the edge of the bed, his left arm, with the fractured clavicle, cradled in his lap, his right elbow resting on his knee, his head bowed, resting in his hand. He started talking to himself then, in whispers too quiet for Pam to understand, but the words sounded fierce and angry, and she soon realized he was swearing; swearing at the unscrupulous pig that was his brother for deserting and abandoning him to a pack of wolves that had been primed for the kill, swearing at himself for agreeing to meet his brother against his better judgment, swearing at his pain, swearing to vent the pent up emotions he had been trying to hold in for so long.

"Boyd?" Pam called out softly, stopping his acrimonious flow of words.

"Pam? Did I wake you up? I'm sorry."

"You didn't wake me. I hadn't fallen back asleep yet. Is everything alright?"

"No. Nothing's alright," he confessed, surprising her again with his honesty, no longer able or willing to hide from her his dejection and despair.

"It's not supposed to be this way, Pam! Right now, I should be thinking about how I've got to get up in an hour so I can go out and shovel the snow and get ready for work. Not thinking about how to breathe and how to move and how to piss! I'm supposed to be feeling excited and happy and looking forward to spring and the baby coming, not pacing the floor bored out of my skull and worrying about our dwindling funds because I can't go to work and all I'm getting are measly disability checks. I'm supposed to be the one helping you, my pregnant wife, making things easier for you, not having you have to help me, like I'm some frail invalid! It's been two weeks! I thought I'd be better than this after two weeks! I feel like I haven't improved at all!"

Pam got up, walked around the bed and sat down next to Boyd. She took his hand in hers. "I don't think you realize how badly you were hurt, Boyd. It takes time to heal. You'll get better! You will! Two weeks really isn't..." Pam stopped in mid-sentence, her eyes dancing with excitement, a smile spreading across her face. "Boyd, feel this!" And she took his hand and placed it on her belly.

The baby was moving inside her, stronger than she had ever felt it before. Rolling, rippling movements spread across her abdomen, as tiny feet, or perhaps it was the baby's hands or even its head, pushed around inside her.

"It's the baby!" Total wonder and amazement lit up Boyd's face, replacing the dark despair that had clouded it. "Look! I can even see his foot making a bulge in your stomach. I can almost hold it. This is so absolutely awesome! Maybe he's trying to tell us something!"

"She's probably telling us we're making too much noise for the middle of the night and we should shut up and go to sleep."

"Maybe he's telling you he didn't like the greasy French fries you had for dinner or that you put too much dill on your scrambled eggs."

"You know what I think, Boyd? I think she's telling you that you need to stop beating yourself up. You've been beaten up enough already. Everything is going to work out fine and you shouldn't worry so much about it. She's saying that you're going to be all better really soon and that you are going to be the best daddy ever."

The baby stopped kicking then and everything was quiet. Pam leaned in close to Boyd. She kissed him, hard, on the mouth, being careful to position her head so she didn't knock his broken nose. She moved her hands slowly down his body. He kissed her in return, deeply, passionately.

They were both breathing hard and fast. Pam knew Boyd must be hurting. He was broken and bruised in so many places. His cracked ribs must be screaming. But she also knew that, right now, at this very moment, he didn't really care.

Scissors beats paper, rock beats scissors, pleasure beats pain.

Poetic License

MOONLIGHT

Paint it pale yellow
Or silvery white
Paint it cobalt
Or dark midnight

Paint descending shimmers
In translucent creams
And blend them at the bottom
Into a nebulous dream

Add tinges of soft blues and grays
Paint a delicate hushed glow
Paint moonlight
Reflecting on snow

Chapter 40

SCARRED LICENSE

Dear sweet lord! She had screamed when she saw her son on the bed in that blue speckled hospital gown. Like a yellow-bellied sissy afraid of a spider on the wall or a snake slithering across the path. Boyd!

His irresistibly handsome face had been an almost unrecognizable disaster. Dark bruises stained it in ugly hues of reds, purples and blacks. One eye had been almost swollen shut; the other eye hazy with pain.

But that was only the visible evidence of the havoc wreaked upon his body by someone's vicious labors. There had been other damage as well, in places she couldn't see, hidden by the blue speckled gown, or deeper, hidden by his skin. Boyd could have been killed!

And then she had nearly fainted, because, almost worse than the fact that her son had been beaten to a pulp, was the reason for the beating. Luckily, her husband, Andy, had noticed her wobble. He put his arms around her and called out her name - 'Erika!' He led her over to a chair and made her sit down.

It was nothing that Boyd had done to cause the assault, unless being decent and loyal could be considered something worthy of blame. But no, the instigator of the attack, the cause of all this pain and suffering was Boyd's very own brother, Erika's second born son - Tom. How could he have done this horrible thing?

Tom had actually called her just the day before, the first time she had heard from him in over three years! She had been happy to hear his voice, hopeful with the possibility that he might have changed, relieved to know that he still existed on the planet. A mother always worries about and loves her children, no matter how estranged or wicked they have become.

He told her he'd been thinking about her, thought she might like to know that he was still alive and kicking. He hadn't offered any other information as to what he had been up to over those three years and Erika hadn't been inclined to ask, didn't even want to know. Experience had taught her that if he didn't bring it up himself, without her pressing him or prodding him, he was probably up to no good.

She had filled him in on the changes the years had brought for herself and the other family members, which weren't that many really. She had retired last year! No longer an RN! She was spending her time now on crafty projects that she tried to sell on ebay, and researching her family tree. She and his father had sold the family homestead and moved into an apartment! And Boyd and his wife, Pam, were expecting a baby in April!

Andy had walked into the room while she was talking, his eye brows raised in an unspoken question mark, curious as to who it was she was talking to in such guardedly cheerful tones. 'Tom' she had mouthed, gesturing that she would hand the phone to him when she was done, giving him a chance to chat with his long lost son.

But Andy had shaken his head, shaping his lips into a large, exaggerated and silent 'NO', slashing his hands sharply in the air under his chin for extra negative emphasis. He had shed too many tears, spent too many sleepless nights, wasted too many years on the ungrateful, worthless, abhorrent nightmare at the other end of the line. His wounds were finally healed. He'd be damned if he let this thing that was supposed to be his son reach in and rip them open again.

But Tom had reached in anyway, reached in by reaching out; contacting his brother and doing what he did best – destroying his family bit by bit, reminding them again, in vivid detail, what a vile and callous monster he was.

That was six weeks ago. Thankfully, Boyd would be able to go back to work in a few more days, finally recovered enough from his ordeal to get his life back on track. None the worse for wear except for a shoulder that would always ache after even the slightest exertion, one tiny scar above his right eyebrow, another at the right corner of his mouth and a nose with a slightly unnatural bend to it.

Six long weeks. Maybe Boyd had recuperated but she couldn't say the same for herself and Andy. They had thrown up a wall between themselves, built of reopened wounds and misdirected blame, of guilt, un-kept promises and silent shame. They aimed accusatory glances at each other, but mostly they aimed these glances inward, at themselves.

Boyd was a wonderful son, a pleasure from the moment he was born. What had she done wrong with Tom? Hadn't she raised them both the same? Why had Tom become so disruptive, disturbed and unbalanced? So evil?

Both she and Andy had tried so hard to do things right by Tom. She knew deep down inside that the way he turned out was neither one of their faults. But knowing this did not take away the deep remorse, regret and sense of failure that filled her till she thought she would detonate and self-combust.

If outward forces had nothing to do with creating this monster, than it must be internal forces, something in the genes, genes that came from her. No matter what she knew, no matter what anybody said, it was her fault. She was to blame.

And she had caused her relationship with Andy to suffer over the years as well. How many times had she rebuffed his tender advances, offered her cheek instead of her lips, turned her back on his smile, tuned out his recounting of his day or his discussions of things that mattered to him, too consumed by the bad seed to react or respond?

Experience had taught Erika many things. She knew this invisible wall she and Andy had built would deconstruct and fall over time because this was not the first time it had been built. It had fallen before and it would fall again. But how long would it take this time? Another week? Another month? Another year?

How long until their wounds healed over once more, leaving in their place a trace of tiny white scars?

Poetic License

WASTED

Clouds tinged pink and feathery
Decorate the azure sky
The sun's radiant fire
Reflected
In morning's golden eye

But I'm stuck behind a city bus
Stop go stop go stop go
Street cleaner in another direction
A constant state of slow

Plans of promise change
Amidst the glances and the stares
Warning me of staying
Preventing me from going anywhere

Young couples like bright suns on the sidewalk
So happy, so vital, so alive
Fragile future spread out before them
Their brightness brings tears to my eyes

But I had this once – this youth
And you!
Eyes held the mischievous gleam of the rogue
Hard lust often turned down and wasted
Why I don't even know

Love still sweet and tender
Warm memories firm and velvety soft
Desire still burns hot and fierce
But abilities have become a little lost

Contents might shift on take off
A sideways glance draws attention away
I've seen enough furtive fingers fiddling
To know things need to be rearranged

Things lost and found connect somehow
Like colors on a wheel
Yellow and red swirl to orange
Yellow and blue to green

Vibrant leaves of yellow gold
Cover morning's pure white snow
Plans of promise wasted
Stop go stop go stop…..
Go

Chapter 41

LICENSE FOR A BIRTHDAY OR TWO

S pring! April! Her birthday! Twenty-One! Legal!
Yes, the magic age of twenty-one, when all concerned were obligated to consider you an adult. Now, to her existing privileges of being able to legally drive or vote or smoke, or get married, get an abortion or enlist in the military without parental consent, she could add the extra bonus of being able to belly up to a bar and order a beer or a vodka martini or a glass of cabernet!

Not that she was much of a drinker. She preferred sparkling water. Or tea. Stumbling around like a word slurring fool didn't appeal to her sensibilities. But her friends at the station had made plans to take her out to Enigma's tonight to celebrate her newly acquired legality. She'd have a drink or two, just to make them happy, but getting ripped was definitely not in her plans.

But before hopping and bopping with the crowd at Enigma's, Mike was taking her out for a little private celebration of their own – dinner at that new upscale Greek place that had just opened downtown! His motto was – When you drink, you eat. When you eat, you drink.

Mike. He worked with Dixie at Channel Twenty and had been part of her Take Out Or Leave It team, along with hunky Jay, Hilary and Dee Dee, before the contest fizzled into oblivion when Dixie went on bereavement leave. He wasn't bad looking, but he was short for a guy, only two inches taller than Dixie herself, and he was not the type that she was usually attracted to. He had a round face, a narrow chin and slightly droopy eyelids that always made his dark grey eyes look a little sad. And he had a scar on his neck - a long thin red line that looked like someone had once tried to slit his throat.

Dixie hadn't noticed the scar initially. She didn't see it when she was introduced to Mike on her first day at Channel Twenty and she didn't notice it for weeks after that. But then, one morning when the team was sitting around the table comparing notes on which breakfast sandwich surpassed the others in takeout-ability, she had spotted it. And once she spotted it, she couldn't keep her eyes off it. There it was, every day, staring back at her and waving 'Here I am! Here I am!'

It wasn't any of her business how Mike had gotten that scar, but possibilities of its origin kept creeping into her mind and poking her like the sharp thorns on a cactus, goading her into trying to determine the truth behind that thin red line. Had he been (or was he still) a bad ass gang member? Did he get cut in a brawl? Had he been attacked in some dark alley while conducting shady business?

Then one day, curiosity won its battle with etiquette.

"How'd you get that scar, Mike?" Dixie blurted out the question seemingly out of nowhere, with no prelude to back it up. It jumped out of her mouth before she could stop it.

Mike had been just about ready to take a bite out of one of the Take Out Or Leave It test subjects when Dixie's question burst into the air. His mouth was wide open, the broiled tilapia with horseradish mayo on a hard roll from Clam City was moving in. Instead, he stopped the impending bite, closed his mouth and set the unbitten sandwich back down, his face grim and serious. He leaned in close to her as if preparing to reveal a dark secret and Dixie leaned in close too, ready to receive proof of his sordid past.

"Drug deal gone bad." He said, not in the whisper that Dixie had expected, but loud enough for everyone to hear!

He had paused for effect, watching the shock and surprise that leapt through Dixie's eyes along with a gratified look of 'I was right! I just knew it!' And then he grinned and laughed and so did Jay, Hilary and Dee Dee. They all knew the truth and this was not it. The joke was on her!

"You shouldn't judge a person by a scar, Dixie! And you can't judge a scar by its location!" Mike chided her gently. "I was in a car accident a couple years ago. Hit me so hard I got thrown right out of my car. A piece of the windshield followed me out and landed right on my neck. I was lucky I didn't get my head cut off!"

How could she have let her imagination convince her that a bunch of obvious hokum could be true? If she had paid attention to anything else about Mike, she would have seen that he was as likely to be a drug dealer or gang member as a lamb was to stalk and kill a rabbit! And Mike had seen right through her.

She hung her head and apologized. After that, she never looked at Mike's scar again. She forgot it was even there.

A few weeks later, her whole world had turned upside down and unraveled. Greg was brutally stabbed and killed and she went home to mourn, to try to come to terms with what was unbelievable, inconceivable, unthinkable.

When she finally came back to work, with her body a little thinner and her eyes a little hollow, Mike had taken it upon himself to help her get re-assimilated. He was thoughtful and understanding and went out of his way to pass by her desk every day with a friendly smile and a cheerful 'good morning'. He would bring her a cup of coffee or offer her half of his sandwich at lunch. He told her silly jokes to make her laugh and dropped blatantly ridiculous suggestions for her next human interest story or audience participation event on her desk, scribbled on strips of florescent copy paper, to make her chuckle.

One night, about a week after her return, Mike had stopped over after work with a package in his hands. It was a remembrance album that he had compiled with all the cards, letters and emails that people had sent to the station offering Dixie their sympathy, love and condolences for her tragic loss. Mike had held her in his arms as she cried.

A strong friendship had grown between them and over the following months Dixie found herself falling in love with Mike and his round face and his grey eyes and she couldn't understand how she had ever overlooked him or thought he wasn't one of the best looking men she had ever seen.

And now here she sat, at her little dinette table, watching as the April day faded to twilight and waiting for Mike's black Nissan to pull into the lot to pick her up for the first leg of her birthday extravaganza.

She couldn't wait! But to tell the truth, the thing she was looking forward to the most was something she had every day. Just to see Mike's face, to feel his body pressed against hers, to hear his voice say her name.

It was just a few months earlier, in February, when Dixie had told Mike how she felt.

His birthday was coming. She wanted to do something special because he had become so special to her so she invited him over for dinner.

"You're going to cook me dinner? Sounds great! Or does cook me dinner mean that you're going to open a can of soup and microwave a couple cups of Kraft Mac and Cheese?" he teased.

"You're too smart! How'd you know?" Dixie teased him back "Now really! What makes you think I can't cook?"

"I've never seen you cook! When we're together and we get hungry we always go out."

"That's because you always say 'Wanna go out? It's on me!' But I can cook. Just you wait and see. It's going to be spectacular! The best meal you ever had."

Mike had showed up in a dark blue gabardine sport coat, with the top two buttons of his shirt undone, and camel colored chinos that almost matched his reddish blond hair.

"Happy birthday, Mike! You're all dressed up! You look so nice!" Dixie complimented and then had to ask, "You know that we're just staying here, right? You remember that I'm doing the cooking?"

"Of course I remember! How could a guy forget a thing like that? But you said the dinner was going to be spectacular, so I thought I should dress the part! Did I make a mistake? Is it really going to be the can of soup now?"

"No! It's not going to be a can of soup!" Dixie laughed. Mike always made her laugh. "Come on! Sit down! Prepare your taste buds for an explosion of flavors to savor!"

And the meal really had been spectacular! She had scoured the internet for menu items to make a meal-to-die for and had gotten all the recipes at yousurecancook.com!

They started with slices of grilled baguette topped with avocado mousse. Next was a watercress and mint salad with walnuts and chopped pears tossed with a garlic and lemon vinaigrette. The main course was chicken and mushroom pot pie in a phyllo dough crust.

At his first bite, Mike's eyes had popped and as each new course was introduced, they kept right on popping with sublime delight.

When the meal was done, Mike leaned back, grinning, and sighed with satisfaction. "Oh, Dixie, that was outstanding! Honestly! It really was the most delicious dinner I ever had!" He started looking around the room then, feigning puzzlement. "Hey, wait a minute! What am I doing still here in your apartment? I thought I was in paradise. Wasn't I just in paradise?"

He stood up and walked over to Dixie, leaned over and kissed her cheek, almost, but not quite, touching her lips. "Thank you, Dixie, for making my birthday so extraordinary."

He lingered there, as if he was going to kiss her again and Dixie held her breath, hoping, wishing, praying that he would. But then he straightened up and started to clear the table.

Dixie jumped up and snatched the dishes right out of his hands. "Don't you worry about those dishes! You're the birthday boy! Go sit back down. I'll clean up! Besides, there's something in the kitchen I don't want you to see yet!"

And Mike did as he was told.

What was out in the kitchen was the 'piece de resistance', the sweet end to her savory masterpiece - a pumpkin bundt cake with maple cream cheese frosting, stuck like a porcupine with twenty-nine birthday candles just waiting for the match to light them up. Twenty-Nine! One for each of the years since Mike's birth and one for good luck.

It took longer to light twenty nine candles than Dixie would have thought.

"What are you doing, Dixie? Do you need help? Should I come out there?" Mike was getting anxious just sitting and waiting. And wondering what could it possibly be that Dixie was up to!

"No! I'm almost done. It'll be just another second. I promise!"

Finally her job was accomplished. Every one of those twenty nine candles was lit! Dixie dimmed the lights and came walking slowly out of the kitchen, the cake a fiery orb in her hands, singing 'Happy Birthday' as off key as she could.

Mike's face glowed, happiness and amazement flickering in his eyes along with the candlelight as she set the cake before him, his job now to blow out all those candles, to accept the new age he had been blessed to attain, and to cut the first slice.

They were talking when the cake first touched their lips. Then the chatting stopped. They had to pause to savor the bliss, their faces brighter than the candles had been, like tiny light bulbs under their skin and the cake the electricity that turned them on.

They both scarfed down two pieces! And when they were done, they smiled with guilty pleasure at their excessive indulgence.

Dixie started laughing then. She couldn't stop! Mike had a bit of frosting his nose and another dab perched in the little dimple above his lip!

"What are you laughing at? What is it?" And Mike laughed too, just because Dixie was laughing. Laughter is, after all, contagious.

Dixie walked over to Mike and wiped the frosting off his nose with her finger. She put her finger in her mouth, "Yum!"

She pushed Mike back in his chair, sat on his lap, and started licking the frosting from his lips and then she kissed him. She let her lips remain there, pressed to his mouth, until his lips understood her message and responded. And once the mutual kiss started, neither one of them wanted it to stop.

After a time, Dixie pulled away from the kiss. She took Mike's face in her hands and gazed into his dark grey eyes, her blue/green eyes twinkling and dancing. She had made the mistake before of keeping her feelings hidden. She had hidden her love from Greg. She had even hidden it from herself. She would not do that again.

"I love you, Mike." she whispered.

"Dixie." Mike breathed her name in reply, his voice trembling, his eyes drunk with love and hunger.

And then Dixie kissed him again. She kissed his lips, his cheeks, his nose and his forehead. And she kissed other places too, places that couldn't give the excuse of having frosting on them.

Sometimes the best gifts are unplanned. Sometimes the best gifts do not come wrapped with bright papers or tied with jaunty bows.

Sometimes the best gifts are saved for last.

Chapter 42

LICENSE FOR THE COMING SPRING

February. The dead of winter. There were driveways to shovel, sidewalks to salt and slow morning commutes as cars crawled over icy roads.

Spring was the farthest thing from Mike's mind, but spring was exactly what Dixie was asking him to think about, as the second in command to her new creative inspiration for the station.

Rebirth and Renewal? Mud and Slush? Beauty or Beast? What does spring mean to you?

She would give people one month before spring's official arrival to compile their thoughts and send them in. It could be a short paragraph or poem, a sentence or even a single word, anything that expressed their personal feelings on the glories or gories of the northern hemisphere's second season.

Then, each day for the week surrounding spring's vernal equinox, she planned to read several of the responses on the morning news. And all of the responses would be available for their perusing pleasure on the Channel Twenty website.

"Don't you think February is too early for thoughts of spring to start rolling around in people's heads?" he tried to reason with her, "It's still the middle of winter!"

"Exactly! That's why it's the perfect time! People are sick of the snow and the cold. They're anxious for warmth and light and color. They want to see flowers and hear birds. No time could be better than February to think about spring!"

And Dixie sent out the appeal to her ever growing and faithful audience in mid-February.

The first week alone, emails cascaded in like an avalanche of winter's hold out snow succumbing to spring's warming climate of change.

'Spring is fickle.
Winter today. Summer tomorrow.
And winter returns again.
Spring is the time
When nature
Can't make up its mind.'
Jeanne A.

Even though Dixie had been right about people and spring, she was still astonished at the magnitude of responses that flooded her inbox.

And Mike couldn't understand that. How could it be that Dixie was always surprised at the tremendous outpouring of support and enthusiasm she received, for all her projects?

First there had been 'Take Out or Leave It'. Restaurants had clamored for a chance to get in on the best take-out food in town action. At December's end it was 'The Closing of the Year', a touchingly bittersweet piece that had the audience laughing and crying at the same time. And calling out for more. Next up was the 'Man Snow, Women Snow' contest, a lighthearted frolic in search of the most unique snow person. Huge successes every one.

And now it was 'Spring!' and the avalanche had just started.

> 'Slush and mud and piles
> of filthy brown snow that look like dirt.
> Spring sucks."
> Amy R.

Somehow, Dixie didn't seem to realize her appeal. She was un-aware that the audience was hungry for as much of Dixie Andrews as they could get. Dixie was a breath of fresh air in a stuffy room, a cold drink on a scorching day, a glimpse of the sun through the rain. Folks hung on her every word, waited anxiously to hear what her next contest or event would be. Dixie was the darling of Channel Twenty News!

But fame did not go to Dixie's head. She didn't even know she had it! She remained as sweet, humble and down to earth as she had ever been.

> 'Dismal skies and bone soaking rain.
> Damp and dreary is the beginning of spring.'
> Tom C.

Another thing Dixie didn't know she had was Mike's heart. He had been in love with her since her first day at Channel Twenty. She had come striding into the room, smiling, vibrant and alive, her eyes bright, her golden hair bouncing around her head. When they were introduced, she had shaken Mike's hand, a strong, confident hand-shake, not the flimsy, weak handshake that most women offered. And as he worked along beside her, as he got to know her better, he lost his heart to her more each day.

He had longed to ask her out - to dinner or a movie or even just for coffee. Both Hilary and Dee Dee said that Dixie told them she had recently broken up with her boyfriend and was currently unat-tached. Well, maybe that's what she was telling other people but she seemed to have forgotten to tell herself. Her vibe told a different story. And Mike wasn't about to try to woo a girl that had 'Taken! Don't touch!' written all over her.

> *'Spring is a time for change when drab winter loosens*
> *its icy grip and the earth comes alive again.'*
> *Jason I.*

So he had kept his feelings to himself, grateful for any time he could get to be near her or work with her on a project and trying not to let her see the love that shone from his eyes or in his smile whenever he looked at her.

> *'The spring sun was so bright as we walked the path*
> *that we took off our jackets, tied them around our waists*
> *and walked only in our T-shirts, soaking up the warmth.*
> *But there was still ice on the puddles! A thin film*
> *that popped and crackled under our feet.'*
> *Diane K.*

And then catastrophe had befallen Dixie. The man she said was not her boyfriend but who really was. The man that she had broken up with but really still loved, died, practically in her arms. And she left the Channel Twenty fold to return home to grieve.

It was a devastated and vulnerable Dixie that returned three weeks later. She tried to put on a good face but Mike could see the sorrow that haunted and dulled her eyes. And Mike offered himself as a friend, his ear if she needed to talk, his shoulder if she needed to cry, to watch out for her and support her on her fragile return to balance. He tried to put some cheer back into her life and bring a smile to her face.

Over the months, as their friendship grew, Mike thought he saw something that hinted at love in Dixie's eyes when she looked at him. She seemed to stand closer to him and let her hand linger on his when they touched. He wanted to tell her that he loved her, draw her to him and kiss her soft lips so badly that it hurt, but he was afraid.

Maybe he was wrong. Maybe he was misinterpreting her feelings. Or maybe it was just too soon. Too soon for Dixie to hear words of love coming from another man's mouth, too soon for her to give her love again.

He should wait. If he had held his love inside this long, he could hold onto it as long as it took, until one day, hopefully, Dixie would have love to give back to him. The most important thing to him now was that Dixie felt happy and safe, that at least she enjoyed his company and thought of him as her friend.

They were wading through the first week of the avalanche when Dixie invited him to her place to celebrate his birthday. She was going to cook for him! A spectacular feast to knock him off his feet!

And after that day, he did have thoughts of the glory and wonder of spring rolling around in his head. He had spring's rebirth and renewal coursing through his veins.

"I love you, Mike" Dixie had whispered.

It was all he had ever wanted. Those words – the best gift of all.

'Spring is a girl
Fresh, vibrant and fair
Colors dance in her eyes
Flowers bloom in her hair
The sun lives in her smile
Her laughter, life giving rain
Spring is a girl
And Dixie is her name'
Mike C.

Chapter 43

LIQUOR LICENSE

The best laid plans………

Her one or two had become three or four. Or was it five? Not to mention the bottle of wine she'd shared with Mike at dinner!

And Jay had agreed to be the designated driver. That plan went out the window too. A more appropriate title for Jay would have been the designated drinker!

"I'll just have one beer," he had promised, "We're going to be here for hours! One beer won't matter!"

But then those beers kept pouring down his throat, one after the other. And they were all having such a great time, they didn't try to stop him. They didn't want to stop him. They were a team, right? Teams worked together, right! It was one for one and all for all!

Dixie remembered the bartender cutting them off and calling a cab for her and her four drunken compadres.

She remembered stumbling around and giggling like a total idiot as she tried to tell the cabbie her address. And shrieking with glee when she realized she had become the word slurring fool she had vowed not to be.

"What was that?" the cabbie had asked, looking at her quizzically, rolling his eyes and shrugging his shoulders, "Come again?"

Mike had stepped forward then, puffing out his chest, confident that his drunken tongue would produce words so much more intelligible than hers had.

Garbled, gobbledygook was what she heard tripping out of his mouth! But somehow the cab driver was able to decipher Mike's inebriated gibberish and the next thing she remembered was being dropped off in the parking lot of her complex with Mike, both of them waving their arms wildly over their heads in an exaggerated goodbye to the remaining three victims of the night as the cab towed them to destinations hopefully known.

Anything that might have happened after that eluded her. Her mind was a complete blank! But they must have gotten into the apartment because here she was, in her own bed, her head aching, her stomach a little queasy. Mike, completely zonked, was sprawled out on the bed beside her. And sunlight - that of the morning or of the afternoon variety, she wasn't quite sure - was drifting through the curtains.

Enigma's had been wild! Totally insane! They talked and they laughed and they danced!

But she almost hadn't made it in. Sounds of the band playing inside had been blasting through the door when she arrived with Mike. It was a cover of Maroon 5's 'Moves Like Jagger'. Greg had covered this song! She could picture him on the stage, his guitar slung over his shoulder, his fingers flying over the strings, his voice strong, his body joining with the beat. Was it possible? Could that be him?

Greg! But she had seen his life slip away, right before her eyes! Her heart had ached till it could ache no more. Part of her wanted to run into Enigma's, into the arms of …. Who? Someone who could not possibly be there? And part of her wanted to run away. Away from memories that were too painful to bear.

Her heart pounded in her chest, her breath caught in her throat, her eyes glassed over. She couldn't get her feet to move in any direction, forward or back. She just stood there, hesitating in the doorway, frozen to her spot.

Mike saw the panicked look in her eyes and somehow he had understood. He knew the desperate, conflicting thoughts that were racing through her head, knew why she stood there, frozen and unmoving. He took her trembling shoulders gently in his hands and looked softly into her eyes.

"It's okay, Dixie. We don't have to go in. We can just go back to your place. I'll text the others that something came up and we can't make it. Don't you worry about a thing."

But then she heard another voice whispering into her ear, barely audible, like words drifting off a butterfly's wings as it fluttered by.

'It's not me in there, Dixie. I'm so sorry. I wish it could be me but it never can be. Go on in. You can do it. It'll be okay. Just hang by Mike. He's a great guy. It's your birthday! And it's gonna be awesome. Celebrate! Celebrate life.' And the whisper faded away.

Mike was looking at her with such tenderness. He put one hand on her shoulder to protect and guide her away from the door. He had his cell phone in his other hand, ready to send the text with their excuses.

But Dixie stopped him. "Mike, wait. You know what? I'll be fine. Really. Come on, let's go in!" And she took Mike's hand in hers and marched into Enigma's and over to the bar where the others were waiting.

"Here she is! The birthday girl!"

And a strawberry margarita was shoved into her hands.

They toasted Dixie and her birthday and the age of twenty-one. They toasted the fickle month of April. They toasted friendship and love and the TV station that made it all possible. They toasted anything and everything that came to their minds.

It really had been an awesome night. Starting with Mike's 'Happy Birthday' kiss when he came to pick her up and ending with waving goodbye to her friends with Mike by her side. An awesome night indeed!

Dixie's still bleary eyes glanced around the bedroom. Mike's jacket lay crumpled on the floor next to the bed, one of his shoes sitting on top of it. One of her shoes was tossed in the corner and the other was on the dresser! Had they pulled off and flung their clothes with reckless abandon, fired up with passion and aching with desire?

But Mike was on top of the covers, fully clothed, except for his jacket and shoes, and a look under the covers revealed her red dress all wrinkled and wrapped around her body, the skirt tangled in her legs. If there had been any flames of desire last night, they had dissolved in the inability of their drunken stupors.

Dixie looked at Mike lying there on his back, his mouth slightly open, his hair tousled and sticking out in all the wrong directions. Darling Mike. She leaned over him and gently kissed his forehead. He stirred slightly and mumbled something indiscernible but he did not wake up. She got out from under the covers and laid down next to him, snuggling close, her head on his shoulder, feeling him breathe, matching the rise and fall of her chest to the rise and fall of his.

Her stomach started to lurch then and she had to rush off to kneel before the porcelain god.

Maybe awesome was the word for last night. But the word for this morning was something else entirely. Next time she'd adhere to her plan and stay within her two drink limit. Better yet, maybe she'd just stick with the sparkling water.

Getting to know the porcelain god did not appeal to her sensibilities.

Chapter 44

LICENSE TO ENTER
THE WORLD

Pam had been looking forward to tonight all week. They were going to Nottingham's for dinner with Lisa and Tony.

At Nottingham's, bawdy wenches, bar maids and young men in forest green tunics would be serving them. The cover of the menu would portray a path through a wooded land of green and brown, inviting them to enter the realm, and the offerings would be written in letters that resembled twigs and underlined with quilled arrows; delectable offerings such as Maid Marian's Corn Chowder, Hood Roast Chicken, Friar Tuck's Soused Onion Etouffee and Sherwood's Forest Vegetable and Tenderloin Skewer. There would be glossy oak slab tables. And, there would be baskets and baskets of her favorite - Robin's Arrow Garlic Bread Sticks.

But now that the day was here, she was thinking she might have to cancel. She had woken up with a backache, a low grade but incessant discomfort that persisted no matter how she stood or sat or lay.

She expected it was because of her elephantine belly. At thirty-eight weeks, it was bulging so far out front that it was throwing her center off balance. And her poor back was probably working overtime in its struggle to keep her upright.

Pam put her left arm over her head and stretched to the right, then switched to her right arm over her head and stretched to the left. She bent forward slightly and then backward. She repeated the sequence several times hoping stretching might ease her pain but her wish remained ungranted. Relief was not hers to be had.

Boyd passed by on his way to the cellar, a screwdriver in his hand, and stopped to watch, grinning with amusement as her pregnant shape made the simple stretches she was attempting look like some slapstick fitness routine.

"What are you doing there, my little Buddha belly?" he snickered at her, his eyes twinkling playfully.

"Don't you dare laugh, Boyd!" she scolded, shaking her finger at him and trying to suppress the betraying smile that kept popping out on her lips to reveal that the scolding was a fake.

"It's my back!" she explained then, taking another stab at stretching this way and that in her search for some kind of comfort, "It's been bothering me since I got up. I thought maybe I could stretch things back into alignment but it doesn't seem to be helping much."

Boyd set the screwdriver down on the table and walked over to Pam, his arms open wide, inviting her into his embrace.

"Come here, Honey. I'll rub it for you."

Pam draped her arms around Boyd's neck and rested her head on his right shoulder. He applied a firm, steady pressure to the small of her back and then started digging in with his fingers, slowly and methodically kneading the muscles around her lower spine.

"Ooooooh yeah!" she sighed, "That's it. That's the spot! Keep rubbing right there. Oooooh yeah."

The massage felt like heaven. Boyd kept rubbing and kneading, the pain was easing, and Pam actually started to drift off standing there with Boyd's shoulder for a pillow, encircled in the warmth of his arms, her thoughts turning to bits of nonsensical fluff, rising and falling on a whim.

The bits of fluff shuddered suddenly and swirled together, materializing again into firm reality. Boyd had stopped rubbing her back and was tenderly kissing the top of her head.

Pam backed out of Boyd's embrace and kissed his cheek. "Thank you, Boyd. You're the sweetest thing."

"So, did it help? Does your back feel better now?" He sounded so hopeful. His face was ready to light up in a mission accomplished glow.

Pam hated to disappoint him.

"It does! It feels lots better." she lied, because as soon as the massage had stopped, the backache returned.

But she wasn't a very good liar. Mission accomplished never made it to Boyd's face.

"You know, if you're going to lie, you have to make the look on your face match the words that come out of your mouth!" he chuckled, rolling his eyes and shaking his head before concern took over his face. "It still hurts, doesn't it? I know you don't like to take anything while you're pregnant but maybe you should this time. Besides, the little bugger's almost due. I don't think a simple over the counter pain reliever will bother him at this point. Come on. Sit down on the couch. Doctor Boyd will get you a Tylenol. And a pillow to stuff behind your back! That might help too."

And he loped off to get the items he prescribed to remedy the Buddha Belly Backache Blues.

Pam fell asleep on the couch with the plush rubber ducky pillow, that Boyd had carried into the room held in front of his face like a smiling and dancing yellow mask, lodged comfortably behind her back and the Tylenol, that he had insisted she take, lodged between the couch cushions where she had stashed it when he wasn't looking.

And when she woke up, she really did feel better. Ready and raring to enter the realm of Nottingham and partake of Robin's Buttery Bread Sticks and the Friar's Onion Etouffee!

At Nottingham's, however, the backache returned, even more aggressive, more insistent that she take note of its angry existence.

Tony and Boyd were talking excitedly about the new microbrewery that had just opened in the old water works building on Chevron Street. Lisa was telling Pam about the Easter egg hunt that she was going to take her kids to at the town hall next weekend.

But Pam kept squirming in her seat and putting her hand behind her lower back so she could press and knead the ache with her fist. She was inattentive and distracted, not holding up her end of the conversation and Lisa noticed.

"Are you alright, Pam? You look so uncomfortable!"

"It's just that I've got this darned backache, that's all. It's been bothering me almost all day. And these chairs aren't helping any. They weren't ergonomically designed for the bowed back of a pregnant lady!"

"A backache, huh?" There was an odd, knowing smile on Lisa's face as if Pam was speaking in code and Lisa possessed the key that released the secret message. "You know what I think? I think you're in labor! That's how it happened with me! A back ache was my first sign."

"But I'm not due for two weeks! And I'm not having any contractions."

"Well, you know the due date they give you is really just an estimate. Think about it! The stick turns blue, you go to the doctor, they ask you when your last period was and then they spout off a due date. Do they ask you how long your cycle is? Do they ask you what day or days you had sex? No! So how do they know when your baby was actually conceived? Besides that, nine months, forty weeks, 280 days, those are just averages anyway! And as for knowing when you're in labor? Contractions may be the best indicator but they're not the only sign. I'm telling you, Pam, I predict that within forty-eight hours you're going to be holding your little bouncing bundle of joy in your arms instead of in your belly!"

Everything Lisa said made sense! Could she really be in labor? Was the little life that had been growing inside her all these months preparing to make an entrance?

Excitement and exhilaration raced through her along with a touch of apprehension. She would be a mother! Life as she now knew it would never be the same again! Was she ready? Was she really ready?

Pam glanced across the table and saw that Boyd was watching her, his eyes soft, a little smile tugging at his lips. She caught his eye, smiling too, and he reached over the table to squeeze her hand.

And then it happened - a tight, cramping spread across her abdomen. A contraction! Lisa was right. She was in labor. This was it! And she was ready. Of course she was.

⌣⟶

They had been at peace here, so tranquil, so content and safe. Floating and rolling, somersaulting and dancing, listening to the music of her calm, steady beat, their own tiny beat a sweet harmony joining in, keeping time.

But now insistent waves were squeezing and pushing and propelling them towards a strange dawn that had appeared in the warm darkness. And part of them wanted to go! To swim with the waves to the light that beckoned and called, that coaxed them away from the known and towards the unknown.

Yet another part of them wanted to stay! To fight the tow and the draw, to cling to the soft protection, to absorb her lulling beat as their own.

But the push and pull of the waves was powerful and strong, and the calm, steady beat had turned fast and the light summoned and lured them with its brilliance.

And they joined with the waves! Pushing, swimming, struggling. Down and down and out and out. And whoosh! The dark known place was left behind and the bright new place was before them.

Whoosh!

And here they were.

⌣⟶

"It's a girl!"

213

A girl! Pam watched, tears of joy and exhaustion trickling from her eyes, as the lifeline that had bound them was cut and her new-born daughter was swaddled in a warm blanket. They put a soft pink cap on her fuzz topped head and placed her into the arms of her loving daddy – pride and exhilaration dueling with bewilderment across his wide eyed face.

Boyd walked as in slow motion over to Pam with his precious bundle and laid her on Pam's chest.

"Here she is, Mommy. Our little daughter." Love and awe were cradled in his words.

"Does she have a name yet?" one of the nurses asked, beaming, caught up herself in the joy and amazement that was birth.

Her name! Pam closed her eyes and smiled, remembering all the nights with the yellow ducky pillow clutched to her chest as she and Boyd mulled over and tossed about name after name after name. All the possibilities that they had rolled around in their mouths and let slide off their tongues, that they had tilted their heads to hear how they resonated and hummed in their ears.

In the end they had settled on names with a history behind them, family names that had been handed down through the generations. She was named after her mother, great-grandmother and great-aunt, after her father and grandfather before her.

"Her name's Pamela! Pamela Andi Boyd ."

And Pam and Pamela lay there, staring with love and wonder into each other's eyes. Their beating hearts kept time together once again. The connection that had been cut was reborn, different but the same, separate but still together.

Now and forever, mother and child.

Chapter 45

CURLY LICENSE

It turned out that the guy belting out the songs at Enigma's on her birthday that night a couple of weeks ago hadn't sounded anything like Greg. He was loud all right but his voice was lame – weak and warbly and a little flat. He kept the place rocking though, and he had played a wicked guitar.

That guitar - it was a dark mahogany Gibson solid body electric, and it reminded Dixie of the dark mahogany Gibson acoustic she had in her closet, pushed way to the back, behind her suitcase. Greg's guitar. The one he had played when he sang her the songs he had written, the one that had waited for him in his car, the one to which he had never returned.

They had given it to her about a week after the funeral. Dixie had answered the chime of the doorbell and there they were, Greg's parents, looking apologetic and somewhat embarrassed that they hadn't called ahead, but mostly looking hollow and empty and lost.

Mr. Grapensteter was like a flash forward image of Greg thirty years in the future, if Greg would have had the chance to get to the future - a little heavier, a little gray, a few wrinkles, but still handsome. He had the guitar case in his hand, clutched between himself and his wife as if to protect it from the brisk, early autumn winds that were blowing that day.

They had come to give the guitar to Dixie. Greg would have wanted her to have it, they said, and they wanted her to have it too. Mr. Grapensteter had held it out to her and she had put her hand on it to take it from him but he had continued to cling to it, not yet brave enough to let it go. This guitar that had been his son's, that his son had touched, that his son had played.

They had held it together for a moment, Dixie and Greg's father, their hands touching, their tear filled eyes locked in understanding, memories of Greg flowing between them, until finally he mustered the strength he needed to release it. Hers now to cherish and treasure, to remember the life and the love that had been.

She had brought it back with her to her apartment, put it in the closet and hadn't looked at it since. Because she couldn't bear to. But it had been calling to her since that night at Enigma's. And it was calling to her now.

Mike was coming to pick her up to take her to a movie but she didn't expect him for at least an hour. Maybe now was the time to heed the guitar's call, let the memories flood her, see if she could remember any of the chords Greg had shown her and then get it put safely back in the closet before Mike arrived.

And what was the reason for that? Getting it put away before Mike arrived? Why didn't she want him to see it? It was funny. When Mike was just her friend, she hadn't hesitated to talk about or mention Greg. But now that Mike was her boyfriend, if she found herself about to say something that had any reference to Greg at all, she would clamp down on Greg's name, force it to stay in her mouth. She would rephrase her sentence, change the subject, pretend she had meant to say something else.

She knew Mike noticed. She wasn't fooling him. He was so attuned to her, to everything she said or did, to every emotion that crossed her face. He'd cock his head and raise his eyebrows. But he didn't say anything.

Dixie retrieved the guitar from the closet and carefully removed it from its case. She ran her hands slowly over the smooth surface, seeing Greg's face reflected in the lacquered shine. She touched the well-worn pick guard, hearing the tap, tap, tap of Greg's pick striking it as he played. She fingered the frets and strummed the strings.

They resonated dully, buzzing and twanging instead of sounding clear and sharp, completely out of tune from long un-use.

Greg had always tuned the guitar by ear. He'd had perfect pitch. Not so Dixie. But he had shown her how you could at least tune a guitar to itself. Just tighten up the low E till it sounded reasonable and then tune the other strings in relation to that. Now, if she could just remember which fret she was supposed to press down on to get started. Was it the fourth or the fifth?

She was sitting on the floor with the guitar still on her lap when she heard Mike's little knock on the door, his key turning in the lock. They had exchanged keys weeks ago since they spent so much time at each other's places. And why not?

She scrambled to get the guitar back into its case before he would see it there and ask her about it, before she would have to talk about Greg in front of him. Too late.

"Hi, Dixie! Hey! A guitar! I didn't even know you had a guitar. You've never mentioned it. Do you play?"

"Not really. I know a few chords, that's all." She spoke in a rush, avoiding Mike's gaze, fumbling to fasten the last latch on the case as fast as she could. "I'm ready! Come on. Let's go!"

"What are you so hyped up about? There's no reason to hurry! I got here early. The movie doesn't start for an hour. Let me take a look at that guitar!"

Dixie balked. She didn't want to take it out of its case again. Her eyes darted around the room, looking at anything except the guitar. She wouldn't let Mike catch her eye.

Mike put his hand under her chin, gently raised her head, made her meet his gaze. "Dixie, what's wrong?" he asked softly, concerned as always for her well-being.

As he looked into her eyes, realization dawned in his. "This was Greg's guitar, wasn't it? You know, you used to talk about him some-times and now you never do, like you think I'm threatened by his memory or something. You don't have to be afraid to talk about him in front of me, Dixie. I know you loved Greg. And love doesn't just disappear when a person dies. You should keep his memory alive and you should talk about him. It doesn't bother me at all. If you can't keep Greg's memory dear to you and love me too, then our love is only a half love. A love that's not quite real."

He paused and Dixie knew he was waiting for her to respond, to give affirmation that the love between Mike and herself was real - was whole, complete, and true.

And that's what she wanted to say! That and so much more! But the words she needed kept speeding around and crashing into each other in her head like bumper cars at the amusement park. She couldn't get them to stop moving, couldn't get them to flow into a sentence, couldn't get them to come out of her mouth. She stood there like a dying fish, terrified and glassy eyed, her mouth opening and closing, her lips flapping, but no sound coming out. Silence. No affirmation. Just silence.

And silence sent a different message.

All the light left Mike's face. He stared for a moment, stunned, and then he closed his eyes, drew in a shaky breath and let it out slowly. When he opened his eyes again, they were moist and fragile. His voice was as fragile as his eyes. "It's not your fault, Dixie. I never meant to rush you or force you into something you weren't ready for. You were so lost and vulnerable. I should have known it was too soon. It's just that… You know I… I should just go."

He walked quickly to the door, his mouth a hard straight line.

No! This was not right! This is not what she wanted! Not what she meant to happen at all! The words cycloning through her head slammed into position and finally Dixie found her voice.

"Mike! Stop!" She ran ahead, forcing herself between Mike and the door, blocking his hand from reaching the knob. "Just because I didn't say anything doesn't mean I didn't have anything to say! I have too much to say! The words were all jumbled and confused and fighting with each other in my head to be the first ones out of my mouth. They wouldn't let me talk! You know, sometimes there are days when you just can't seem to think straight….curly days! And some days are curlier than others."

"Dixie, you don't have to try and explain anything to me. Please, just get the hell out of my way. Let me go. I don't want to hear you babbling about words fighting in your head and days that aren't straight." Attuned had flown out the window. Anger followed sadness and despair.

"But I do have to explain! Because you were right. I have been afraid to talk about Greg around you. I think it's because I felt like it was taboo. I was breaking an unwritten law. I had told you I loved you, and now any other love was just supposed to vanish. And maybe it wasn't so much that I wasn't supposed to let you see this other love, but that I wasn't supposed to let myself see it. I was supposed to pretend it didn't exist or that it never existed. But now, you've made me see straight again, like you always seem to do. I don't have to hide anything from you. And I don't have to hide anything from myself either."

"Great. That's great, Dixie. So I was right. I'm right about a lot of things. So what? What does that get me? Nothing. It gets me burnt, that's what it does. It mucks up my life. It makes everyone else see the path through the trees and then they desert and run. They leave me stranded alone in the forest."

"But you're not right now, Mike! Now you've got it all wrong. I'm not leaving you anywhere. You're not listening to what I'm trying to tell you!"

"What are you trying to tell me, Dixie? Spit it out! Straighten out your damn curly day! Because I can't take this anymore."

"I'm trying to tell you that I do love you! Not a half love, not a partial love, not a love that's not ready yet. I love you totally and completely. A whole love!"

Mike closed his eyes again and sighed so deeply Dixie thought he had stopped breathing all together. He ran his hand through his hair and across his face, leaving it to rest over his eyes. Finally he looked at her - relieved, exhausted. A vague hint of lightness trying to push away the left over despair and anger that weren't quite ready to leave him. His heart not quite sure if it was safe to fuse the crack that had started to form there.

"Couldn't you have started out with that, Dixie, instead of dragging me through hell first?"

"Oh, Mike. I'm sorry." And Dixie started to cry. "Sometimes I'm just so stupid and nothing goes right. I don't know why...."

"Shhhhhh. Don't cry, Dixie." Mike interrupted, tenderness and understanding making a tentative comeback. "You're never stupid. Sometimes you're just....curly." And the tease of a smile breezed across his lips and through his eyes.

He folded his arms around her then and they stood there, clinging to each other, rocking back and forth, zeroing their minds, letting themselves feel safe again in each other's arms.

Chapter 46

INTRODUCTORY LICENSE

Dixie was coming home for the long 4th of July weekend! And she was bringing her new boyfriend, Mike!

Lainey couldn't wait to see her beloved daughter. It had been months! And she was so eager to meet this wonderful young man that had gone from friend to best friend to boyfriend and had re-brightened Dixie's life. Dinner should be something fantastic! Something to welcome and impress.

Lainey knew she wasn't the most imaginative cook in the world. She tended to veer towards the traditional, the tried and true. And the 4th of July always meant picnic foods to her. Hot dogs and hamburgers on the grill were a must. And there had to be macaroni salad and potato salad!

But that didn't mean the salads and other accompaniments had to be boring. She could put a creative spin on them! If she really put her mind to it, she could be imaginative. For example, instead of plain deviled eggs, she could make horseradish deviled eggs. Instead of plain mayo on the sliced tomatoes, she could make a pesto mayo! She could add chopped jalapeños to her artichoke dip. Chunks of avocadoes and sliced black olives would taste great in the macaroni salad. And what about adding bacon and chives to the potato salad and substituting sour cream for half of the mayonnaise?

Another thing Lainey wanted for the weekend, besides delicious sustenance, was smooth sailing. There should be no reminders of past sorrows, no tears, no conflict, no tension and so she had come up with a list of common sense 'rules' that Joe and the twins had all agreed made good sense and had pledged to follow.

Common Sense Rule #1 – Don't mention Greg or play or sing any songs that Greg might have covered! It would bring sadness and heartache to Dixie. And it would bring tension to Mike, as the one who was following in someone else's footsteps.

Common Sense Rule #2 – Don't make a mistake and, out of habit, call new boyfriend Mike by old boyfriend Greg's name!

Common Sense Rule #3 – Don't ask Mike too many questions all at the same time! Be discreet! Space them out, sprinkled casually throughout normal conversation so as not too make it obvious that you are dying to learn his whole life story - past, present and future - all in the space of the first half hour!

Common Sense Rule #4 – (For Joe. Lainey know how he could be!) Don't set unrealistically high standards that you expect Mike to live up to before you deem him worthy of Dixie's affections or your own good graces. In other words – Be friendly! Be nice!

Common Sense Rule #5 – (For Owen and Gabe, the bedlam twins) Be polite. Introduce yourselves. Act like civilized young men, not like a couple of chimps. No teasing. And no practical jokes!

Now the day was here! Lainey had red, white and blue napkins and paper plates. She had a cake with whipped cream frosting, topped with drizzles of blueberry syrup and sliced strawberries.

The food was all prepared. The rules were refreshed in everyone's minds.

And there was a black Nissan pulling into the driveway. It must be Mike's car!

"Joe! Boys! Dixie and Mike are here!"

Lainey flung open the screen door and rushed out to greet her eagerly awaited guests, Joe right behind her. The twins came bounding down the stairs.

"Dixie!" she and Joe called out in unison, both of them throwing their arms around Dixie's neck, hugging her and kissing her and hugging her again.

Then she turned to the young man with the reddish blond hair and gray eyes who was standing off to the side grinning as he watched them. "Mike! It's so good to meet you."

And she threw her arms around his neck and hugged him too.

Joe shook Mike's hand and patted him on the shoulder. "Come on in, Mike! Make yourself at home! Want a beer?"

So far so good!

Joe had agreed to Lainey's common sense rules just to make her happy. He did agree with rules #1 and #2 about not mentioning Greg. Now that was common sense.

And #3 was maybe ok. Actually no! On second thought, that one made no sense at all! How could you converse with someone you didn't really know if you didn't ask questions? What would they talk about? The weather?

But rule #4? That one was simply unnecessary. What made Lainey think he was going to be anything except friendly and nice? Well, maybe he did have a tendency to be tough on Dixie's boyfriends, to make like the KGB and try to dig out of them what they were all about and what their intentions were. There had been the short lived Seth. The even shorter lived Hunter. And then there had been Greg.

He had been tough on them all. Made them prove themselves to him. But that was his duty as a caring father. He didn't want some high testosterone young male taking advantage of his daughter.

It would be different with Mike. He almost felt like he knew the guy already. Every phone call with Dixie for the past four months had seemed to consist of nothing but sentences that included the word 'Mike'. Of course, all these glowing reports were from Dixie's point of view. He had to form his own opinion. Uncover his own facts. But he'd do it in a nice, friendly way!

And there was the black Nissan pulling into the driveway. They were here! His little golden nugget and her new beau.

After all the greetings and introductions, after all the hubbub and excited commotion, they were finally settled around the picnic table in the back yard. They had their drinks and their red, white and blue plates and Lainey's delicious array of appetizers spread before them.

And Joe started right in with the questions. "So, what do you do at Channel Twenty, Mike?" He was surprised to hear an acerbic sharpness to his words, not the friendly sound that he had meant his voice to carry.

"I'm the Account Executive," Mike said pleasantly, but he stared Joe right in the eye. It was obvious that he had heard the bite in Joe's question. "I develop relationships between the station and local business leaders and solicit advertising commitments from them. But we're just a small station. Jobs overlap. Sometimes I help out the camera crew or do copy writing. And sometimes I help Dixie with her projects. That's always a lot of fun!"

Mike glanced at Dixie, smiling, and Dixie smiled back. Joe could see the love flowing between them, reflected in two pairs of shining eyes.

"I liked her take-out food contest idea!" Owen piped up, "She got to stuff her face and get paid for it!"

Mike laughed. "The perfect job, huh! She's working on another really good one now. It's called The Evolution of the American Swimsuit-

From Completely Covered to Nearly Naked. And she's planning on modeling the different suits too!"

"Nearly naked? Who's nearly naked?" Gabe had been paying more attention to the food than the conversation. He was all ears now!

His brother elbowed him in the side and shot him a grin.

"Swimsuits over the years. That sounds like fun! But where are you going to get the old fashioned suits?" Lainey wondered.

"Mike knows a fashion designer in town who agreed to make the swimsuits in exchange for air time. I gave them photos and drawings of the suits I'm going to need and I gave them my size for the women's suits and Mike's size for the men's suits." Dixie looked at Mike as she said this, a playful twinkle in her eye.

"What!" Mike's eyes mushroomed and seemed to catch fire. He nearly choked on his deviled egg and then on the swig of beer he gulped trying to wash down the egg. "You're kidding aren't you? You never told me…. I don't want ….. Come on, Dixie!!"

Dixie smiled and laughed as she watched Mike squirm. But her face was set. She wasn't joking! "It's going to be fun! Just wait and see. And you're going to look so cute in that red and black striped suit!"

Resigned acceptance was the last look on Mike's face. He knew he was stuck. There was no way out of it.

"Looks like she's got you on the hook, Mike," Joe chuckled, "So, aside from having to model swimsuits on TV, how do you like your job? Have you been there long?" And there was that bite creeping into his voice again. It seemed to slip out of his mouth of its own accord. He was glad that neither Lainey nor Dixie seemed to notice it. And he wished that Mike didn't.

"Oh, I love it. And I work with a bunch of awesome people. There's always something exciting and interesting going on, creativity flying through the air, pushing your limits. I've been there five years. Started shortly after I graduated from college."

And then Mike kept right on talking. He knew that was what Joe was looking for – information on this man who dared to touch his daughter.

"I went to Penn State. Got my BA in Advertising and Public Relations and then moved up here when Channel Twenty offered me the job. And then last year, I bought a house in the village that was up for foreclosure. I've been fixing it up. It's a really slow process but I think it's starting to look pretty good! Right now I'm ripping out the old carpeting and installing hardwood floors. I got a surprise when I got the carpeting up though. The floors themselves weren't in that good a shape so I had to start by putting down four by eight sheets of quarter inch plywood underlayment. Dixie's been a big help. We've got a real system going. I measure, cut and place the sheets and Dixie secures them with the nail gun."

And then Joe almost lost sight of his mission. Instead of digging in and prying out more information about Mike, he was about to ask for more information on the hardwood flooring! But Lainey opened her mouth before he did with a great question. The one he should have been ready to ask next but almost let slip by. Except she asked it with a warm and pleasant curiosity, not the cold bite that had taken over Joe's tongue.

"A Penn State graduate, huh? Are you from Pennsylvania, Mike? What about your parents? Do you get to see them much?" Lainey asked, smiling.

"I am from PA but I haven't been back there since I moved to New York." Mike paused and Joe was surprised to notice tears form and then reabsorb in Mike's eyes.

When Mike spoke again, his voice was hushed. "Both my parents are dead. My Dad died when I was sixteen of pancreatic cancer. It took the doctors months to find out what was wrong with him and when they finally figured it out, it was too late to do anything about it. He withered away to nothing right before our eyes. And my Mom died about a week after I got out of college. Broadsided by some woman in a pickup truck that ran a red light."

"Oh, Mike. I'm so sorry. I didn't know. That must have been so hard for you." Lainey's eyes wavered behind tears.

"It was hard. I was devastated. At least I still had my mom after my dad died. But after my mom died? I felt like I'd been tossed overboard without a life jacket and there was no one to throw me a rope. I don't have any brothers and sisters either. I felt totally alone. And I just couldn't understand it. How could this happen? Why did it happen? Why did it have to be both of them? But there are no answers to those questions. And death? Death is something the living can never understand. Not really. All we know is that someone we loved was here and then, suddenly, they're gone. And all we can do miss them."

Joe sat there quietly, watching the other hushed faces around the picnic table, thinking, as they probably were, about what Mike had said. Thinking about those that he had loved that death had stolen. He watched Mike reach across the table, searching for Dixie's hand. He saw the tenderness in their touch, the compassion in their gazes, both offering and seeking support for the tragic losses that had touched each of their young lives.

Mike looked up then and the two men's eyes caught. Joe saw something else in Mike's gray eyes. A haunted look crisscrossed the sadness of loss. There was something tortured there that connected with Joe's own tormented past and spoke to his soul.

There would be no more steely-eyed alpha male with an inquisitor's cutting edge. Joe understood this young man now. Conclusion reached. Opinion formed.

"Bro! You're doing it all wrong! Keep your leg straight. Don't bend your knee!" Owen's sudden, sharp critique of his brother's karate moves rang out, snapping those still around the table out of their contemplations and back to life.

Sad musings had not occupied the twins for long. Resilient, they had slipped away from the table unnoticed to practice sparring techniques out in the yard in exaggerated slow motion.

"You know, Mike, I want to know more about that hardwood flooring you're putting in. I've been thinking about putting it in our dining room but I haven't committed to the idea yet. Are you using real hardwoods or those engineered wood planks?"

"Hey, Joe?" Lainey interrupted before Mike could answer, "That sounds like it could end up being a long conversation. Do you think you could get the grill started first? We really have to get dinner going if we want to go see the fireworks later."

"Let me grab a couple beers, Mr. Andrews, and I'll meet you over by the grill. I can fill you in on everything I know about hardwood floors while you flip the meat!"

"Sounds like a plan, Mike!"

Joe had known he was going to like this guy. And he did. He liked him a lot.

Chapter 47

FIREWORKS LICENSE

Mike had never liked fireworks. They reminded him of the bad part of his life, when he had lived with the woman that bore him and the ugly man with the hairy fingers and the dirty cracked nails. And of how those hairy, dirty hands had looked gripping the stained leather belt and yanking it taut between them so that it went 'snap!'

They reminded him of how that belt had first gone 'crack' and then 'slap' when it hit his naked backside and how the cracks and the slaps and the ensuing cries that had torn out of his mouth all mixed together and disappeared into the loud booms and bangs and pows of the fireworks that were going on in the park across the street.

They reminded him of how the red and blue and yellow dazzles of light that had ignited the room and danced on the walls had seemed synchronized to the flashes that ignited inside his head with each crack of that belt and with each sear of pain. And how he had squeezed his eyes shut so tightly that the tears couldn't even escape.

And they reminded him of how the woman that had borne him had screamed at him the next morning about all the work she was going to have to do now because of him. How hard it was going to be to get the blood stains out of his sheets. And how hard it was going to be for her to come up with a good excuse to explain to the doctor why a five year old's bottom was bloody and raw. And if he would have just gone to bed, like the ugly man had told him, instead of gawking out the window at those god damn fireworks, none of this would have happened.

Ever since then he had avoided fireworks. Feigned illness, made up excuses, anything so that he would not have to look at them and watch as their exploding colors lit the fuse on dreaded memories of the horror, pain and fear that had been his early childhood.

But now here he was, in the Flint Hill High School football field with Dixie, his neck getting stiff from being bent back for so long as he stared heavenward.

Flash, Sparkle, Soar, Fly, Loop, Cascade!!!

Pop, pop, pop!! Boom!! Bam!! Crackle!! Pow!!!!!!!!!!!!!!!!!

Fireworks on the 4th of July.

The crowd ooohed and aaaahed as the night's own pinpoints of natural brilliance were overshadowed by soaring rainbow bursts of man-made stars that shimmered and crackled before they spiraled back down to the earth, accompanied by loud bangs and pops and smoking trails. And Mike tried to smile and look like he was enjoying the display as much as the rest of them.

Dixie would squeeze his arm with cheery anticipation as each new launch whistled up into the dark sky. She would shout out in elation as the colored lights escaped their prison and flung themselves into the night. She would stick her fingers in her ears when the booms and bams erupted too loudly. And the smile never left her lips or her sparkling eyes the whole time.

"Ooooooh! Wasn't that one beautiful, Mike?"

"All blue! What do you think of that one, Mike? I think it's my favorite so far!"

"Oh wow! Look, it's filling up the entire sky! And now shooting stars! I've never seen anything like it! Have you?"

In answer to any of her questions, Mike just smiled or shook his head or pointed upward. And Dixie was so excited and awestruck, so intent on seeing what was coming next, that she didn't even notice that there were never any actual words coming out of his mouth.

Every now and then she would turn to him and kiss his cheek, her face flushed and radiant. Mike could feel her joy vibrating right though her lips.

Mike glanced around at all the others crowded about him. Happy, smiling faces were everywhere. People enjoying the spectacle and the camaraderie. People having a good time.

He thought about the good time he'd been having with Dixie's family back at the house. Dixie's Mom and Dad were great. Her brothers were great too, in a teenager kind of way. And then he started thinking about his own family. Not his birth mother and the ugly man, but his real family. The wonderful couple that had adopted him.

And Mike had an epiphany! For all these years he'd been looking at fireworks the wrong way! Letting them claw up the wrong memories!

That night twenty-three years ago? The night of the fireworks and the beating? That hadn't been his first beating but it had been the worst. His brain was fog. His eyes, streaming, gluey orbs. His heart, a dull drum pounding in time with his agony. He was pain. And pain was him.

In the morning he couldn't even walk. When his 'mother' finally stopped screaming at him, she had dragged him by one arm, thrown him, like an unwanted inconvenience, into the car, and taken him to the emergency hospital.

Then she transformed! Like an actress on the stage. She pretended she cared. She wrapped him in a blanket and carried him in her arms as if she loved him. She painted worry and concern on her face. And she concocted a story to cover up the crime.

But no one believed her.

After that he had gone to live with the Chatelains. And his whole life changed. Instead of torment, pain and fear, there was love, patience and understanding. The Chatelains became his real mother and father and the agony of his existence became a happy and wonderful life.

And that's what fireworks should remind him of! Not of the day that he had gotten the worst beating of his life but of the day that his life had been saved. They should remind him of the day his suffering ended and his life truly began.

The grand finale was exploding into the air! Night became day! Glittering, glimmering sparkles shimmered and showered the sky. Bangs and booms and bams hammered the celebration home.

Mike twirled Dixie to face him, his face smiling, his eyes bright. "Whoa, those were really great fireworks. It was like I was seeing them for the first time in my life. It was watching you watch them that I liked best though. Watching all those colors sparkling in your eyes."

Chapter 48

LICENSE TO BE EMMA

"Dixie? Dixie Andrews! Is that you?" Emma rushed over to the girl with the short golden hair and tapped her on the shoulder.

"Mrs. Baxter! Hi!"

"It's good to see you, Dixie! That was quite the fireworks display wasn't it! Loud though. My ears are still ringing! So, what have you been up to since you graduated from Duckwood Community? Please! Tell me you've been able to put your degree and that tremendous talent and creativity you have to good use."

"I have! I'm working at a small TV station upstate. Creative Assistant! I just love it."

"Wonderful! They're lucky to have you. I'll never forget that little film you made. Marzipan Fever. So clever. How in the world did you ever come up with an idea like that? It was a masterpiece, Dixie."

"Thank you! It was a lot of fun making it. I think my brothers still have the fan blade antlers stuffed in their closet." Dixie laughed, blushing. "Oh! You know, I should have introduced you! This is my boyfriend, Mike. Mike, this is Mrs. Baxter. She was one of my teachers at Duckwood Community College. My favorite teacher!"

"It's nice to meet you, Mike. So, you're Dixie's boyfriend. You must have been the purple haired hero in Marzipan Fever! Oh, no... Wait a minute.... I'm so sorry.... I just remembered... I heard about.... You can't be..... Oh, I am so sorry. Please, forgive me." And Emma rushed away, flustered, embarrassed, appalled by her stupidity.

She had stuck her foot in her mouth again. Said the wrong thing. She had been doing that too frequently these days. In front of her students when she was teaching a class, in front of her colleagues at meetings. A scatterbrained, forgetful fool. Maybe now was the time. She should retire, like Caleb had done.

Caleb had retired almost a year ago. He was so happy! Instead of grumping around the house and frowning all the time, he smiled and whistled. He brought out his pencils and pastels and started drawing again. Scenes of places of interest around the town - The east courtyard at Duckwood Community College, geese on the pond at Cobbs Hill Park, patrons munching on hot dogs from a street vendor's cart outside the Hall of Justice downtown.

She would come home from work every day to hear the radio tuned to the jazz station and find Caleb humming along as he put the finishing touches on dinner. And they started going to bed together again. She would fall asleep with her head on Caleb's shoulder, thinking of nothing except how soft and warm his skin was under her hand as she rubbed his chest and how good life could be.

They had been sitting at the table after dinner one night having tea and amaretto pound cake, when Caleb had looked at her and smiled. But it was an odd smile - kind of confused, kind of sad. The cup had dropped out of his hand, bounced off the table and shattered on the floor. The tea had spread out in a puddle, soaking the napkins brown and dripping over the edge. And Caleb had keeled over, dead. Heart attack.

He'd had three weeks to be the happiest he had been in years. And then it was over.

Forty-two years they'd been together! Married for forty of those forty-two years! And now he was gone and she was alone.

She had done her best to recoup herself - gone back to the classroom, gotten used to having grief as her constant companion. And she had decided to start that book she had always dreamed of writing. Only instead of a book of carefree fiction for young adults as she had originally planned, it would be a novel about relationships and stress and corporate America's involvement in the destruction of the human spirit.

It was giving her trouble though. She had plenty of ideas but she was having a hard time coming up with the right words to express what she really wanted to say. She could feel the perfect word hovering in her head, trying to materialize, sitting on the threshold but then it would deconstruct and float away before she could catch it, before she could make it flow through the pen or tap out on the keys.

One thing she was not having a hard time with was the characters. She had them all mapped out in her head, each one loosely based on real people that she knew or had known. The main character, the star of the book, would be based on her dear Caleb. She was going to call him Carl. Emma would be called Emily. And Dunbar and Bexley Eco-Systems, where Caleb used to work, would be The Dickhead and Bastard Company.

Dickhead and Bastard! Emma laughed.

But it was not a happy sound.

Poetic License

GONE

It only takes a second
It's odd how things can change
Normal is rear-ended
And things are not the same

Confusion bends the brain waves
The heart beat speeds and slows
Legs buckle and collapse
The breath catches in the throat

And those that remain
Stand stranded
Lost and alone
Scrabbling
To make sense of the senseless
Wondering
Where life's essence has gone

Chapter 49

LICENSE IN A WHISPER

Life whispered in my ears today! It woke me with the joyous chirping of sparrows and the cooing of a dove, and the delicate light of the orange rising sun.

I watched the cream swirl white in my coffee, the eggs pop and sizzle as they hit the hot griddle, the butter run in melted delight on my toast. And I closed my eyes as I savored the warmth and the flavors and the textures of breakfast on my tongue.

A painting emerged from my hands today! Created from an image frozen in time by my camera one October morning years ago - autumn's last leaves dropped on winter's first fallen snow. The leaves were sun-kissed gold, the snow crystalline and pure, blinding white, the tree furrowed and dark, and the sky an unbelievably brilliant azure blue.

It was a masterpiece! A testament to life's immense beauty. A glimpse of perfection in balance, contrast, color and light.

I had encapsulated heaven! I felt so fulfilled! This was what I was meant for, to create beauty and share it with my fellow man.

At least I could share it with Emma. Now, at least I could do that. Awe and wonder would move across her face. And pride. She would be so proud of me.

How many past days had I wasted? Days when morning's tentative hope had faded to dull disappointment and ended with bitterness and anger. And all I wanted to do was go home to my Emma! But I arrived with anger deforming my features and plastered to my words.

If I started out with anger, how could she trust the smile that might follow?

If one side of my mouth blasted, accused and criticized and the other side of my mouth told her I loved her, how did she know which side was lying and which was the side she should believe?

But we got past all that. I left the bitterness and anger behind. Morning's hope and anticipation became a day filled with happiness and contentment at night.

In the end it's the little things that matter most. They explode with importance. They remind me of what I will miss the most. They tell me why it was good to be alive:

Sunlight sneaking through the maple's green canopy, leaving dappled patterns on the ground.

The hush in the air as the sun dips to meet the horizon and the sky is filled color - radiant oranges, purples, pinks and blues.

Red breasted robin trilling an evening song.

The perfectly smooth and creamy surface of peanut butter in a newly opened jar.

Chocolate, rich and dark, melting on my tongue.

Tea running warm down my throat.

The fine wisps of gray at Emma's temple and mingled in her chestnut hair.

Emma's eyes sparkling and crinkling at the corners when she laughed.

The way my heart sang for Emma.

I tried to smile. I'm not sure it came out right. I hope she could see it. I hope she could see my love for her shining in my eyes as life pounded in me one last time and then kissed me goodbye.

Chapter 50

FAMILY LICENSE

"Bye!" Dixie shouted out the window, waving as the four figures in the driveway waved back. "I'll call you when we get home so you know we're safe. Love you!!"

It had been a wonderful weekend. It was so good to see her Mom and Dad. And even her brothers! They hadn't done one devilish thing. Well, they did hide the bowl of French onion dip and then try to make her believe it had never been there. But that was nothing compared to pranks from the past like substituting vinegar for mouthwash!

She had, surprisingly, actually enjoyed Owen and Gabe's company. Imagine that.

"You know, I'm really going to miss them. But I'm looking forward to getting back too. It's like I'm happy and sad at the same time. So, what did you think, Mike? How did you like my parental units?"

"They're awesome. You've got a great family, Dixie. I really had a good time. You're dad reminds me of my dad - hands on, intense, but with a good sense of humor and an easy laugh. Once he was sure of my honorable intentions and pulled the Glock away from my head, I think we really connected."

"The Glock? What're you talking about?" Dixie squinched her eyes and crinkled her nose, totally confused.

Mike laughed, "Never mind. It's a guy thing."

"Whatever you say! So, now we're headed to Bunderby to visit Pam and Boyd! It should only take about three hours to get there.

Set the GPS for Elm Street. You don't even need to enter a house number. All we have to do is look for flowers. Lots and lots of flowers! Wait till you see it! It's like a fairyland at the end of the rainbow!

"Pam and Boyd are great, Mike. You're going to like them. I told them we'd only stay an hour or so though because they've got the new little baby and everything. Pam forwarded me pictures! Baby Pamela. She's the most adorable little thing."

"I bet she is." Mike replied with a quick smile and glance in her direction and then he was quiet, eyes on the road.

They drove along in silence for a bit. Dixie watched the scenery zip by on her right and fellow travelers zip by on her left. She was just about to mention the funny license plate on the car up ahead of them, 'I M ZANY', when Mike started talking again.

"I've been thinking a lot about families this weekend, Dixie. Thinking about how lucky we both are to have had good parents that love us and care about us. Thinking about how easy that is to take for granted."

'Family', 'Lucky', 'Good' – Those were all positive words, with a happy connotation. But Mike's tone was not happy. He seemed edgy, tense. Dixie sensed that he was headed into uneasy territory and his next words confirmed this.

"Parents aren't all the same, you know. There's the good, the bad and the ugly. And I know about all three."

'The good, the bad and the ugly', 'He knew about all three'. Her stomach screwed up into a knot. She started to feel a little tense herself. Maybe even a little scared.

"I'm adopted, Dixie. George and Mary Chatelain weren't my blood parents. They adopted me when I was five. I've wanted to tell you so many times but I always chicken out. Not because being adopted is a bad thing. It was the best thing that ever happened to me! But because I was afraid of the questions you might ask and the memories I would have to dig up of the hell I lived in before they rescued me.

"The people, if you could even call them people, that I lived with before the Chatelains were nothing that anyone would ever call parents. They belonged to a different genre, the inhuman kind. I was just a little boy, Dixie! And every smile I ever had was torn right off my face." Pain and anger filled Mike's voice.

"The Chatelains might not have been my birth parents but as far as I'm concerned they were my real parents, my only parents, the best parents any kid could ever have. And those other 'things' that I lived with? I'm going to bury them again, as far down as I can, because they don't deserve to occupy even one speck of space in my brain. But I just wanted you to know, Dixie. As the woman I love, I thought you should know."

Emotions pulsed strong in Dixie's veins – horror at what she could only imagine had been done to innocence, gratefulness to two saviors she never knew and that she could never meet, love for this man beside her who must have suffered so much.

Dixie reached for Mike's hand that was clenched into a tight fist on the seat between them. She un-balled his fingers, brought them to her lips and kissed them gently. She held his hand to her cheek and felt it's warmth tremble on her skin, and then she kissed it again, brushing away the tear that had fallen on it with her lips.

"I love you, Mike." The words resonated with intensity, carrying more meaning than they ever had before.

And that was all she said. It was all that mattered really.

Love.

Chapter 51

LICENSE FOR A VISIT

N aptime was precious. Two or so uninterrupted hours! And there were so many things she could fill those hours with. She could pay some bills or do some house cleaning, maybe fit in a little gardening or do the laundry. Laundry. There was always laundry. Lots and lots of laundry! Or she could just relax with a cup of tea and read a magazine or catch up on emails. When she did that though, it usually ended up that she dozed off herself, her head thrown back and her mouth wide open.

Pam usually put Pamela down for her afternoon nap at 2:00 and she woke up about 4:00. 'Usually' was the key word here. If there was one thing Pam was learning, it was not to get used to anything. As soon as you thought things had settled into a pattern that you could count on and plan around, that's when it changed. Babies didn't care about clocks or timetables. They had no preconceived agenda. Every day was simply a day to be alive! To look and listen and feel! And to soak up the love showered upon them.

But today, Pam had really been hoping she could count on 'usually'. Dixie was stopping by for a short visit with her boyfriend, Mike, on the way back from spending the July 4th weekend with her folks! Expected time of arrival – 4:00. If the baby went down at 2:00 for a two hour nap, Pam could get the house in order while she slept. And when Pamela woke up at 4:00 she would be her brightest and sweetest little angel self, ready to impress and thrill a new set of admirers.

Unfortunately, today was not a day for plans to come to fruition. Pamela had not gone down for her nap until 2:45 and Dixie had just called to say that they should be arriving in less than fifteen minutes. The house was still a mess! Boyd had vacuumed earlier, but there were still dirty dishes in the sink. And she didn't expect Pamela to be up for another hour!

Well, maybe it was better that way anyway. They could chat a little and get comfortable before baby commotion entered the picture. And if worse came to worse, Dixie could at least catch a glimpse of a sleeping cherub before she had to leave.

Pam hoped they would stay longer than an hour, though. Dixie had stressed that it was to be a short visit because they didn't want to be an inconvenience. Didn't she know that she could never be an inconvenience? Besides, they hadn't seen each other since October and there was so much to talk about! Sure, there was Facebook and they texted, called and emailed from time to time, but that was nothing like real face to face conversation. And they needed time to get to know Mike!

Boyd was going to try and convince them to stay for dinner. He was out back now prepping the grill for a homemade grilled pizza! How could they turn that down?

And what was that little cooing sound she heard? Was that baby Pamela? Her little darling was waking up at the perfect time after all.

Waking up time was precious.

"Dixie!"

"Pam!"

Mike had never seen two women happier to see each other. Their smiles were so wide they almost didn't fit on their faces. They were like two sisters that had been best friends their whole lives, reunited now after too much time spent apart. But Mike knew Pam and Dixie weren't sisters and he also knew they hadn't known each other for very long either. It was one of those things that happen sometimes.

Two people that just click and form an instant bond. Reincarnated souls perhaps – connected through eons of time.

"You cut your hair!" Dixie squealed, holding Pam at arm's length after they embraced.

"Pamela's fingers were always getting tangled in it and pulling it right out of my head! I was getting tired of it anyways. Short is easier. You know what I mean! And no dangly earrings either. Nothing but simple posts. Babies are so curious! Pamela grabs for anything within her reach. And the last thing I want is for my earrings to get ripped right through my ear lobes!"

"Well, the pixie cut really suits you. And I like the blond highlights in your bangs!"

A slim, good looking guy with bright eyes and an infectious smile, that Mike had to assume was Boyd, came down the hall then carrying a pink and green frocked baby in his arms.

Dixie rushed over to him, squealing again. But Boyd was not the object of her squeals. It was the baby she was after.

"There she is! Little Pamela! What a cutie!" And she scooped the tiny girl out of Boyd's arms, oohing and aahing over her wide eyed face.

Boyd looked at Mike and rolled his eyes. The smile never left his face, though. Mike figured he was used to being ignored over the baby.

He clasped Mike's hand in a firm shake. "Hey, Mike. Do you get the feeling that they don't even know we're here?"

"Hey, Boyd." Mike returned the handshake, grinning himself. "Huh? Who? Is there anyone else here besides two and a half women?"

Mike stood there with Boyd, shrugging and smiling, as they watched Pam and Dixie make a fuss over each other and over baby Pamela, whose little face started to pucker up and flush red. And then she was crying, desperate to get out of the strange arms holding her captive and into the known and loving arms of her mother.

"Oh, little darling. Hush, hush now. Here's Mommy. That's just Auntie Dixie. No need to cry," Pam cooed as she took Pamela into her own arms.

Was this the lot of men then, to be forgotten in the face of baby-dom? Finally Mike saw realization dawn in two pairs of eyes. Pam headed towards him, embarrassment all over her face.

"Oh my god! Mike! I've completely forgotten about you. I guess I got carried away! I'm so sorry!" She took one of his hands in hers and leaned in to kiss his cheek, the baby balanced on her hip. "It's so good to meet you."

"What? You forgot about me? I was so busy watching the baby change from a sunny, pink dumpling into a frowning, red dumpling that I didn't even notice!" Mike laughed. "It's great to meet you too."

And Dixie, flushed with embarrassment herself, rushed over to Boyd.

"Oh no! Boyd! I haven't even said hello to you yet! You know I'm glad to see you, too. I really am! I didn't mean to ignore you." Dixie hugged Boyd warmly and kissed him right on the lips.

Mike wasn't sure whose face was redder after that - the baby's, Dixie's, or Boyd's?

It was amazing really, the transformation between the devastat-ed, haunted girl he had met in October and the fresh-faced, vibrant girl that was in the kitchen with Pam now, putting a salad together while Pam fed the baby. Boyd couldn't get over it.

Dixie was actually a lot like Pam. Both of them effervescent and wonderstruck with the glory of being alive, refusing to enter-tain or acknowledge the bad unless forced, focusing on the good instead. It was almost like they were twins! Twins - thirteen years apart.

Boyd shook his head and smiled. It was great to see Dixie happy. Happy and in love.

He grabbed two beers out of the fridge, stuffed them into bright green can cozies and walked out to the patio. The aroma of baking dough and red sauce was just starting to waft from the grill. The lure of a pizza on the grill had done its job. It had hooked their visitors into staying for dinner, just like he knew it would.

Mike had his nose in the bouquet of Gerbera daisies in the center of the patio table, trying to get a whiff of their scent. Boyd handed him one of the beers.

"Here you go, Mike. Pop the top on a nice cold one!"

"Hey! Thanks! Man, this is one great yard you've got here, Boyd. It's like a park! My yard looks just like it!" Mike paused then, a twinkle in his eye, and then he laughed. "Minus the flowers, bushes, trees and patio! Yeah! All I've got is half dead grass and a lot of good intentions."

"At least you can say you've got grass. You should have seen this place when we first moved in. It was a real dump! Inside and out. A total disaster. Me and Pam busted our asses fixing it up. But, you know, there's nothing like hard work to let you know you're alive. When your back is aching and you barely have the strength to strip your clothes off, what else are you but alive? And then later, you can sit back and marvel at what you accomplished."

Mike nodded his head in agreement. "I'm inspired! If I can get my house to look half as good as this, it would be so awesome! I've only had it a year, though. I figured I'd start on the inside and work my way out."

"If I was you, I'd do it the opposite, Mike. Start on the outside first. Things take time to grow. Get things planted and while they're taking root and spreading their wings, you can be refurbishing the kitchen and painting the walls."

"That's good advice. Now that you say it, it makes a lot of sense. But it's already too late. I already painted the walls and I just started putting in hardwood floors. I've got to finish that before I start on another project."

"Why? Your floors aren't going anywhere. Take a weekend or two and plant trees and bushes. You can go back to the floors anytime."

The girls came out then, smiling and laughing. Pam was carrying Pamela and Dixie was carrying the salad and a bottle of chardonnay from Cayuga Lake Winery.

Boyd saw Dixie glance in Mike's direction. He saw Mike catch her glance. Suddenly her face seemed softly luminescent; her eyes took on a tenderness, as if she was being kissed. And Mike looked the same way.

Boyd looked at Pam and Pamela then, with tender eyes of his own. He walked over to his little family, encircled them in his arms, and kissed first the tops of both their heads and then both their cheeks.

This was what life was all about, wasn't it?

Family and friends. Smiles and laughter. Happiness and love.

And it was so good to be alive.

Dixie was gazing out the open kitchen window as the summer breeze blew in, marveling at the myriad colors and textures that made up Pam's gardens. Her hands dipped in and out of soapy suds as she washed the dishes. There weren't many. They had used paper plates and bowls.

"What are you doing? Never mind those dishes, Dixie!" Pam had protested when Dixie pulled out the dishpan from under the sink.

But Dixie had insisted. Now Pam was off with the baby, giving her a bath and getting her ready for bed.

"Just leave the dishes in the drainer to dry," Pam had instructed, "I'll put them away later."

She could see Mike, still out on the patio with Boyd. The last rays of the sun were shining on his hair, accentuating the reddish in the blond and making him look almost like a carrot top. Their topic of discussion was patio construction and maintenance.

"I spray the seams between the pavers with weed killer in late spring and put on an application of concrete sealer every fall. Keeps it looking good and protects it from the freezing and thawing roller-coaster of these crazy upstate winters." Boyd was telling Mike.

Mike had a look of concentration, probably hoping he would remember all the details and advice for some future day when he fulfilled his dream of having a patio of his own.

Dixie was stuffed. The pizza had been awesome. So unique compared to traditional oven baked pizza. She liked the slightly smoky flavor it got from the grill. But the thing she had loved best about it was the char on the eggplant, zucchini and spinach that Boyd had topped it with. And the cheese! Lots of melty mozzarella! She must have had three pieces!

She was having such a great time. Everybody was. It made her wonder – Why had she waited so long to visit? It's not like Pam and Boyd lived that far away. It was only an hour or so's drive from her apartment! She would have to make a point of visiting more often.

Another thing she wondered was what would have happened to her if Pam had never taken her home that October day last year. Would she have ever gotten over her sorrow and her guilt? Would she still be walking around like a hollow shell with no insides and a dead heart? Would she have brushed off Mike's attempts at friendship, so sure that she was the cause of tragedy and death, so full of self-loathing, that she would never let anyone in? Would she have ever let herself know love again?

She owed Pam and Boyd so much. And her parents, too. And Mike. Her sweet, darling Mike. How could she ever repay these angels in her life?

By always being there for them, just the way they had been there for her. By never passing up an opportunity to tell them she loved them. By never settling for 'good enough' and striving to be the best that she could be, letting them see that she had been worth it. That's how.

And she intended to do just that.

Chapter 52

LICENSE IN A NIGHTMARE

They had surfaced. And he couldn't get them to go back down.

He'd wake in the middle of the night wet with sweat even though the room was cool; his heart wild in his chest, his stomach knotted in terror.

His dreams always started out normally abnormal; He was playing chess but all of his pieces were pawns. They crawled across the board towards their opponent, the mission lost before it had barely begun; He was standing by water with a long rope, trying to tie a knot. The square knot mantra repeated itself over and over in his head. Right over left and under. Left over right and under; A jigsaw puzzle was scattered all over a green carpeted floor. The top of the box showed the pieces would fit together into an image of the dashboard of a car. He was sprawled on the green carpet, searching and searching for the fourth corner piece.

But, differently as all the dreams began, they all ended the same; With the glowering face of the ugly man; With a belt being pulled through the loops on a pair of jeans; With the sound of a 'snap' and fear so strong he couldn't breathe; With screams and tears and pain.

The rest of the night he'd pace the floor or lay there sleepless, tossing and turning, his mind racing past the memories he thought he had left behind him long ago. Wondering why they were here, after all this time, trying to force themselves upon him again and why he couldn't find the heavy stones he needed to sink them back down into oblivion.

The daylight hours he spent trying to follow his normal routine. But his eyes felt too hot, too moist and too wide. And he couldn't seem to concentrate.

It had been like this every night for over a week. He was exhausted and desperate but he was afraid now to even try to sleep.

He had always been able to handle any problems that came his way. He was independent. He was his own man. But that wasn't working for him now.

Mike knew he needed help. And if he didn't get it, he honestly thought he might die.

If Dixie had to describe Mike's personality in one word, the word she would select was 'confident'. Mike was his own man. He knew who he was, why he was, where he was and how he was.

But that word would not describe him lately. He seemed insecure and unsure of himself, impatient and unfocused. Something was wrong.

She had her suspicions. It might have something to do with the abused early childhood he had revealed to her. She tried to draw him out, let him know she was there for him but he would barely admit to there being a problem and he certainly didn't want to discuss it. All he would say was that he was having trouble sleeping.

She would venture to say that he wasn't sleeping at all! His eyes were blood shot and dopey looking but at the same time wide open and big as quarters from all the coffee he was suddenly guzzling every day. She was getting increasing worried about him.

Now it was Friday. Mike had spent most of the day out of the office, making the rounds, drumming up advertising commitments from clients. She always met him at his house after work on Fridays. They usually went out to eat or to a movie. Sometimes they just stayed home and worked on the hardwood floor installation. But she had different plans tonight.

She was going to make him tell her what was wrong. She was going to be the angel that it had become so obvious he desperately needed.

She tapped on the door to announce her arrival and then let herself in with the key. Mike usually arrived just a few minutes before her. She would find him, still wearing his dress shirt and tie, sorting through his mail or grabbing a cold drink out of the fridge – his face happy and bright at the sight of her.

But today she was surprised to see him wearing cargo shorts and a plain white t-shirt. He must have gotten home early! He was sitting at the kitchen table, looking at a photo album. There was no happy look on his face. He didn't even look up.

She walked over to him, put her arms around him in a big hug and kissed his cheek. It was wet.

"Mike? Are you alright?" She didn't know why she even asked him that. She already knew he wasn't.

He ignored the question. "Did I ever show you this album, Dixie?" he asked instead, his voice jittery and hoarse, "This is me when I was ten with my parents at Brocade Amusement Park. And this is me shooting some hoops in the driveway with my best friend, Mark. Here's my Mom and Dad in front of our house when all the rose bushes were in bloom. They were beautiful, those roses, but my mother was always disappointed. They didn't have any smell."

He kept flipping the pages of the album absently, quiet for a moment. The pages were shaking as he turned them.

"I don't have any pictures of my real mother or the piece of scum she lived with. And I don't care either. But they've been trying to force me into thinking about them all week. Giving me nightmares. I've tried so hard to ignore them! I can't sleep. I'm so tired I can't think. I just can't do it anymore!

"I stopped at Psychology Associates this morning to get them to renew the ad they've been running. I told the guy that you were doing a piece on nightmares and I was helping you with the research and would he mind if I asked him a few hypothetical questions. I think he knew I was lying. About the hypothetical part anyway. He knew I was asking for myself. Any asshole can see I'm a total freaking mess.

"You know what he said?" Mike was straining to keep his voice calm. Dixie sensed what he really wanted to do was scream the words. "He said if nightmares are caused by a past trauma, the trauma has to be acknowledged and relived. Relive it instead of trying to hide from it. Make myself remember all the horrible details! I don't know if I can do it, Dixie! I don't want to do it!"

Mike's t-shirt was moving in and out, in and out with the beating of his heart. His eyes wavered - desolate, frantic and lost.

Dixie put her hand gently on Mike's shoulder. "Come on, Mike. Let's go sit on the couch. It's more comfortable than this hard kitchen chair." She kept her voice soft and even, a soothing counterpoint to Mike's despair.

She took him by the hand, led him over to the couch and made him sit down. She sat down next to him and held both of his hands in hers.

"Maybe you can tell me about it, Mike. I'll sit right here. Right next to you. You can relive it with me."

He hesitated, searching her face with his desperate eyes. And then he did tell her. In graphic detail. Dixie had to force herself to stay composed, not to weep, not to plead with him to stop.

Until he was five and a half, he had lived with his birth mother and some man that wasn't his real father. At least he didn't think it was his real father. Mike was supposed to call him Ray. To himself Mike called him 'the ugly man'.

There were a few good days that he could remember in those five years, days when some kind of love for his little boy self seemed to exist. They would smile at him or surprise him with a new toy or take him out for an ice cream sundae. They would say 'Ooops!' with a little chuckle when his spaghetti slid off his fork and landed on the floor instead of in his mouth and simply wipe it up for him, instead of screeching 'Watch what the fuck you're doing you little bastard!' and whacking him so hard he fell right out of his chair.

But he had a hard time trusting those scattered good days. And if there were too many good days in a row, and he had started to trust, that made the bad times and the pain that followed so much more unbearably worse.

They never spanked him or scolded him for his 'wrongdoings'. They beat him. And there were so many beatings.

He had been beaten for not finishing his pancakes and for spilling his milk. He had been beaten for getting cookie crumbs on the couch, for coming in from the backyard with mud on his sneakers and for turning on the TV too loud. He was beaten for laughing because his mother had lipstick on her teeth, for crying when the ugly man ripped all the pages out of his coloring book, and for wetting the bed, even though they had locked him in his bedroom and wouldn't let him out. And sometimes he got a beating for nothing, just because he was there.

His mother would haul-off and slap him across the face, leaving hand shaped welts, hot and red on his tender cheeks. Or yank his pants down around his ankles and beat his little ass with a wooden spoon, till those cheeks were hot and red too.

But the ugly man always used his belt. He'd grab Mike by the arm, practically ripping his shoulder right out of its socket. He'd roar about the mess Mike had made or the trouble Mike had caused or the order Mike hadn't obeyed, while he pulled the belt through the loops of his jeans. And Mike would be crying and shaking and begging and promising he'd be good. Next time he'd be good! But the ugly man didn't care. Mike would hear the snap of that belt being pulled taut anyway. He'd hear it cut the air as it whizzed towards him. And the ugly man whipped that leather so hard across Mike's back or on his bottom that he almost passed out. Over and over and over again.

And there were other things too. Once, the two of them burned him with cigarettes. They snatched him as he toddled by, the stinking things hanging out of their mouths, the ends glowing red as they sucked down the smoke. And then they took that hot glowing end and pressed it onto his arm. And they laughed when he screamed. 'Look how cute, Ray! A perfectly round little red dot!' he remembered his mother saying. They held him down and did it again and again; just to watch those perfectly round red circles burn onto his white skin.

"How could they do those things to me, Dixie? I was just a little boy. And I tried so hard to be good. I really did! I tried so hard! But nothing was good. Not to them. My stomach was always in a knot. I was always afraid. Afraid that the next thing I did…. There would be that belt….. Fear and pain. That's all I had. That's what life was. And all I wanted was for them to love me."

Mike leaned his head forward and closed his eyes, taking in deep breaths that came out shuddering and shallow. His hands had been shaking the whole time he talked. Now they were still.

"Oh, Mike, I am so sorry," Dixie said softly, determined to keep her voice steady and her own hands from shaking, "You were good. You know you were. They were the bad ones. They didn't even know what good was. Or what love was either. They were monsters, not people. With no eyes and no hearts. And you were a wonder that they didn't deserve.

"But you were saved! I wish I could have met them, George and Mary Chatelain, your Mom and Dad. They must have been the most marvelous people. They saved you and loved you. And me and everyone else in your life now, we are all blessed, because we get to have you and know you and love you with all our hearts."

Dixie stood up and reached for Mike's hand. This time she led him into the bedroom. She pulled his shirt over his head, undid his shorts and tucked him into the bed. She kissed his eyelids closed and then climbed in behind him, pulling the soft plush blanket tight around them and encircling him with her arms.

And finally, Mike slept. He slept straight through till morning, untroubled, his face smooth and at peace. The battle was over. The better man had won.

Chapter 53

NUMBER TWENTY-SIX LICENSE

Joe knew Lainey was more than disappointed. She had called to make the dinner reservation at their favorite restaurant and instead of a friendly voice at the other end of the line, she had gotten a recorded message announcing that the number she had dialed was no longer in service.

A quick Google search had turned up the sad fact that Emeralds had bitten the dust shortly after their last visit several years ago.

Secretly, Joe was glad. He knew Lainey loved the place. And he loved Lainey, so he led her to believe that he thought Emeralds was the place to dine as well. But in truth, he considered it uppity, too trendy and geared towards the affluent.

Lainey would always sit there, awed and dreamy, as the waiter proclaimed the evening's specials and exotic sounding foodstuffs flowed smooth off his tongue.

And Joe would sit there smiling and nodding, trying to turn his bafflement into his best simulation of knowledgeable enthusiasm instead.

But what were those things the waiter was rattling off?

Arugula gremolata. Garlic crostini. Smooth chipotle aioli. Haricot vert. Rosemary demi-glace.

Were they sauces? Side dishes? Seasonings?

Lainey would order something like Pecan Crusted Pork Medallions served with a cabernet peppercorn demi-glace, accompanied by haricot vert drizzled with garlic infused butter and porcini dusted pommes frites with a rich tomato aioli on the side.

Did she really know what was she ordering?

And Joe would search the menu for something he thought he recognized, like the Flat Iron Rib Eye with a creamy gorgonzola mash.

Surely, that must be a steak with mashed potatoes!

Then, when her meal arrived, Lainey's eyes would practically pop out of her head. They became basins of sparkling delight, as if heaven had just been set before her.

To Joe it looked like nothing more than a few small pieces of pork in a pool of brown gravy, green beans and French fries, all arranged like a work of art with drizzles and dollops of creamy sauces on a fancy plate.

His meal would arrive on a fancy plate too, with the steak already cut into strips, fanned out in a semi-circle and sprinkled with several different kinds of mushrooms. There was a sprig of greenery sticking out of the potatoes.

Joe would have preferred to cut his own steak! But he figured he knew why they served it that way. To make the piece of meat look larger! Joe was sure that if he reassembled the strips, his steak wouldn't be any bigger than Lainey's pork medallions!

Who did they think they were fooling? Not him! And apparently not anyone anymore!

Now a new place was going to have to be decided upon. If it was up to Joe, he would select a down to earth restaurant where he could get a thick cut of prime rib or a tender, juicy steak cooked medium rare, a baked potato and a salad. A normal place that called gravy 'gravy' and mayonnaise 'mayonnaise' and didn't charge double just because they called it a reduction or a remoulade.

But the fancy fooler was the type of place that made Lainey happy, especially when they were going out to celebrate something special. And, bottom line? If that was what made her happy, then it made Joe happy too.

"Don't you worry about it, Sugar Girl," he told her, "I will personally take it upon myself to find another place befitting the wondrous occasion of our twenty sixth wedding anniversary. You just leave it to me."

After getting recommendations from some of his co-workers and checking out websites and menus online for high class trendiness and aioli, demi-glace, haricots, and frites availability, he settled on The Crystal Inn.

It was a huge success.

Poetic License

JOE AND LAINEY AND HONEYMOON #26

It was the perfect place, the perfect night
There were white cloth napkins
There was candlelight
And Joe and Lainey feasted
Till they could feast no more

Their appetites to whet
They started with
Salmon croquettes
Topped with creamy dollops
Of lemon caper aioli

There was crusty baguette bread
With a garlic butter spread
And a salute
With raised glasses of chardonnay
Here's to us!
You and me!
On this, our 26th anniversary!

Next to tantalize their palette
Arriving on a crystal plate
And tasting just fabulous
Was a crisp iceberg wedge
With warm bacon dressing
And crumbles of tangy blue cheese

Then the waiter, with a flair
For the main course did declare
They should have the most delicious
Pan seared scallops
On a bed of angel hair

The finishing touch
Before they went on their way
Was red raspberry coulis
Lightly drizzled
Over airy coconut meringues

Click each course upon arrival
Click on Joe's happy smile
And click on Lainey's smile too
Click on her candlelit green eyes
Click on the kiss
Joe planted on her lips
That the waiter took by surprise

The very next day
When Lainey went out to shop
To the photo kiosk Joe did trot
Select, edit, print
And last night's clicks
Were now photos in the palm of his hand

Back home again
Joe hurried then
There was no time to waste
A surprise to prepare before Lainey's return
And her sweet lips again he did taste

Down from the shelf he took it
Their anniversary album
Leather bound and gold inscribed
And to the next unused page he did flip it
It was there his plan would come alive

With glue stick in hand
He! Joe himself!
The photos inside did affix
And in rainbow colors
He titled it
Honeymoon #26

When Lainey through the door did come
She spotted the open book
She dropped all her bags
And quick as a flash
Into Joe's arms she did jump

She kissed him all over his face
Love singing in her heart
And with tender tears and a grin
She made a proclamation
There was no doubt in her mind
Joe was the world's best husband
And would be hers till the end of all time

They smiled and they laughed
And around the room they danced
Giddy and light as two balloons
Each day was a celebration

A joyous confirmation
Of their love
And their never ending
Honeymoon

Chapter 54

LICENSE TO BE GRANDMA

There was nothing better than waking up to birdsong! It made Erika want to jump out of bed, run out the door into the yard and raise up her arms to the glory of the morning! It made her want to grab her pruners and her garden trowel and her v-bladed weeder and stick her hands into the sun kissed soil.

But into what yard would she run? That was what she missed most about not having the house any more – the yard. The only soil she would be sticking her hands into these days was in the pots she had out on the patio.

And, certainly, she could go out there! She could venture off her patio and out onto the grass, let the dew wet the bottoms of her feet and raise her face to the sun. But there could be hundreds of pair of eyes watching her! Wondering what she was doing out there in her nighty. Wondering if she was crazy.

Better to just sit at the little patio table and sip her coffee, watching the sparrows and chickadees flit and fly and hop. Watching the robins run across the grass, leaning forward on their skinny bird legs, and then stopping with their heads tilted to the side, listening for breakfast's tiny clicks and buzzes or hums. Fast as lightening they'd lunge and then stand there with their prize dangling from their mouth before they swallowed it down. Tiny raptors they were, the last vestiges of dinosaurs gone by.

Maybe she didn't have a yard to garden in and greet the morning in any longer but there were other things to look forward to now. Like Mondays, Wednesdays and Fridays! Those were her favorite days of the week! Those were the days the daughter-in-law of her dreams worked at the diner from ten till five and Erika got to baby sit her sweet little dumpling!

Pam would drop baby Pamela off on her way to work and then Boyd would pick her up on his way home. That gave Erika six hours of pure and simple joy to spend with her little angel.

Just the sight of Pamela sent warm waves traveling through her veins, like melted chocolate, sweet and creamy, coating her insides with love.

When it was naptime, Erika loved to sit in the rocking chair with Pamela and watch her fall asleep in her arms. She'd just sit there and gaze in awe at the baby's angel fine hair and the way it fell on her forehead and over the top of her button ears. Her heart would sigh at her delicate eyelids framed by feathery lashes and marvel at her silky smooth skin and the look of complete peace and serenity on her little cherub's face. It was like heaven on earth.

Andy said she was spoiling the baby by letting her sleep in her arms so often. He said the baby needed to learn to rely on herself and become independent. Rely on herself? Become independent? She was only three months old for heaven's sake! Much too young for words as big as that. And much too young to be spoiled either.

Andy wasn't fooling her though. She saw how tenderly he held the baby and the glow in his eyes when he looked at her. She could see his wheels turning, imagining when she got older how he would push her on the swing or pull her in the wagon. How he would buy her ice cream and hot dogs and watch her twirl around and do somersaults. Erika was pretty sure that the person who would be the biggest spoiler of their grandchild in the years to come would be none other than Grandpa Andy himself!

He even bought a plaque that he had hung up in the kitchen one day, the biggest grin on his face that she had ever seen.

'GRANDCHILDREN SPOILED HERE'

There was another plaque that she had seen at The Fair Weather Gift Shop. Next time she stopped in there she was going to snatch it up.

'GRANDMA'S THE NAME. SPOILING'S THE GAME'

Maybe she could find one that said something specific about Grandpas too. Or maybe she could make one. That would be even better! She was into crafty things lately! And wouldn't that just make Andy's day?

'Awesome', 'Insane' - These were words of the times. The ones today's young people used to express something so great, so fantastic that they couldn't contain their enthusiasm.

Like when kids used to say 'cool' or 'groovy' or, way back in the day, when they used to say 'the cat's pajamas'.

'Awesome' and 'Insane' were not words she usually used. In fact they were not words she used at all!

But what other words could she use now? How could she possibly describe it any other way? There was simply no other was to say it!

Being a grandmother was totally, unbelievably, insanely awesome!

Really, there was just nothing else like it.

Chapter 55

LICENSE IN GRAY ASH

Bigwigs seemed totally dark after the bright sunshine of the August day outside. Boyd peered into the dimly lit interior until his eyes adjusted to the change in light. Déjà vu.

The place was almost completely empty. There was no group of 'mulanyans' at the far end of the bar, no one sitting at any of the tables, just a couple of unsavory types with their backs to the door, their derrieres hanging over the edges of their adjacent stools. They must have been buds since they sat side by side instead of spaced a respectable distance apart like strangers would normally sit, but there was no conversation between them. They sat hunched over their beers, lost in whatever addled thoughts they might have been capable of having.

Boyd sat down on the same barstool he'd sat on in January, when he'd come to meet his brother. The bartender headed his way and Boyd recognized him as Marko, the same bartender that had been there in January too. Maybe he was the owner. Who else would still be working in a dump like this seven plus months later?

"What'll yah have, Dude?" Marko asked with little enthusiasm.

"Bring me a beer. Something in a bottle. Do you have any Sam Adams?"

"Yeah, sure, coming right up. You know, you look familiar. You been in here before?"

"Maybe." Boyd stared him in the eye, willing him to remember, waiting for Marko's memory to jog into place and picture Boyd's face at the receiving end of a hard thrown punch. "Maybe not."

"Well, if you don't know, I sure don't." And Marko walked to the other end of the bar for the beer.

Boyd reached into the bag he had with him and pulled out a plain cardboard box, the size of a tissue cube. He placed the box on the bar in front of him, right where the four shot glasses filled with the mystery whiskies had been lined up on that wintery January day, whiskies that his brother had tried to force down his throat.

"You pulled your stunts one too many times, Tom," Boyd said to the box, "And now here you are."

It was a week ago that Boyd had stopped at his parent's place after work to pick up baby Pamela. He was whispering sweet nothings into her tiny ear and tickling her little belly. She was smiling her wide and toothless grin, giggling and squealing with glee. Each dimple and coo melted Boyd's heart.

"I made a tuna casserole for you to take home, Boyd!" his mother said cheerfully from the kitchen, "Now neither one of you will have to cook tonight! All you have to do is stick it in the oven. 375 for half an hour."

"Thanks, Mom. Was Pamela a good girl today?"

"Oh, my little dumpling's always a good girl. A total pleasure!"

And then the doorbell had rung. Who could that be? And his mother had skipped happily to the door like a little girl herself. Maybe it was a friend of hers stopping by. She could show off her darling granddaughter to them!

Boyd heard a deep voice saying something he couldn't make out and then the loud, unexpected sound of something clattering as it hit the floor. He rushed to the door to see what had happened, with Pamela balanced on his hip. His father came hurrying out of the bathroom, drying his hands on a towel, concerned as to what the sudden commotion was all about.

It was the casserole dish that had fallen, spilling saucy tuna, peas, mushrooms and noodles at his mother's feet. She had forgotten to set it down and had carried it with her to the door in her excitement to greet a friend, but there was no friend at the door to greet. Instead, it was a police officer that stood there, looking grim and uncomfortable. He had come to deliver unwelcome news. Tom was dead.

It had happened in a bar in Northboro, Pennsylvania. Tom had been his usual bastard self - drunk, unruly, getting in peoples' faces, pushing the wrong buttons. A fight had broken out and Tom had fled out the door like the coward that he was. But in his stupor, he had tripped on the threshold, stumbled and fell, ramming his head into a fire hydrant and cracking it wide open. Passersby had tried to help, an ambulance had arrived in less than five minutes, but there was no saving Tom. Death had been almost instantaneous.

Boyd had just stood there at the news, frozen, his face a blank mask. Some kind of emotion churned inside him but he didn't know what it was – Sorrow? Jubilation? Relief?

His father had been as frozen as Boyd was, staring straight ahead with vacant, dead eyes. Finally he shook his head, closed his eyes and when he opened them again, tears that had pooled behind his lids trickled down his cheeks and dripped off his chin. He wiped them away, almost angrily, with the side of his hand.

Boyd's mother had rushed, flustered, into the kitchen for a towel to clean up the mess she'd made. She dropped to her knees by the spilled casserole, the towel pressed instead to her face, hiding her anguish, muffling her sobs, soaking up her tears.

They cried, not so much over the life that had been lost or because of what Tom was, as they cried over the life that had been wasted, of what Tom wasn't, of what they had hoped he still might become, of what there was no chance of his becoming now.

Boyd made the three hour drive down to Northboro the next day, to positively identify and take possession of the body. His parents had instructed him to have the body cremated and to then scatter the ashes in a place befitting Tom's memory.

The Northboro police gave Boyd everything that his brother had had on him, which was nothing but a worn leather wallet and its contents - two twenty dollar bills, an expired New York State Driver's License and a scrap of paper with two phone numbers scribbled on it. One said 'Mom and Dad', the other said 'Boyd'.

⟶

"Hey, Marko. Keep your eye on my beer. I gotta take a leak."

"No problem, Dude."

Boyd picked up the box and headed for the men's room. The putrid stench of dried piss and old barf met his nostrils, filthy walls inked and etched with words from the pen or the knife met his eyes, proclaiming Veronica K. to be the best fuck in town, urging him to call Tammy for a good time or advising the best way to increase the size of his junk.

The door to the stall hung crooked and unclosable, ripped half way off its hinges. He walked in anyway and lifted the smear stained seat with the toe of his shoe. He opened the cardboard box and slowly started to pour its contents into the bowl, watching as the course gray ash that had been his brother sank to the bottom, falling like gravel and dirt through the water. Several times he pushed down the flusher with his foot to make sure the cremains didn't clog up the pipes.

The empty box, he dropped down onto the tacky floor, smashed it flat, and shoved it into the corner along with the strips of toilet tissue, crumpled towel paper and empty cigarette packs that spewed and overflowed from the pail meant to hold them. Then, he washed his hands and went back out to his beer.

"I'm in the mood for a shot," he informed Marko who was bullshitting with a newcomer several stools down, "Got any scotch?"

"Of course I've got scotch! This is a bar, you know. I run a fine establishment here," Marko replied, looking offended. He reached to the top shelf and brought down a bottle labeled White Horse Blended Scotch Whiskey.

"Pour shots all around, for yourself too. I want to make a toast."

Once the shots were poured, Boyd raised his glass in the air, indicating that his four bar mates should do the same. "To my brother, Tom. And to this fine establishment we have the pleasure of imbibing in."

"To Tom and this fine establishment!" the others mimicked, looking a little confused since they didn't know who the hell Tom was or what fine establishment this joker could possibly be referring to, and Marko looking pleased with the compliment to Bigwigs, even though he knew it was a fake.

And down their hatches the golden colored liquid flowed. Boyd grimaced as the whiskey burned its way down his throat, like fire water, or like gasoline. White Horse my ass. He drank down his last swig of beer and stood to leave.

"Thanks," he said to Marko, who was grimacing himself.

Boyd reached into his back pocket and pulled out the two twenties, smacked them down onto the bar and walked out of Bigwigs and into the day. Out of the dark and into the light; the bright sun making him squint, bringing tears to his eyes.

Chapter 56

LICENSE FOR A PROPOSAL

D ixie lay, flopped like a rag doll, on the ground in Mike's back yard, her eyes closed. Closed partly because she barely had enough energy to keep them open and partly to block out the bright sun that shone down on her from the bluer than blue late summer sky.

Mike lay next to her, equally flopped, his own eyes closed. Dixie thought he might have even fallen asleep. Finally she mustered the strength to sit up. She heard Mike mumble something and she grabbed his arm to pull him up into a sitting position beside her.

"Oooww!" he complained, wincing a little as he rubbed his upper right arm and shoulder with his left hand. And then he smiled.

They had started at 7:00 that morning. For the next eight hours they had dug and lifted and raked and watered and sweated. And now the fruits of their labors were spread out before them - A maple tree, two blue spruce and six variegated dogwoods planted in the back yard, and a crabapple, a forsythia and two boxwoods planted in the front.

"Look at it, Mike! It looks awesome already! Just imagine how it's going to look in the future as things grow. And in the spring the crabapple will be pink and the forsythia will be yellow. It'll be beautiful. I can't wait!"

"I'm going to take some pictures and email them to Boyd. I want him to see I took his advice. Maybe almost two months later than he thought I should, but I still got it done this year instead of waiting till next! I'll send him pictures of the almost finished hardwood floor too.

"Yeah, you know, for some reason I got a lot done this summer," he continued, trying to feign confusion. But he couldn't keep the glint of a tease from his eyes. And the smile that he tried to hold in kept popping out onto his lips despite his efforts. "I really don't know what that reason could be though. Do you have any idea what that reason could be, Dixie?"

Mike gave way to his smile and leaned in close to give Dixie a kiss but stopped short, his lips barely touching hers before he pulled away.

"Was that supposed to be a kiss? Don't I deserve something more major for all my help than a kiss that felt like a mosquito buzzing by my lips?" She tried to sound slighted but she laughed instead. She knew the reason for the peck instead of the smooch.

"Oh Dixie, you do! You deserve way better than that. And I promise, once I change from smelly, slick and salty into suave and sophisticated, I will give you the proper thank you that you most definitely deserve."

"Me first!" Dixie shouted, jumping up and bolting for the sliding screen door, looking behind her at Mike as she ran. "I'm getting suave and sophisticated first!"

She rushed inside, laughing, and headed for the bathroom and the relief of a nice cool shower.

The water flowed from the showerhead in a refreshing cascade. It washed cool over her sweaty upturned face, ran warm down the rest of her body and hit her feet almost hot. She was a sun, changing the temperature of the water on contact with her abundant solar power.

Suddenly the shower curtain slid open.

"I figured we'd save water," Mike said innocently as he stepped into the tub behind her.

So they took turns. While one of them soaped up, the other one rinsed. While one shampooed, the other conditioned.

Dixie didn't think they saved any water though.

It was running the whole time Mike gave her the proper thank you that she did most assuredly deserve.

Later, they headed up to Elwanger Beach Park for some ice cream.

The line at Crocus Hill Creamery was long. It snaked down the sidewalk and along the edge of the parking lot for what must have been half a mile. Everybody seemed to have had the same idea as Mike and Dixie. Enjoy summer's warmth while it was still here. It was almost September, and although still officially summer, once September hit, the air always had an underlying touch of coolness to it regardless of how warm the thermometer declared it to be.

But efficiency was a top priority at Crocus Hill. The line moved quickly and soon they had their cones in hand; two scoops for Mike - Chocolate Brownie Blitz on the bottom and Eggnog on the top. And one scoop of Elderberry for Dixie.

They sat at a picnic table licking their cones as the day began to wane and the clouds took on shadings of pink and orange with the glow of the descending sun. Seagulls glided above or ambled about on the sparse grass or in the sand, screaming at each other and fighting over scraps of hot dog buns, stale potato chips and orange cheese puffs that had been left behind by messy picnickers.

One gull was struggling to pilfer a half-eaten ear of corn away from a group that was pecking at it together and claim it for its selfish own. Shrill shrieks and screeches accompanied jabbing beaks and sharp, taloned claws as they all fought now to gain independent ownership of the prized cob.

Dixie chuckled to herself at the spectacle. Winning for any one bird seemed a dicey prospect but she was rooting for the gull that had the gray head and one gray wing. He seemed to have a more diplomatic approach to the quest for cob-dom. There was reasoning in his screeches and he did less jabbing.

What a day it had been! Not only had the weather been perfect - Bright and warm with cotton ball fluffs of cloud drifting across a magnificent blue sky, but she had spent the entire day at Mike's side; useful, productive, creating beauty from plainness, soaking in nature's wonders, reveling in sweetness, and embraced by love.

And now she started to get nervous. Because things were so perfect. Because perfect was what she had been waiting for. Because the perfect day was the perfect time.

Three weeks ago she had called her father to broach the subject of what she proposed to do.

"Hey, Dad!"

"Hi, Dixie! What's up?"

"Can I get your opinion on something?"

"Sure. I've got plenty of opinions. Which one do you want?"

And his response had been more than positive.

"I say go for it! I think it's a great idea. I'm with you one hundred percent. You're your own woman, Dixie. Good for you!"

But behind all his words of approval and encouragement, Dixie had felt like he wanted to laugh! She could picture him, trying not to grin and then, when he remembered that she couldn't see him, letting that smile out, so big it almost fell off his face. And once he let the smile out, now he had to work at holding his laugh in.

What would have made him have a reaction like that? It made no sense! Surely, she must have been imagining it.

She was gazing off into the distance wondering about this curiosity when she realized Mike was asking her something.

"So, do you want to, Dixie?"

"Want to what?"

"Go on the Merry-Go-Round!"

"Okay! Yeah, let's go! Sounds like fun!"

Mike took her hand in his and they walked the path that led to the carousel.

The perfect day, the perfect time and now the perfect place! Flittering flutters started to tumble about in Dixie's stomach. Her heart began to pound. As they waited in line for the ride, Dixie rehearsed in her mind what she was going to say. She made a conscious effort to keep part of her mind attuned to Mike's possible conversation but he was quiet, content just to stand by her side holding her hand and watching the horses, pigs, goats and rabbits go up and down, up and down and round and round.

Normally, Dixie would be watching the carved and painted animals too, trying to decide which one was her favorite, the one she would make a mad dash for when it was her turn to ride. But today was a different kind of day. Round and round was good. Up and down did not fit her plan. This time she was going to suggest they sit together in one of the carriages instead.

When the merry-go-round stopped and the line was moving forward to board, those words were just about to pop out of her mouth when Mike beat her to it!

"Let's sit in the carriage, Dixie." And he rushed over to it, hoping no one else would get there before him.

She scooted in beside him just as the calliope began to play and the wooden animals all about them jerked to life for their roundabout gallivant, her heart beating even faster than it had been before.

"Mike, I've been ..." Dixie started to speak the words she had rehearsed only Mike had started talking at the very same time.

Not talking really, but singing! Quietly, so the only person that could hear him was Dixie. "*And the seasons they go round and round and the painted ponies go up and down. We're captive on the carousel of time.* Have you ever heard that song before, Dixie? The Circle Game by Joni Mitchell? It's a classic. Joni compares life, time, to a merry-go-round. Each year of your life is one rotation on the carousel. And I wanted to ask you, Dixie, if you'd ride on that carousel of time, together, with me?"

Mike reached into the left pocket of his cargo shorts then and pulled out a little cream colored velvet box. He cupped her chin in his right hand, leaned in close and kissed her lips softly. Then he opened the velvet box. Inside the box was a ring - a simple diamond set in white gold bordered by two glittering green emeralds.

"Will you marry me, Dixie?" His voice was hushed, hopeful, and full of love.

It was so beautiful. So perfect. All of it. Everything. Mike's words. Mike's voice. Mike's face. The ring.

"Oh, Mike," she whispered, love welling up in her heart along with the tears that were welling up in her eyes.

And she was going to say yes. Of course she was going to say yes! But before she could form the word, she started to chuckle and the chuckle became a little laugh and then she tilted her head back and laughed out loud.

Now she understood her father's reaction. Mike must have called him to ask for her hand before Dixie had called him to ask his opinion. Her father had known the whole story. And now so did she.

But Mike had no idea why she was laughing! He was staring at her, incredulous, bewildered, confused.

Before he could get the wrong idea and his bewilderment started to turn to hurt. Before he could start to think she was having another 'curly' day, she took his face in both her hands and kissed him. Then she reached into her purse and brought out a plain white box, about the same size as the velvet box that Mike had taken out of his pocket.

She opened it. Inside was a gold band shaped like the encircled twig of a tree.

"Darling, darling Mike. You have taken my heart. And now, you have taken the words right out of my mouth. I was going to ask you the same thing. Will you marry me, Mike?"

Smiling and laughing, they put the rings on each other's fingers, 'yes' sparkling in dual eyes and whispered from dual mouths.

And then, as the merry-go-round continued its journey round and round, they kissed.

They were still kissing when the carousel stopped. Their ride on the merry-go-round at Elwanger Beach Park was over. But a new revolution on the carousel of life had just begun.

Chapter 57

LICENSE FOR SEPTEMBER

And here it was, September.

And the air was warm and chill at the same time.

Last year this day had been on a Friday.

And this year it was on a Saturday instead.

At this time last year, on a Friday night, he should have been playing to a packed house at the Lyell Road Tavern or Stoney's.

Instead he had come to sing to her.

And he had stood right there, next to the couch, with his dark mahogany guitar and his green t-shirt and his tight jeans, with his hazel eyes and crooked smile and tousled sandy hair.

And she had sat right there, on one of the dinette chairs, listening to him sing, watching the emotions pour out and overtake his face, his voice laughing the words or crying them, cradling them or chewing them up and spitting them out, feeling those emotions pour then into her.

And he had made her realize she still loved him.

And she had let him leave anyway.

And the next morning? How could it be true? How could it possibly be true?

She had rushed to the hospital. He had been so weak, his skin so pale. Almost as colorless as the white sheets on bed, as colorless as the white walls.

But he had still smiled at her. And he had squeezed her hand.

And then....And then....

And he used to have purple hair and he used to play in a band and he used to wink at her in the crowd. He used to snort sometimes when he laughed and eat his French fries with gravy and guzzle his beer. And he used to run his hands so slowly down her body and kiss her so tenderly that she swooned.

But not now. Not since that day last September. Not anymore.

Dixie hadn't been aware, not on a conscious level, that this was the exact one year anniversary of that devastating weekend. But the knowledge of it must have been keeping time in the back of her mind because when she looked, sleepy eyed, out at the little patch of petunias across from her window, the purple and white striped ones had stood out, bolder and brighter than all the others. And she had pictured Greg's Malibu parked there. And she had known.

Sobs burst from her mouth, instantaneous and uncontrollable. They filled her ears and vibrated in her chest, too low and too deep to possibly be coming from her own throat, yet somehow they were.

She wandered from room to room, aimless, untethered, desolate and lost, barely able to see through the torrent issuing from her eyes and missing Greg so much that it hurt.

Then, as suddenly as the tears and the sobs had started, they stopped, leaving her with a dull, consuming emptiness that made it hard for her to breathe.

She wished Mike was here with her now. On Saturdays, she usually woke up with him at his place but last night Mike had to wine and dine clients so she had gone out for a burger with Dee Dee and Hilary after work and then slept at home. And she had woken up alone. And today was not a good day to be alone.

She had her phone in her hand, ready to call Mike, when she heard a little tap on her door and the key turning in the lock and there he was.

"Mike! I was just going to call you. I'm so glad you're here." Dixie ran into his arms and laid her head on his shoulder. "Today's...." Her voice faltered and cracked, hovering on the edge of tears.

"I know, Dixie. I know what today is." Mike's tenderness and compassion were like a balm, spreading solace over the ache in her soul.

She stood there, silent, not moving, letting the protective circle of his arms comfort her, while he stroked her hair.

"Mike?" she whispered softly after a time.

"Yeah?" Mike whispered softly back.

"Will you take me to Betty's Pantry? There's something I have to do there."

"Anything you want, Angel."

Dixie moved slowly out of Mike's embrace and went to the closet, rummaging around and moving things out of the way, searching for something, while she explained to Mike what it was she wanted to do.

"I painted a memorial to Greg on the side of Betty's Pantry last year, right at the spot where......, where everything changed. It's probably faded over the course of the year, in the snow and rain and wind and sun. And I don't want it to fade away. I want to do it over again. Make it fresh and new."

Finally she found what she had been looking for - the template she had made, the thick purple paint and the stiff brush.

It was not nearly as faded as Dixie thought it would be. The inch and a half high letters were still completely legible, still completely purple. Mostly it was just dirty - splashed with muddy water and stained by salty slush and the dried and splattered remains of a soda that had spewed on it from someone's accidently dropped cup.

Luckily, Dixie had thought to bring a jug of water and a couple of sponges. And afterwards, when the wall was clean and the paint was refreshed, she had stood before it with her head bowed, clinging tightly to Mike's hand.

She had spent the day remembering Greg, missing his existence, mourning his loss. She had drawn strength and support from Mike's presence and his unconditional love. But suddenly she found herself relaxing her grip, extricating her hand from Mike's, giving herself space.

There was something else she had to do. Here in this spot, where Greg had stood for one last moment still vital and strong, just before the blade of a knife took everything away from him, what she needed now was some time alone. She needed to do more than remember Greg. She needed to talk to him.

"Mike, would you mind..," she started to ask but her request remained unfinished. Somehow Mike seemed to know what she needed almost before she knew herself.

"I think you need a little time alone, Dixie. I'll wait for you inside the restaurant. You take as much time as you need." He put his arm around her shoulder, gave her a little hug and kissed the side of her face and then he walked away.

Dixie took a deep breath. She sat down, cross legged, on the black pavement, her hands in her lap, her back against the gray wall right next to the purple letters, and closed her eyes.

And the words that had been collecting in her head and in her heart all day came tumbling out, searching for a wave length to carry them to the ears of the one that she had lost.

Betty herself was pouring Mike a cup of coffee when Dixie slid into the seat across from him fifteen minutes later. Betty did a double take when she realized who it was.

"Oh my goodness! Dixie Andrews! I can't tell you how much I enjoy your segments on the daily news! They really make my day. To what do I owe this honor?" Betty was glowing, all smiles and sunlight.

Suddenly a cloud seemed to drift across Betty's face, blocking the sun of her smile. She was looking at Dixie's hands, had noticed the few flecks of purple paint on them and the somber look on Dixie's face.

"It's been a year hasn't it? Oh, honey, I'm so sorry. For that to have happened in my parking lot. I've always felt that somehow it was my fault." Betty stood there, shaking her head slowly back and forth and clucking her tongue against the back of her teeth.

"Listen," she finally continued, "you and your friend order whatever you like. It's on me today."

"You don't have to do that, Betty!" Dixie objected.

"Stop fussing. I know I don't have to do that. I don't have to do anything. I want to do it! And just to let you know, our lunch special today is a Turkey Reuben with Fries.

"It's really good!" she added, a partial smile returning to her face.

"Is it too late for biscuits and sausage gravy?"

"Honey, it's never too late for biscuits and sausage gravy! You've got it!" Betty turned to Mike then, "And what about you? What would you like besides the coffee?"

"The coffee's really good by the way! And to eat, hmmm, I guess ……." Mike began but before he could inform her of his stomach's desire, Betty started talking again.

"You know, you look really familiar. Maybe I saw you... Oh! I know! Aren't you the one that modeled the swimsuits with Dixie?" Betty chuckled.

"Yeah, that was me alright." Mike chuckled too, rolling his eyes at the embarrassing memory of it.

"What a hoot that was! Those old timey time swimsuits really cracked me up. And, not to embarrass you anymore than I can see you already are, but when you came out in that skimpy little Speedo, your face was so red! I nearly peed my pants I laughed so hard!"

All three of them were laughing now.

"Betty, I should introduce you. This is my fiancé, Mike Chatelain."

"Your fiancé! How wonderful! Well, congratulations to the both of you. So then, Mike, have you decided what you want yet?"

"Since you made it sound so good, I'll have that Turkey Reuben special but could I get it with onion rings instead of fries?"

"You've got it!" And Betty hurried off to turn in their order.

"How come you didn't get the biscuits and sausage gravy too, Mike? You said it was your absolute favorite during the Take Out or Leave It Contest!"

"It was my favorite! But you already ordered it! I figured I'd get to taste yours."

"Oh no! Mine is mine! If you want a taste, you're going to have to order your own!"

"Seriously? Well, if that's the way you're going to be, don't even think about trying to snatch one of my onion rings!"

It was just small talk, gentle teasing, surface skimming. Dixie could see Mike watching her closely, gauging sadness versus sparkle, ready to offer support, understanding, or even protection, if she still needed it.

So much love for Mike surged up within her she thought she'd float away, a love filled balloon sailing up to join the clouds. Soaring up and then smiling down! Just like her words to Greg had soared heavenward in the parking lot minutes before.

'I miss you, Greg. Every day. I did so many things wrong, made so many mistakes. And I am so thankful that at least I got the chance to tell you I loved you and that you didn't have to leave this world not knowing. Thankful that love was the last thing your ears heard and that your heart felt.

'I saw you, you know. Like an ethereal mist leaving your body. I felt you, like downy feathers brushing my cheek. And I heard you. Softer than a whisper breathing in my ear and fluttering in my heart.

I got your message. That you expected me to go on. Do you know how hard that was? To go on? I almost couldn't do it! But I had angels living right here on earth that helped me and I did go on living, just like you wanted me to.

'I'm engaged to one of those angels now! Mike! I'm in love and I'm happy! Mostly. But sometimes I wonder what would have happened if you hadn't died? What my life would be like? Would we have gotten back together? Would it would be you I was going to marry now instead of Mike? But wondering about things that can never be doesn't help anybody. It's going backwards instead of forwards. And going backwards isn't good for you.

'You were my first love, Greg. There will always be a spot in my heart that's yours. A place where I keep my love for you safe and forever. I'll never forget you, Greg. Never.'

A light breeze had started up while Dixie was talking, ricocheting off the wall of the building and moving the little fly-away hairs at her temple, making them tickle the side of face. She kept brushing them away with her fingers, slightly annoyed. But then a different thought entered her mind. She stopped brushing away the little hairs and sat still. The faint essence of a tickle moved softly down her face to her lips and hovered there, like a delicate kiss. It moved across her nose and touched her closed eyelids, first one and then the other. It drifted down touching her hands and she tried to touch it back, to hold it, but there was nothing there to grasp. And then the sensation was gone.

Dixie had never told anyone about the ethereal mist, the feathery kiss, the butterfly whisper that she had experienced in the hospital room after Greg died. Who would believe she had seen a ghost? Not a ghost really but a transcendental presence.

She could just imagine the look on people's faces if she did tell them. They would probably nod their heads in false sincerity and pretend that they believed her. But they would just be humoring her, a silly girl, who had been lost in grief, reaching for straws. Behind their hands they would scoff and roll their eyes at the absurdity of it all.

But she knew what she saw. She knew what she felt.

She had felt it outside Enigma's on her birthday too.

And she had felt it today.

Betty returned then with their lunches. The lovely aroma of the sausage gravy steamed up into Dixie's face from her heaping plate.

Hungrily, she gathered up a mouthful onto her fork. And reached across the table with it. The first taste for Mike.

And there was Mike, pushing his basket of onion rings towards her. To share.

Smiles spread across their faces as they dug in.

"Mike?" Dixie asked, suddenly serious, her blue/green eyes gazing across the table into Mike's eyes of grey, "Do you believe in ghosts?"

The trace of an understanding smile touched Mike's lips. He gazed back at her, his eyes as serious as her own.

"I don't know if I've ever actually experienced one but I believe they're out there. I believe in the possibility." Mike paused, staring into her eyes.

"Tell me about it, Dixie," he whispered softly.

Poetic License

G **G**ravity has no hold on me
   I float like a balloon
   Unhindered
   Softer than a whisper
   But a whisper needs breath
   And breath I have left behind

H **H**igher and higher I float
   Surrounded by calm, acceptance and serenity
   Still, although up is where I go
   Down is where I look
   I see
   But my living eyes are closed

O **O**nes that I have loved
   I see them on the ground
   They look up as I look down
   They wale inconsolable
   So much grief, so much sorrow
   I ache to comfort them
   Try to tell them my soul is at peace and free
   But words no longer belong to me

S **S**till they weep
   Time is what they need
   Time will blend their heartache and sorrow
   Into a new normalcy, a happy tomorrow
   Burning tears and anguished sobs
   Will be replaced by nostalgic memories
   Whenever their thoughts turn to me

T Time passes differently here
   Minutes and smells
   Colors and days
   Music and shapes
   They all combine
   I float content
   And hope they know I watch over them
   In the twinkle of the stars
   In the warmth of the sun
   Love and life go on
   In more ways than one

Chapter 58

REVOKED LICENSE

Ten hours a day, six days a week Kayla worked at the deli, slicing lunchmeats and measuring out salads. But she didn't mind the long hours. It gave her something to do and kept her out a trouble.

She always had lots of customers in her line. They liked her because she smiled and chatted with them, all friendly like. Being friendly was something she never was before she got cleaned up and straightened out but she liked to be friendly now.

The boss might give her the old evil eye, nod his head in the direction of the line that was getting longer and longer with people waiting to order their ham and bologna and potato salad. 'Quit your jabbering and get back to slicing, Vester!' Those eyes would warn. 'Or else!'

Or else what? Kayla wasn't too worried. She was the best worker he had. She was always on time and never once in the six years she'd worked there had she ever even missed one day.

Another reason she had lots of customers in her line was because sometimes, after the order had been weighed and she had slapped on the price sticker, if she was sure the boss wasn't looking, she'd wink and throw on a extra slice of turkey breast or another little spoon a pasta salad. And that was because she was trying to be nice now, like she had never been before either. Even before she got hooked, Kayla had never been nice.

Getting hooked changed you. Getting cleaned up changed you too. But getting older changed you most, made you see things different, made you know all what you done wrong before and made you want to do better now.

And Kayla had done lots wrong. She tried not to think about it too much. It ate her insides out, made her want to scream, made her want to sit with her head in her hands and cry forever. How could that person a been her? How could she a done the things she done?

So now she tried to be friendly and nice and kind to everyone to make up for them bad things. And she tried especially hard to be nice to children. They'd come into the deli with their little hands tucked into the hand a their mom or dad, most a them looking bored and dying to get out a there. And Kayla would smile and offer them a sucker from the basket by the register.

Their eyes would light up and they'd reach into that basket searching for their favorite, which most times would be one a them red, cherry ones. The ones Kayla hated, that tasted like sickening sweet cough medicine and made her wanna gag. They nearly never picked her favorite, the sunny yellow lemon ones.

Kayla used to have a kid once. A little boy. But she lost him more than twenty years ago. And when she made the kids at the deli smile it made her glad and sad at the same time because it made her think a him.

Then one day, when she was off on a vacation visiting her cousin out a state, she seen him on a TV morning show! Her son! Her heart about stopped dead and then it started beating so fast she thought it might jump right out a her mouth. She couldn't hardly breathe!

She tried telling herself she had a be wrong, so her heart would settle down. But that didn't work because she knew she was right. There was no one else it could be but him! He was taller and older a course, but he still had the exact same round face and gray eyes. And he had the same mouth! Except on the TV he was smiling, like what she never made him do before she lost him when they took him away from her.

He was one a the bad things she done. She made him cry instead a smile. She broke wooden spoons on his little backside. She scratched the jagged end across his skin till he bled. And she didn't care how much he cried or how loud he screamed. And she let the guy she lived with beat him too, till he was near unconscious, for nothing more than using the red crayon for the sky instead a the blue one.

And she got to thinking she should contact her son somehow. Apologize for the terrible things she done to him and let him know how awful sorry she was. Tell him she was so thankful he turned out ok in spite a her, with happiness and goodness and love and success in his life. Tell him she was a changed person now, good and kind instead a mean and cruel. And ask him if he could ever forgive her.

She found out his new last name, because it sure wouldn't a stayed Vester once he got adopted. And she found out the address of the TV station where he worked.

She started that letter so many times.

'Dear Mike Chatelain,'

But she always ripped it up. He had enough scars. On the outside, probably. On the inside, for certain.

He didn't need no reminders a her.

Chapter 59

LICENSE FOR BEGINNINGS IN AN END

BUT.........
(October)

Hot house tomatoes. Lainey didn't know why she even bought them. As red and ripe as they looked on the outside, when you cut into them, they were unappetizingly pale and juiceless, with a dry, mushy texture and a taste that hovered between yuck and nonexistent. Nothing like the plump, succulent tomatoes she bought by the peck at farmer's markets and road side stands during the summer.

Yet here she was, slicing the deceptive things into wedges and tossing them on top of the lettuce she had already broken up into the salad bowl. What would a salad be without tomatoes?

As she stood slicing and tossing, Lainey heard the side door open and close and felt a wisp of cool autumn air blow across the back of her neck. Someone was home. Out of the corner of her eye she perceived height and dark hair coming towards her. It was probably Joe. Or it could be Gabriel. It was hard to tell these days. Gabe had sprouted up as tall as his father and he had always had the same dark curly hair. It was funny, now that Gabriel was a man/boy, he and Joe looked more alike, more like twins, than Gabe and Owen, the real twins, did!

She had actually mistaken Gabriel for Joe several times now. There was really no harm done if she called out over her shoulder

'Hi Joe! How was work today?' Or 'Did you remember to stop at the bank on your way home, Joe?' or 'Joe, can you get the rest of the cork out of this wine bottle? It broke off in the corkscrew!' only to hear Gabe snort behind her like she was an idiot or was losing her mind to senility.

But once, as she had stood at the kitchen counter writing out her grocery list, she had been so sure it was Joe coming up behind her that she had turned around with a 'come hither' look on her face, her hands reaching towards his crotch area, ready to caress the object that resided there.

Only it had not been Joe! There stood Gabriel! Her heart had leapt up into her throat! Horror, shock and embarrassment flooded over her like hot water. She pulled back her hand so fast it was a blur. She erased the sexy look from her face and replaced it with an innocent smile.

Luckily Gabriel, chow hound that he was, was too busy trying to see what it was she was doing at the counter, if it involved food and if there might be some delectable morsel he could stuff in his face, to even notice. Thank the lord above!

That was not a mistake she had any intention of making again! Be sure of your target. Never assume anything. Those were her mottos now.

She was turning around to see exactly which dark haired household member was coming towards her when excited chatter erupted from their mouth.

"Hey Mom! You know what? She had them! Seven of them!"

No question now. It was definitely Gabe. But she turned all the way around anyway. The momentum of the turn was behind her. Easier to keep going than to try and stop.

"She who? Had what?"

"Moonlady! Stace's dog. She had seven puppies!"

"Is that right." Lainey was cautious in her response. She thought she knew where Gabe was going with this and she didn't want to encourage him. But, to tell the truth, her interest was piqued. After three years of doglessness, she had found herself starting to long for a pooch again. Life without a dog was almost like a salad without tomatoes! But still, she wasn't entirely sure she wanted to make the commitment.

"They're so tiny and cute. Five males and two females. Three of them look like springer spaniels, brown and white, just like Moonlady. Two are brown and black and two are all black. Except one of the black ones has three white paws. The black ones look kind of like labs so it must have been Jack down at the end of the street that gave Moonlady the bone and knocked her up."

Gabe's face turned redder than the deceptive tomatoes when that statement blundered out of his mouth. Lainey clamped her mouth shut, doing her best to force the chuckle that was bubbling in her belly and tickling her lips to stay put and pretend that she didn't notice the slang that had just erupted from her son's mouth. Gabe was already embarrassed beyond words that he had made not one but two inappropriate sexual references in front of his mother. It wouldn't do to embarrass him even more.

Once she felt certain that the chuckle was stifled, what she wanted to do next was ask Gabe for more doggie details. Which puppy did he like best? Was the one with the white paws a boy or a girl? How long till they would be weaned from their mother? But she kept her eager interest stifled too.

"Oh, really," was all she said, keeping her voice flat and unenthused, as if she was barely paying attention to the doggie news.

"So, anyway, I was wondering....." Gabe plowed ahead to his now unmistakable intended destination, "You know they have to find homes for them and I was thinking..... Mom, can we take one of them?"

Owen came bursting into the kitchen then, out of breath and windblown. Lainey saw him catch his brother's eye in an unspoken question. She saw Gabe shake his head slightly. She could imagine the entire conversation that must have just passed between them without a word being spoken.

'Did you ask her yet, Bro? What did she say? Is there any chance? Did you tell her we'd take care of it?'

'Told her. Waiting for an answer. Be cool, dude! Got it under control.'

Twins. What amazing things they were.

"When your father gets back from the hardware store we'll talk about it, okay?" was the practical answer she gave.

She tried to sound leery about the whole prospect but ....

IS.........
(November)

Her valiant little soldier was on the move. Belly flat on the floor, pushing with her polka dotted knees and purple socked feet, pulling with her elbows, she was just inches from her target - the sewing chest that Pam had left on the floor next to the chair when she'd had to make a mad dash for the bathroom.

Pam swooped in like a hawk, scooping Pamela up into protective arms and smooching her geranium pink cheeks.

"Oh no you don't my little cupcake! That's Mommy's. Not for Pamela."

She blew gurgley air bubbles into Pamela's soft belly and laughed out loud as Pamela squealed and squirmed and giggled, her entire body a smile.

Seven months old already. Seventeen pounds! It was amazing how fast she grew and how much she had changed in so short a time. Smiling and laughing, sitting up and crawling, babbling confidences and the details of her day in a language that bordered on the understandable. Pam could swear there were at least some real words in those babblings. Perhaps in French or Spanish or Dolphin or Bluejay!

"You know what, my little darling? Mommy needs to find Daddy! Do you know where Daddy is, Pamela? Maybe he's in the cellar. Come on, let's go look! Let's go look for Daddy!" Excitement was sprinkled on her every word.

Pam started eagerly towards the cellar with Pamela's diaper clad bottom balanced in the crook of her elbow.

Two words halted her cellar destined stride. Two soft, hesitant words, which were really one word spoken with imperfect perfection.

"Daaah dee."

That word did not border on the understandable. It was under-standable! Daddy! Had Pamela just said 'Daddy'?

"Who are we going to go find, Pamela? Daddy? Are we going to go find Daddy? Where's Daddy?"

"Daaah dee!" Spoken with confidence now. Spoken with glee.

"That's right! Oh, you little dumpling you!"

Pam bounded to the cellar. "Boyd! Hey Boyd! Are you down there?" She shouted with her head stuck through the open door but she was already halfway down the stairs before the question was halfway out of her mouth, Pamela clinging to her neck like a little monkey singing 'daaah dee, daaah dee, daaah dee' all the way down.

Boyd was standing over by the work bench sifting through his coffee can stash of screws. Perturbed concentration clouded his face as he combed his fingers through the varied assortment, pulling out one hopeful possibility after another and tossing them back in - too long, too thick, wrong head.

He glanced up at the commotion of a babbling, excited whirl-wind rushing towards him. Annoyed vexation transformed to sun-shine and light.

Pamela loosened her hold on Pam's neck and stretched out her arms, reaching as far as she could and struggling to get away from her mother and over to her father. And Pam struggled just as hard in the other direction, to hold her back, to keep baby Pamela in her arms and not let her fall on the floor! Seventeen pounds became twenty-seven, thirty-seven, and forty seven!

Boyd leapt to the rescue, snatching Pamela up, up and away as she squealed with delight, just before Pam thought her aching arms would sag like a rubber band and collapse with the strain.

"Boyd, did you hear that?" she asked, her excitement slightly tempered by discomfort as she shook her arms to ease out the ache. "Pamela was saying Daddy! Her first word! Listen. Pamela, who's this? Is this Daddy? Say Daddy Pamela!"

Pamela was silent. She just stared with her wide brown eyes. Not even a babble escaped her bow shaped lips.

Boyd laughed and kissed her chubby cheek. "Oh, looks like my little girl's showing her stubborn side. Did you say Daddy, Pamela? Am I Daddy?"

Nothing but a smile.

"I swear, she really did say it, Boyd. As clear as can be. 'Dahdee'. So, what are you doing down here anyway? Did something break?" Pam inclined her head towards the screw can, sitting temporarily abandoned on the edge of the work table.

"Well, I came down to get a new light bulb for the bathroom. But then the buzzer went off on the dryer so I took the clothes out and then the washer went into spin cycle but it was unbalanced and shaking all over so I lifted the lid to redistribute the clothes and then a screw popped out of the hinge and I couldn't find it for the life of me, so now here I am looking for a replacement! If it isn't one thing, it's another!"

Pam picked up the coffee can and peered into its screw filled depths. "Maybe I'll have better luck. What kind of screw do you need?"

"I'll have to tell you that later," he whispered slyly, a scoundrel's grin spreading across his face and glinting in his eyes. "When the baby goes down for her nap."

Pam grinned herself. "What a dirty minded boy you are! Always trying to get me into trouble."

Happiness and love swirled through her. Pam leaned around Pamela, who was sitting quietly content in her father's arms, and kissed Boyd's mouth. She meant it to be a long, slow kiss; tender and warm, revealing all the love for him that beat in her heart. Instead it was a little peck. She just remembered! There was something else! The original reason she had been searching for Boyd.

'Dahdee' had sidetracked her, screws had sidetracked her, love had sidetracked her. But, when it came right down to it, those sidetracks were the reason there was a destination in the first place.

"You know Dixie asked me to be a bridesmaid for her wedding and I told her yes. But now I think I'm going to have to bow out."

"Why would you have to do that?"

"She plans on getting married next July and that's eight months from now."

"So?"

"Well, I'm pretty sure I'm going to have a conflict of interest eight months from now."

"A conflict of interest? How can you suddenly have something else going on the same day as Dixie's wedding? Just change the date on whatever it is!"

"Oh Boyd. Being a bridesmaid is more than just showing up on the day of the wedding! Besides, I can't change the date. Actually, the date is indeterminate. All I know is......."

TO.........
(February)

There were lots of girls that Owen thought were cute. Sara and Jess in his homeroom, Megan whose locker was right next to his, and Andrea who sat in front of him in Science class.

Besides being cute, Jess was built. A rack like a couple melons! He tried not to stare, but it was hard to keep his eyes off her. She bounced when she walked and jiggled when she laughed.

Megan liked to wear wild colors and streak her hair. Owen liked it best when she streaked it blue because it matched her eyes. She was always dropping her books or her pen and Owen liked to watch her when she bent down to pick them up, especially if she was wearing a short skirt. Her panties were color coordinated.

Andrea had the sunniest smile and she smiled all the time. There had been a few times now, when Andrea had been passing papers back and smiling at him, that her hand had unexpectedly touched his. He had felt himself rising to the occasion.

He was glad he was sitting down. Nothing could be worse than having Andrea, or anyone else for that matter, see that he was pitching a tent.

But the girl Owen really liked was Emelda from his karate class! Just a glimpse of her and his heart started beating like a snare drum, loud and fast. His hands even got sweaty.

Emelda's skin was smooth and golden, like toast, even in the winter. Not white as a sheet of paper like Owen's. She usually had her dark hair tied back so it didn't get in her way, but if she let it loose, it swayed when she moved and draped over her shoulders like a waterfall glinting in the sun.

With her golden toast skin and espresso brown hair, you'd think she'd have brown eyes too. But she didn't. Her eyes were green. Green, with flecks of gold.

Owen knew there were gold flecks in her green eyes because whenever Master Amos set them up to spar against each other she would only be inches away from him. And she stared him down with those gold flecked eyes of hers. And she always won.

He liked to tell himself that he let her win, because he didn't want to be too forceful and chance hurting her. Or, that she won because he couldn't concentrate, distracted as he was by her nearness and her beauty.

But the truth of it was, she won because she was kick-ass good.

And Owen really liked that about her. That she was all up into karate, just like he was; intense and precise in her moves, not wimpy and half assed like most of the other girls in the class.

And he really liked her name too. Emelda. It was exotic and uncommon. She probably got a lot of flak for that name, though. Just like he got flak for his name sometimes. What kid these days was named Owen?

But he didn't let it bother him any. He just shrugged it off and stole the bullies' ammunition. He joked about his name right along with them. Owen didn't know what they thought they were trying to prove when they got in his face about his name but the only thing they ended up proving was that they were assholes.

Owen could tell Emelda was the same way. She wouldn't let some bully making fun of her name faze her. She was strong, inside and out. Strong and beautiful and smart.

And he was in love. Every minute he got to spend in her presence was ecstasy. He needed more of those minutes! Maybe he could ask her if she wanted to come over to his house and practice katas, perfect their punches and kicks!

But how would she get there? They were both years away from driving. One of her parents would have to bring her over. Like little kids in elementary school getting together for a playdate. Could anything possibly be stupider than that?

But at least he'd be with her! He could watch the way her lips moved when she talked and hear her laugh. He could smell her sweetness and see her green eyes flash as they bore into him if they sparred - focused, anticipating his next move.

Oh man! It would be so totally, seriously, awesome! He should do it! He should ask her over!

But first he needed to get up the balls to ………..

YOU……..
(April)

Cooking was not Mike's strong suit. Sure, he could boil pasta, heat up a jar of sauce and throw together a salad. He could make sandwiches and grill hot dogs and hamburgers. He could cook eggs – hardboiled, scrambled or fried. But to actually follow a recipe and make something like Chicken Fricassee or Spinach Soufflé? That was a different thing entirely.

A different thing that he was trying to do now. The cookbook was spread open on the counter before him. And the plan was that when Dixie returned from clothes shopping with the birthday gift card her parents had sent, she would be greeted by the delicious aromas of the wondrous birthday celebration meal Mike had prepared just for her with his own two hands.

Wondrous, but simple. He didn't want to screw himself by delving too deeply into the gourmet. His first thought had been to galvanize her senses, make something truly stupendous like he had seen in a magazine at the dentist's office - Crispy Roast

Duck surrounded by fingerling potatoes, Blanched Asparagus with Béarnaise Sauce and Apple Prune Compote. But he could see it ending with himself drowning in a quagmire of inexperience and unknown cooking terms. He could imagine Dixie's squinched up face when she walked through the door into greasy smoke and the smell of burnt.

Instead, he had let common sense take over. *Elementary Asian* was the name of the cookbook. Hot and Sour Soup, Chicken Vegetable Stir Fry, and Jasmine Rice was the name of the game. Slice, chop, sauté, boil, can opener. Those were terms he could handle.

And if the dinner didn't turn out as good as he hoped, he could fall back on the gift bag he had hidden behind the couch. Inside, the grapevine and field flowers wreath and the bracelet of polished red-banded agate that he had seen catch Dixie's eye at the Artisan Works Mall a couple weeks ago.

Mike taste tested the soup. Not too bad! Maybe a little flat and lacking intensity, but not bad at all. And if they started with a few glasses of sake first, Dixie probably wouldn't even notice!

It was amazing how a conversation rolled and spun and traveled. First they were discussing whether sake was best warmed, chilled or room temperature. Then they were experimenting with chopstick holding techniques and laughing as slithery noodles and straw mushrooms plopped back into their hot and sour soup. Next they were wondering about all the steps involved in the production of seaweed wrappers. And then, somehow, they were talking about how many kids they would have and if Keiko was a good name for a girl.

"Keiko Chatelain. Do you think that goes? Hey, how about Edelweiss? That has a ring to it, doesn't it?" Dixie face was half light-hearted and half concentration as she tried to firm her chopsticks up on a baby corn nugget from the stir fry Mike had just spooned out onto her plate.

"By 'ring' do you mean yodel? What do you say we defer back to forks? I don't think we're quite getting the hang of these chopsticks. I know I'm not." Mike paused then, his head tilted, his eyes opening from his own squint of concentration into a wide question mark. "Why are we talking about baby names? Are you trying to tell me something, Dixie?"

"What? No! I'm just having fun! Thinking of our glorious future! Looking forward to someday! You and me and little Edelweiss!"

Her laugh was light and carefree like glass chimes tinkling in a breeze. Mike could almost see the dreamy vision of a golden haired toddler capering in her shining eyes.

But what if she had said 'yes'? So what if the wedding wasn't until July. So what if a baby hadn't been in their immediate plans. The gleam dotting the question mark in his eyes would have turned into a grin.

Suddenly Dixie's eyes misted over and bulged out in a reddening face. She had just managed to snag the baby corn and some bean sprouts and get them into her mouth.

"Whoa!" She puffed her cheeks and blew out air. "Lots of wasabi!"

"Did I make it too hot for you? Try eating some rice!"

Not what he had hoped. Not wondrous. Maybe now was the time for the gift bag. Or maybe he should bring out the cupcakes he had picked up at Dimetri Bakery and decorated with a fortune cookie pressed into the frosting on top of each one.

"It's okay! I'm okay. Really! Whoa!" Dixie grabbed for a tissue, wiped her eyes and blew her nose. "I'm telling you, if you have a stuffy nose, wasabi would be the thing to eat! It really clears out your nasal passages! It's completely different than the heat you get from hot peppers. Hot peppers make your mouth feel like it's on fire but wasabi shoots the fire right up your nose instead!"

"I better add a few notes to the recipe in case I dare to make it again – 'Watch the Wasabi', 'Fire in the Hole!', 'A.k.a Enter the Dragon Stir Fry'!"

Dixie laughed as he quipped, her eyes bright again, her whole face a smile. And she picked up her chopsticks and went in for another bite.

"Are you sure you want more? You don't have to eat it if you don't like it. I can handle rejection. Maybe I can rinse off some of the sauce or something."

"Mike!" Dixie set her chopsticks back down, releasing wasabi sauced snow peas and chicken back onto her plate and put her hand on top of Mike's. "I didn't say I didn't like it. I said it was a lot of wasabi. I love it! I really, really do. And I love that you cooked it just for me. Everything's great! The soup, the stir fry. Everything. Seriously! I'm not being glib. I think this is the best stir fry ever. I like feeling like a dragon!"

Mike shook his head, chuckling and grinning. Warmth spread through him that had nothing to do with his heavy hand on the wasabi powder. His Dixie. His bright faced hot smokin' dragon girl. God he loved her.

He jumped out of his chair then and came back with more sake. And two forks.

"Here! It'll be easier to keep the dragons stoked with these."

And the conversation turned to dragons, and wound around to grapevines and grapes, and to pondering if dragons would eat grapes. It travelled to misspelled fortunes and Chinese translations and somehow arrived at wondering if The Wedding March was available on a calliope roll and if anyone would think it odd that they were getting married in a park by a merry-go-round.

Eventually it wandered into soft sounds and lone syllables that flowed into words only they knew the meaning of. And that meaning was love.

Dixie was in the shower, singing 'Cover Me Up', the next morning when Mike opened the door a crack and stuck his head into the swirling fog of humidity that was the bathroom.

"Whew! Steamy! Can you even breathe in here? I'm leaving now, Dixie. I've got that early breakfast meeting with Howl The Moon Coffee. See you at the office. Love You!"

"Bye Mike! Good luck with the sales pitch. Love you too!"

And she was on the phone when he walked in after his meeting a couple hours later, her honey swirls bobbing about her head as she nodded in agreement with whoever held the other end of the line. She waved at him, a sunflower blowing in the breeze, and aimed an air kiss in his direction.

Beaming, Mike strode over, set a cup of her favorite caramel cream latte on her desk, and gave her the thumbs up. Howl had committed to a month of ad time to start, split between morning and evening time blocks.

Still beaming, he cruised the office passing the word that steaming elixirs to soothe everyone's caffeine cravings were in the break room. In addition to Dixie's favorite cuppa, he had brought in two 96 ounce Traveler Boxes so all could share in the glow of success. One box was Howl the Moon's signature brew, the dark roasted Wolf Pack Aphrodisiac and the other, the lighter bodied Brazilian Moonlight Blend.

And what was coffee without an 'and'? There was also a giant box of Crescent Moon Blueberry Almond Scones.

When he finally got to his desk, he found it there, resting on his keyboard with a few other pieces of snail mail. A plain white envelope hand addressed to Channel Twenty and marked 'PERSONAL - ATTENTION MIKE CHATELAIN'. The top left hand corner was conspicuously empty, the sender of the envelope a mystery.

What's up with this? Curious, he scrabbled around in his drawer until he found the letter opener, slit the envelope open and pulled out the contents - a letter, hand written on a sheet of lined paper with a blotchy pen, messy letters scrawled across the page.

'Dear Mike Chatelain,

I saw you on a TV morning show one day last July when I was visiting my cousin out a state. My heart about stopped dead and then it started beating so fast I couldn't hardly breathe. I knew you...........'

LOVE........
(July)

Summer. A time for fireflies, barefoot beaches, and juicy watermelon picnics. A time when love bloomed like wildflowers and basked in the sun.

Dixie had been thinking a lot about love this summer. And the question had popped into her head one day while she was driving, along with a word. MNT were the letters on the license plate ahead of her. 'Moment' was the word that popped. And the question – Could anyone say the exact moment when they had fallen in love?

Mike said he could. He said his love for her started the moment he first saw her; vibrant, smiling, confident - a bright eyed, golden haired vision in a sea green dress and a long beaded necklace that glinted when it caught the light. And that was it for him. He was in awe. Hooked, smitten, gone. Head over heels in love.

Her mom said the same thing about falling in love with her father. It was love at first sight. A thunderclap! A burst of light! Cupid's arrow!

Her father thought it was a dumb question. Who cared if love came swooping in on blazing wings all at once in one identifiable moment or if it crept in slowly a smidgen at a time? All he knew was that he did love Lainey and that was all that mattered to him.

The Channel Twenty audience had a lot to say when she posed the question to them.

'Love. Did it creep in or dart? Was it the tortoise or the hare?'

*'Hare - Love always starts like a speeding freight train for me.
And then it jumps the tracks.' Still single after all these years*

'Blank - Love is love.' June D.

*'Tortoise - Love is like the morning sun. It rises slowly, slowly,
and then it bursts into life.' Clare B.*

'Tortoise – First single notes and then a song.' Madeline L.

'Hare – Fireworks, Baby. Fireworks' Felix G.

'Neither – Never been in love. Don't give a shit.' SYZMADRS

*'Both – The hare brings infatuation first. Then the tortoise
brings the love home.' Becky T.*

Dixie herself would have to say 'tortoise'. There was no one big defining moment blaring to the heavens that she had fallen in love with Mike. Just lots of little moments. Bits, flashing in the background and building on each other without her realizing, until love was just there, warming her soul and dancing in her heart.

And she thought about those bits as she stood hidden from view behind the carousel in the shade of a big maple, her flowing white dress with the emerald green sash fluttering in the breeze.

Compassion and protection in gently encircled arms; a playful wink and silliness on a scrap of colored paper; a take-out sandwich, a thin, red line and a gentle admonition; a seed, a sprout, a flowering vine.

And there it was! Her cue! The calliope had started!

And there was her father, kissing her cheek and putting his arm in hers.

And there was Mike, waiting for her at the end of the petal strewn runner, more handsome than she had ever seen him. Her beloved. Her darling. Her Mike.

Summer. A time for merry-go-rounds, hotdogs and toasts with glasses of pink champagne.

A time when love........

Poetic License

A BLANK PAGE AND A PEN

Spring pink leaves
Glow in the spotlight
Of the sun's last refracting rays
The sky explodes with color
At the end of the day

White starry jasmine
Honeys the emerging night
Scent set free
And drifting
In day's fading light

A page is turned
Night's dark curtain falls
Moon and stars
Embroidered
In shades of white and gold

Day will come again
A blank page
Waiting for a pen
And ever changing colors
To fill the hours in

Day to night
Night to day
A blank page and a pen

Lives may fade
Circumstances change
But the story never ends

Chapter 60

LICENSE ON A BLANK PAGE
(Chorus, Cadence, Coda)

He had accepted it. He had to. There was no possible way to change it. But always he hovered near, in case she needed him.

Not that there was anything he could do except feather lightness against her cheek or whisper softness in her ear. He had gathered himself several times to do those things and it had seemed to bring her comfort. And in whatever odd way you could say that he could feel, this had made him happy.

Colors and hours had passed. Days and shapes. And he had been content. But this day was different. She was white and happiness emanated off her brighter than the sun that shone above her head. Others that had meant something to him were gathered there too, dressed in jubilation and gaiety.

And memories of life crashed through him.

He had been someone. He had smiled and laughed. He had hoped and dreamed. He had loved and been loved. And it had all been taken away from him.

Sadness engulfed him. It ached, intense and raw, in the place that had once been his beating heart.

Why can't that be me standing next to her now, in the pebble gray tuxedo and white tie, nerves and excitement jittering in my stomach and elation racing through my blood stream?

Why can't that be me holding her hand and putting the gold band on her finger, love's sweet music trembling between us?

Rain fell softly from the cloudless sky. She that was Dixie looked up. She let the gentle drops fall on her sun kissed face. Understanding swam in her eyes. She knew the rain was tears. She knew it was me.

She turned to he that was Mike beside her and kissed him, her lips moist with the warm rain. But it was really me she was kissing. For one moment, it was me. And then she gave all the tenderness and love in her kiss back to Mike. And that was as it should be.

Because Mike was the one that made her blue/green eyes sparkle and shine now, the one that she loved, totally and completely, the one that loved her, always and forever. He was the one she would share her todays and tomorrows with, dream with, as they headed into the bright but uncertain future.

Because Dixie and Mike had a future. Dixie and Mike were alive.

And he was not.

Melodies and days go by. Minutes and scents. He accepted what he was and floated, content, as below him life's chorus went on; Rising and falling, ebbing and flowing -

An elusive song.

ACKNOWLEDGEMENTS

Many people helped me turn *License* into the book that it became - Family and friends, neighbors, casual acquaintances, and unsuspecting strangers sipping coffee or wine at open mic nights and poetry readings. Their input meant more to me than they will ever know. I send them my sincere and heartfelt thanks.

Of all of those that helped me in ways large and small, there were four individuals on whom I depended the most. Their support was as priceless to me as they are themselves. Special thanks and eternal gratitude I send to them – my indispensable core:

Jeanne Colt - dear friend and neighbor, who eagerly awaited and faithfully read each and every chapter as I dropped them at her door and gave me her honest opinions, criticisms and praises and (usually) a big 'thumbs up'.

Peter Rivoli - intermittent editor at large, whose knowledge of the young tongue brought twenty-something conversation into the modern age.

Joshua Rivoli - my most precise editor, whose recommendations and guidance untangled confusion, unearthed missteps and made dull moments shine.

Joseph Rivoli - promoter, inspiration and partner in crime, whose faith and love, contributions and confidences, unlimited patience and untiring ear can be seen in the eyes of every character and the polish on every word.

Finally, many thanks to ARiZona and the slow and snowy February day that started it all.

ABOUT THE AUTHOR

Diane Rivoli lives in beautiful Upstate New York where she enjoys the changing of the seasons, puttering in the garden, cooking gourmet meals, entertaining family and friends, singing at the top of her lungs and walking nature trails or suburban sidewalks hand-in-hand with her husband, Joseph.

She also enjoys visits to the now empty nest by the two grown sons that vacated years ago, the daughter-in-law of her dreams, and the schnoodle that masquerades as her grand-daughter.

License is her first book.

www.dianerivoli.com

dianerivoli@yahoo.com

68974742R00194

Made in the USA
Middletown, DE
18 September 2019